SOMEONE LIKE YOU

A BECOMING US NOVEL

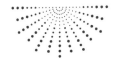

BRITTNEY SAHIN

EMKO MEDIA

Someone Like You

By: Brittney Sahin

Published by: EmKo Media, LLC

Copyright © 2017 EmKo Media, LLC

Second edition © 2019

This book is an original publication of Brittney Sahin.

Editor: Cassie Cox, Joy Editing

Proofreaders: Joy Editing; Emily at Lawerence Editing

Cover Designer: Mayhem Cover Creations

Photo license: Shutterstock

Paperback ISBN-13: 9781947717916

Sign up to receive exclusive excerpts and bonus material, as well as take part in great giveaways. Get alerted when books are released. Sign up at: brittneysahin.com.

❀ Created with Vellum

For Carlene, Jen, and Whitney. Thank you for everything.

PROLOGUE

NOAH

Why the hell isn't she answering?

"Yo, we're ready to roll out at zero one. We're meeting up in ten to go over the mission once more. You good?" Craig's in the doorway, casually leaning inside the frame with crossed arms.

"Yeah, sure," I mumble.

His forehead creases as he straightens his stance and drops his arms. He knows something's up with me. We're a team, one unit; we can read each other.

But *is* something wrong with me?

I've had a bad feeling in the pit of my stomach for weeks, and it's not about the mission. I never get nervous on ops. I live for them. We were trained at BUD/S to remove fear from the equation, so I know going into Iran in a couple of hours isn't what has me rattled.

"I'll meet up with y'all in five. Just trying to see Cindy and Lily before we leave." I turn back to the laptop screen and end the unanswered Skype call once again, killing the annoying beeping sound before I try one last time.

"All right."

I lean back in the chair and narrow my eyes when the call finally connects, and my daughter's face fills the screen. Lily's long blond hair is draped in front of her shoulders, and her huge emerald-green eyes trap me, giving me a serious ache in my chest. It's been months since I've been home. She's almost five, and I've been away from her more than I've been with her. She's the reason I'm not sure if I'll re-enlist when the time comes in four months.

But she's also why I do what I do—to protect her, to try to make the world a little better for when she grows up.

"Hi, baby girl. I miss you." My index finger goes to the laptop screen as if I can actually touch her tiny palm as she waves, her dimples popping as she smiles.

"Hiya, Daddy. I miss you too. Mommy is packing. She says we're going to see the Big Apple."

I lean in closer. "Where's Mamma? Can you put Mamma on, baby girl?"

"Okay, Daddy. Love you."

"Love you more." I kiss two fingers and press them to the screen, and Lily does the same. It's our ritual goodbye.

A moment later, Cindy is on camera, and I've lost sight of Lily. Now I'm certain as to why I've been hanging on the damn edge.

My wife.

She's been off for a while, but I haven't wanted to admit it. With the way her brows pinch together and her lips draw tight, I can tell she's holding something back from me, something I don't want to hear.

I catch a glimpse of my mother's old record player off to the right behind her. It's closed and probably collecting dust. When we first got married I would play my mother's jazz music and dance around the living room, trying to get Cindy to move with me. She always hated that record player. She'd shirk away and raise her palms, insisting I was crazy for wanting to dance in the middle of the day just because it was a rainy afternoon.

Not once did she dance with me.

My gaze snaps back to Cindy as she wets her glossy pink lips and brushes her dyed blond hair to her back. Her green eyes aren't on mine. She looks past me as if someone is standing behind my chair. I almost peek over my shoulder just to be sure I'm alone.

"Where are you going? What's Lily talking about? Another trip to your mom's?" My body tenses as an unnatural pull of stress ropes me in, and I grind my knuckles against my thigh. "Cindy?"

She finally looks at me.

I almost regret it, because the look in her eyes…well, it's as if she's a ghost.

"Noah."

My name used to sound good when she said it, but now it's as though the word has become an inconvenience, my existence a nuisance.

"I don't have much time," I say as anticipation cuts me open. Give me a terrorist to face any day, but a pissed off wife…not so much.

"When are you coming home?" She knows the answer to that because I can never give her definitive dates.

"I don't know. Maybe sooner than I thought." I didn't think the raid in Iran would happen this month, so I'll probably get back to Virginia in a matter of weeks.

"Well, I'm going away for a little while…so, uh, we won't be here when you get back."

I blink like a damn fool as I try to make sense of that.

"What do you mean?" I stand, needing to be on my feet

for this conversation. I brace against the desk, palms down, a grimace spreading across my face.

"We're leaving. I've already had a lawyer draw up the paperwork. The law requires us to be separated for a year before we can get a divorce, but because of your unique situation, they're allowing me to take Lily out of state. If you want to contest it, you can, but please don't." Her voice doesn't even quaver. There's not an ounce of remorse or fear, no emotion at all. Just…hollowness. An empty vessel of what used to be there.

My wife is gone. When did that happen?

I grit my teeth and stare at her, assessing the situation, trying to figure out how to get through this as if she's an op and I want to minimalize the collateral damage.

She won't look at me again. "I wanted to tell you when you came home, but I don't think I'm strong enough to face you in person. I just want what's best for Lily."

"What's best for Lily?" My heart thrashes as I take a deep breath, trying to calm myself the hell down.

As a SEAL, I'm trained for the unknown. I can turn any object into a weapon—if I remain calm, that is. *If* I keep my shit together.

But let me tell you what I'm not trained in—keeping my wife happy while I put my life on the line every day. And no, I never got instructions on how to deal with the intense blow she's delivered.

"You're not taking Lily anywhere." I bow my head, knowing I'm on the other side of the world and can't do a damn thing about it. Hell, I'm about to go into dangerous enemy territory and might not even make it out alive.

My skin crawls, and my body slightly trembles. I've never once, in all my goddamn years as a SEAL, thought about the possibility of not coming home. You can't think like that because it puts your men at risk and takes your eyes off the end game, the goal.

What is Cindy doing to me?

I pinch the tight skin at my throat and close my eyes. I have to keep my shit together for my men, for the mission. "Please, can we talk about this when I get back? I'll be able to call you in a few days. Don't go anywhere or do anything before then. Give me your word. We've been together for thirteen years. You can't just drop this on me right before I'm about to go—"

"I'm sorry to do this to you, but this is your fault." She actually looks annoyed instead of sad. A scowl mars the pretty features of her face. "You were only going to be in the military for four years. This wasn't supposed to turn into your life. I-I can't handle this anymore."

"Are you asking me to choose? Are you at least giving me an option?" My eyes flicker open at the possibility that I might be able to save my marriage. I just need to give up being a SEAL.

You know, give up breathing...

I take another breath as if it might be my last, stealing time as I wait for her response.

"It's too late for us. Lily needs a family. A better home life."

My fist pounds the metal desk, shaking the laptop, as I bite out, "I am her family."

Cindy covers her face with both hands. "I'm sorry, but we're going to New York."

I stumble back a step. "What the hell is in New York?"

Is Cindy following her old dream of being an actress? If that's what she wants, I can sacrifice—I can do something—but dammit, the woman isn't giving me a choice.

Her hands fall from her face, showcasing her dead eyes.

No tears. Not even a hint of sheen over her green irises. "I met someone."

The words are so low it sounds like a coo from her lips as chills rake my spine.

"Say that again." My heart isn't beating fast like it probably should be. Instead, it's like a slow drumbeat. So slow I wonder if it's still working.

She's standing now, her arms folded over the blue sweater that has the word NAVY on it.

My sweater. Is she fucking kidding me? She's going to tell me she's leaving me for some asshole while wearing my goddamn sweater? A sweater that represents what she apparently hates about me—the military.

I can't even look at her anymore.

"I didn't mean for it to happen. He's a stock broker," she says it casually as though she isn't shattering my world right now. "I met him while at my mom's, and now he's transferring to New York, and I—"

"Are you screwing him? For how long?" This has to be a nightmare. It can't be real. I face monsters in the dark. Hell, in daylight too. People who blow themselves up to kill soldiers and civilians...but when I finally look at her again, *she* is now what I can't handle.

"A year."

I slump back into the chair, and my palms press against my fatigues.

She cheated on me even while I was home. My stomach shakes a little, and I think I might puke.

"He's taking a job on Wall Street, and he asked Lily and me to come with him. He has money. He has the ability to give me—I mean, Lily, the life she deserves."

Thirteen fucking years.

Gone.

"This has been a long time coming, you know that. You don't love me anymore. You love being a SEAL. You'd rather be off in a war zone than home with me. I need someone who can take care of Lily and me. Provide a safe and stable home."

There's a high-pitched ringing in my ears, and I clench my jaw tightly as I try to formulate the words to say.

"We gotta move." Craig is back in the doorway. "Noah?"

"Not now," I rasp.

"Go, Noah. There's nothing left to say for now. You'll get the papers when you're portside. Call me when you're in Virginia, and we'll chat." Cindy spoke as if we were discussing getting a cup of coffee together. Is she out of her mind?

"Wait."

But it's too late. She's already ended the call, and I have to resist the compulsion to break something.

Calm. Cool. Collected. The three Cs—the normal me. But not right now. Cindy has ripped out my heart, and I can't even fight back.

"You okay, man?" Craig comes toward me as I push my fingers to my temples, where an intense throbbing gathers.

"No, man. No, I'm not."

And that means I might be putting my team at risk when my boots hit the ground in Iran.

1

NOAH

ELEVEN MONTHS LATER

"Don't bail on me now. You need to get out and have some fun."

I slouch down on the couch on the deck of my boat and tip back the last of my beer. "I get out plenty."

My cousin shakes his head and opens his hands palms up, then he faces the towering buildings to our left. "You need to experience the real New York, not the dive bars you go to for a quick beer." Cam leans back against the railing and folds his arms, attempting to stare me down. Yeah, good luck with that.

"I'm not a nightclub kind of guy." I rest my empty bottle on my thigh. "Besides, I'm in New York for one reason only."

Lily.

Of course, I only get to see Lily on Sundays, and it's always at Cindy's rich uptown loft. Her boyfriend is never home when I pick up Lily, and so far, I haven't met the son of a bitch. Cindy must realize my self-control has limits.

But I put a smile on for Lily, and I suck it up. I do it for her. And Cindy and I have agreed that once we're officially divorced and I get a home—not living on a boat at the docks on the Hudson—I can have Lily on the weekends. I'm trying to scratch together enough cash to do right by my daughter.

I don't know why the hell I put up with Cindy's bullshit. Why I let my ex dictate what happens. A woman I'm still married to for another three weeks, five days, and fourteen hours—yes, I'm counting down.

As much as I hate Cindy for what she did to our family, I know that allowing my anger to consume me won't do Lily any good. Well, not every damn moment of the day, at least.

"You've been in this city for six months now, and I don't think you've even begun to discover it. Just give me one night, cuz." Cam pats his black, gelled, spiky hair and cocks his head to the side as he studies me. He's only twenty-five. Seven years younger than me. His concept of the real world has always been a little different than mine, and age doesn't have anything to do with that.

When you've seen and done the shit I have, it changes your perspective.

"One night."

Hooking up is the last thing on my mind, and I know that's the real reason Cam wants me to go out. He thinks it'll be good for me to screw half of New York to get Cindy out of my head. Yeah, well, I don't miss my ex. I miss having a family to come home to, but I can never miss someone who could cheat on me and break apart our family like she did—and right before I was about to jump out of a plane into Iran. Give me a break, what kind of woman with a heart does that shit?

"You're thinking about her, aren't you?"

Thirteen years for what?

"Hell no." My mind drifts to the few women I did have sex with last winter—my so-called revenge sex.

I didn't enjoy it, though. It was too soon. Call me old-fashioned, but after being with someone for a decade plus… well, it's not that easy to turn off the switch, even if Cindy did cheat on me with the jackass William Fletcher. Jesus. Even his name sounds like some Upper West Side rich fucker.

Money. It's about money, and Cindy still can't look me in the eyes and tell me anything different. I should have known better back when we first met in high school. She came from a wealthy family. Her sixteenth birthday gift was a Mercedes, and mine was a shooting lesson at the gun range from Pops. I think she dated me just to piss off her parents, but somehow she fell in love with me.

I clear my throat and rub my palms together while lifting my gaze up to see the Freedom Tower. It's a thing of beauty, with the perfect octagon at the center. LED lights behind the stainless-steel panels illuminate the structure. I joined the military to pay for school so I could become an architect, but once I became a SEAL, I forgot all about the dream of creating my own structures.

"Noah?"

Cam's in front of me, but I keep my eyes on the building. I can almost see the ghost of the World Trade Towers in its midst, and I have to swallow the sudden knot in my throat, knowing I'll no longer be going abroad to stop terrorists. Instead, I'm about to drink an overpriced cocktail.

"Where are we going?" I stand and toss my beer in the recycling bin before facing him.

A sneaky smile meets his lips. "Well, I have a friend who can get us into Club Y. He's the bouncer, and we can bypass the line."

"Great. Sounds like fun," I say while rolling my eyes, but I probably shouldn't be a dick to him. Cam's only trying to help me get back out there again.

11

"But you can't go like that."

"Like what?" I'm in jeans and a black tee.

"This is New York."

As though that's supposed to mean something to me.

Cam holds up his hands. "Fine. Fine. But at least lose those dirty work boots."

* * *

I SCRATCH AT THE STUBBLE ON MY JAW, AND MY HAND SLIDES down to my throat, where I pinch at the skin there. I'm mentally preparing myself for what I'm about to do. Enter a club named one letter, and it has an honest-to-God red velvet rope. I thought that was for the movies.

"We're good to go in. Come on." Cam motions for me to follow him, and we walk past the long line.

I nod my thanks to the bouncer and follow Cam into the club. It's not what I was expecting. A dark hallway, lit only by a strand of lights trailing along the sides as if I'm at the movie theater in search of my seats.

Oh, and it gets better. Once we reach the end of the hall, there's a door painted a variety of colors—swirls of red, pink, bright orange, and something close to green without looking like geese shit. And I have to wonder if we're about to cross into Neverland or that place where Alice follows the rabbit down the hole. Okay, so maybe I've watched too many kids' movies, but I'm just not ready for this scene. When we walk through the door, it's like I'm tripping on acid, even though I've never done drugs aside from accidentally eating Cindy's hash brownies back in my senior year.

No, I'm not some schoolboy saint, and I don't currently perform miracles, but I'm not a fan of altering my mental state.

"What do you think?" Cam smiles at me and slaps his hands together.

All I can do is squint as I try to gain visibility in the room. I need my night vision goggles for clubbing in New York.

Is the place on fire, or do they purposely fill the room with so much smoke people can barely breathe? And what the hell is with the people dangling from the ceiling from what looks like hula hoops? And are they naked?

I do a double-take at a pretty brunette, but the two guys on either side of her…well, seeing a guy's junk on display isn't exactly what I'd call a good Thursday night.

"I can't do this." I turn away before Cam can rebut and make my way back out to the street, where I suck in a breath to clear my lungs.

"Give it a chance. Come on, let's go back in."

I face Cam and cringe at the idea of subjugating myself to that place again. Nope, it's not going to happen. I tip my chin toward the bar across the street. "Let's grab a drink over there. And then you head into Wonderland, and I'll go to bed."

Cam laughs and slaps a hand to his chest, his fake Rolex glinting beneath the city lights. I hope one day Cam can make enough money to buy himself some stupidly expensive watch if that's what will make him happy, but to be honest, if my cousin first learns to stop trying to impress other people and just live for himself, that would be a big improvement.

Maybe that difference between us doesn't have to do with age. When I was twenty-five, I was on a US destroyer—no need for pretending.

My mind races to my broken marriage again. To a woman I'd thought I loved. Maybe love doesn't exist. Well, at least not for me. Maybe Cindy's right and, aside from loving my daughter, I can only ever love being a SEAL.

Am I addicted to the fight?

"Okay, so maybe this place has a few perks," Cam says once we're inside the bar across from Club Y.

"Yeah, like being able to see," I say before cracking a smile.

"Whoa, wait a second." Cam sticks his arm out in front of my chest. "Do you see that chick talking to the bartender?"

I follow his gaze to a woman in a pair of white dress slacks and a red silk sleeveless blouse. Red and white. Like a Fourth of July gift. Her hair, the color of a dark golden honey, is swept up into a high ponytail, pulled so tight I wonder if it's giving her a headache. I can't see all of her face, only her profile, but she's definitely hot. And entirely out of poor Cam's league.

"Dude, I have to talk to that woman. She's got that hot secretary look." Cam rolls his shoulders back and pushes his chest forward a little, trying to gain another inch. He tucks his hands into his gray slacks, his eyes still zoned in on the woman at the bar.

"Why does she have to be a secretary? Maybe she's the boss."

Cam looks over his shoulder at me with an "are you kidding me" look. "When did you become so goddamn progressive? And if she's a boss, I'd be happy to bend her over her desk."

"Yeah, I really didn't need that visual image."

"Wish me luck." Cam pats me on the back and moves toward the woman.

I stand off to the side of the bar, near a high-top table, and observe with amusement, waiting for what I assume to be lightning-quick rejection.

The woman is facing him dead-on now, and it gives me the chance to look her over and see how little of a chance

Cam has. Not that Cam's a bad-looking guy, but his youth and inexperience, coupled with his crass behavior, won't go far with a woman like her. Tall, firm body, her shoulders squared back with an edge of obvious confidence. She has curves in all the right places.

I start for the bar, unable to stop myself.

Her eyes drift away from Cam and meet mine as I come up next to him. Her eyes are a light blue-gray. Like the color of slate.

"You okay?" I'm not even sure who I'm asking. The words just fall from my lips and hit the counter with a heavy thud.

"You were just leaving, right?" she asks Cam and raises a perfectly arched brow before turning from the both of us and facing the bar again. She reaches for the stem of her martini glass and looks at the TV screen on the wall, above the rows of liquor bottles.

Cam nods toward a few women who have come to the bar at the other end and starts their way.

I should follow, but I don't. "Sorry about him. I hope he didn't say anything offensive."

"Nothing I haven't heard before," she says while glancing over her shoulder at me for a fleeting moment.

"Right. Well, can I buy you a drink to make up for it?" I have no clue why I'm still standing here, but damned if I can get myself to move.

"Ohhh, I get it." She slips her hand free from her glass and faces me. "Is this some party trick of yours? One of you approaches and acts like an ass and the other guy steps in for the rescue? It's kind of a tired routine, don't you think?"

Her pale eyes draw me in before my attention dips down to her lips. No lipstick or gloss. Just full, natural lips. Lips I suddenly want to pull between my teeth to see if she tastes as good as she smells.

This is new for me. This feeling of being drawn to another woman. Even after almost a year of separation, I can't help but notice the tinge of guilt coiling inside me over being attracted to another woman. Sure, I had those random rebound hookups, but those were out of anger.

"No, it's not a routine," I say.

"Well, you're not my type." Her eyes wander to my hand, which is pressed to the counter at my side.

"And what's your type?" I look at her. "Some guy in Armani with a money clip packed with more bills than I have in my bank account?"

Shit. Cindy's in my head and this woman is fast becoming my target, someone I suddenly want to hate.

Although Miss Fourth of July looks nothing like my ex, she certainly reeks of money. Her clothes probably cost more than my rent at the docks. Not that I'm paying that much thanks to a friend.

But the huge Prada bag on the bar stool next to her could buy my meals for a month. And the bag is another reminder of Cindy, because the only reason why I know it's Prada is because Cindy's mom bought her a similar purse on our ten-year anniversary—as if that wasn't enough to make me feel like shit. Yes, thank you, mother-in-law, for outdoing me about ten times over on my goddamn anniversary.

The woman stares at me with parted lips, not saying anything, and I get the feeling that isn't the norm for her. There's a slight bit of red pulling at her cheeks when she finds my eyes again.

"Well, I hate to break it to you, lady, but you're not exactly my type either." Okay, so I don't even know what my

SOMEONE LIKE YOU

type is anymore, but I'm not in the right state of mind to find out.

"Ah. You really are clever, aren't you?" The woman's smiling now. Her white teeth tease between her lips, but it's the sexy way her eyes and nose smile too that has me swallowing.

"Oh yeah? How so?" I place a hand on my chest, forgetting Cindy for the moment. Hell, the way this woman is looking at me right now, I can barely remember my own name.

"You're trying to make me want what I can't have. You, in this case."

I didn't expect that. Women don't talk like this where I grew up, but I guess New York is a whole other ball game.

"Oh really?" I'm keeping up this charade longer than I have any business to. "So you have everything you want in life, huh?"

She wets her lips briefly. "I do, in fact." Her eyes drift away from mine, an attempt to hide a lie.

I step closer and bend my neck a little so our eyes meet again. "You sure about that?"

She sucks in a noticeable breath, and when I realize I have her roped in—right the hell where any man would want a woman—I back up and turn away. Because I know a woman like her can be dangerous, and right now, I have one person I need to focus on. That's Lily.

Cam's drinking a beer alone when I move toward him.

"You struck out too? Didn't you flex your biceps or something? Or at least tell her you're a SEAL? Works like a charm for me. Women drop their panties when I mention that."

"Oh, and when did you become military?" I can't imagine

17

my pretty boy cousin ever even breaking a sweat, let alone shooting a gun in the desert.

"We're in New York, baby. I can be whoever I want to be on a night like this."

"Yeah, call me baby one more time."

He laughs and drinks more of his beer.

"And just a tip, most SEALs don't go around telling people who they are."

We live in the shadows like spooks in the CIA. Long hair, beards, it doesn't matter. We're designed to blend in. We're not like soldiers, and our wives can't talk about what we do, not that they're allowed to know much.

Well, I *was* living that life.

Past fucking tense.

"Anyway, I'm out of practice with this whole dating thing," I say and steal a quick glance at the woman at the bar.

She rubs the tip of her heel against the back of her slacks, which pulls the material up a little, the ankle strap of her heel briefly on display.

"Nah, it's just the type of women who hang out in this place. Rich and—"

"Classy," I finish for him as two women walk by. I'm not in the mood to defend Cam if a woman has the urge to knock him in the face with her three-carat diamond ring.

"Yeah, sure," he grumbles. "Can we please go back to Club Y?" Cam bumps his fist to my shoulder.

"You can go. I'm going to bed."

"It's eleven."

"Exactly. It's late."

I still get up at 5:00 a.m. to do drills. I run ten miles and work out before the sun even rises. I can't shake the routine, and I don't really feel like letting go. I'm not sure if I'm prepared to face the reality that I'm no longer military.

18

A *civilian*.

The word doesn't sound right. I roll it around in my mouth and taste the word almost every day, trying to absorb it into my system.

I'm still not there yet. I'm still a SEAL in my head. In my blood.

I start for the door, not wanting Cam to try to talk me into going to Club Yo-Yo, which should be the name, but I can't stop myself from getting one last glimpse of Miss Fourth of July.

A guy is approaching her, and I have some strange desire to go play interference, but when he kisses her cheek and motions toward a table, I realize they know each other. Of course a woman like that is taken. And the guy's probably wearing Armani.

But as she walks over to a table with him, she peers my way and our eyes connect. There's something between us— something I don't remember feeling for a long damn time.

But it doesn't matter. We're from two different worlds, and I'll never see her again.

2

GRACE

"I don't want to hear that. Get the job done or I'll find someone else!" I kick off my heels beneath the desk and wait for my contractor to respond.

"But the materials we ordered can't come in for two more weeks, ma'am, so—"

"That won't work. Sorry, Bill. I'll send you a check for the little work you've done, but you're fired." I end the call and lean back in my leather chair.

"Oh, thank God! The bitch is back." Rachel's walking toward me, carrying two cups. She sets my usual latte in front of me and slips into the seat on the other side of my desk. "I've missed you. The *real* you. You've been acting all crazy —you know, nice—for the last month or so since you came back from that trip. But it's you again. It's really you," she says with her typical exaggerated flair. "The Queen Bee."

"You're so fired."

I chuckle as Rachel holds up three fingers. This is the third time I've fired her as my personal assistant this month.

"You're lucky we're friends." I shake my head.

"And my friend is finally back. I hope this is goodbye to Miss Nice Girl." She sips her drink and winks at me.

I perk a brow. "How many other names do you have for me?"

She smiles. "Wouldn't you like to know. Now…who pissed you off?"

"The company I hired to redesign my loft." I reach for my coffee, needing the energy boost.

"Really? And I recommended them. Damn."

"I need someone to fix my place up soon. It's a mess. My friend, Jessica, got her home remodeled a few months ago, and it looks phenomenal. I should have gone with the company she suggested."

"Jessica Scott?"

"Yeah, why?"

"When you see her, please find out when her delicious brother, Luke, will be back in town. Maybe you can arrange for a little bump in between the two of us."

"And you know he's not the kind of guy to settle down."

She waves and is already back on her feet. "Did I say anything about settling down? Hell, a good roll in the hay with him would be just fine."

"A roll in the hay?" I chuckle.

"Luke's from Nashville—that accent just gives me the chills." She shakes her body a little as if shivers are darting through her.

"Anyway…"

Rachel pushes her red-rimmed glasses higher on her nose. "But what about you? How was your date last night? Patrick, right?"

I try not to smile as I think about my night.

"Oh. That good? I didn't think you'd enjoy a date your

21

father forced you to go on." Her eyes widen as she presses her palms on my desk and leans forward. "Well? Details."

God, if only it was Patrick I was thinking about and not the hot guy in the black tee who'd rendered me nearly speechless last night.

For some inexplicable reason, I can't get the man from the bar out of my head. The rich baritone of his voice, his incredible royal blue eyes, and his strong forearms—the veins slightly prominent. So much strength emanated from him, and some part of me wanted him to pull me into his arms and have his way with me last night.

He did in my head. Once in bed, then again in the shower this morning.

I must be losing my mind. Working way too much. Men don't make me self-combust from a few words and a couple of hot looks. They have to earn my desire, and it usually takes a long time. It's been so long I wonder if anything other than my vibrator will ever produce an orgasm again.

"Did you and Patrick sleep together?" Rachel pushes away from the desk and clasps her hands together. "I didn't see that coming."

I recoil in disgust, remembering Patrick in his Armani suit, and the words of my mystery man pop into my head. God, the sexy guy had me all wrong and yet right at the same time. "No. God no."

"Since you've been acting so strange lately, I wasn't sure."

I touch my stomach when I remember my trip last month to Athens. My eyes flash shut, my body growing tense as I sink back into my chair.

"Well, who're you thinking about that has your cheeks all red?"

I let go of my thoughts, pushing them away as I do every

time they creep up to strangle me. I open my eyes and release an exaggerated sigh while arching my shoulders back. "A stranger."

I can't help but wonder if Bar Guy is military. The way he stood with authority, the pensive look in his eyes—a look of a man who has witnessed a world of pain. I've never been with a soldier before, but there's something about the uniform and combat boots that's such a turn-on.

Of course, Dad would have a heart attack if I showed up to dinner with anyone in something other than a suit.

"No one dates Grace Parker-King without being worthy," my father likes to say, and by "worthy," he means uber rich.

And yes, my name is hyphenated. My parents joined their last names together on our birth certificates. It's obnoxious, I know. I should do what my brothers Cade and Corbin did and drop the Parker part of the name.

"Earth to Grace?" Rachel's at my side now, snapping her fingers in my face.

"What?"

"Who's this stranger who has your panties soaked right now?"

I stand, forgetting I'm not wearing my heels anymore, and I go around to the front of my desk. "Not your business."

"Since when? Come on, I know all your sordid past details."

"Sordid?" I laugh. "Sure. I'm about as vanilla as they come."

"Yeah, well, you're dying for a little kink. Hell, you need it."

Rachel is a bit wilder than me. And by wild, I mean she likes to get tied up and spanked. And for some godforsaken reason, she thinks I need to hear about it.

I elbow her in the ribs and smile. "Can you just call Jessica and get the name of that designer for me?"

"So I'm not fired?"

"Guess not."

"But first tell me who—" Rachel stops at the sight of dear ol' Dad in the doorway. "Mr. King."

She nods at my father and retreats from the office after a quick sympathy glance my way. I may be known as the Queen Bee, but Dad...well, he's the king, and the fact that his name is King only makes him think he's actually royalty. I'm waiting for the day when he has a red carpet installed in the hallway to his office.

He closes the door and shoves his hands into his pants pockets, and the way he eyes me suggests he's talked to Patrick. "Did you really have to knee him in the groin? Do you know who his father is?"

I roll my eyes.

Yeah, a duke. Patrick only told me twenty times, at least.

But he's also a Taylor.

"Well, the man still needs to take no for no."

"I'm sure you misunderstood his intentions. I think you should give him another chance. This is a good match for you."

Yes, sticking his tongue down my throat and trying for a second attempt after I told him no sounds super accidental.

I huff and head back to my desk. "Why would you want me dating the son of our number one competitor? Looking to steal some trade secrets?"

He doesn't say anything.

"He couldn't meet me until after eleven at night, and it was at some sketchy bar," I add. "Kind of weird, right?"

"He'd just gotten in from London, and he probably didn't want to be recognized by the media."

"The media?" I laugh. "Does he think he's Prince William or something?" *Give me a break.* "Maybe I can find my own dates from now on. Try some dating site. Millionaires dot com." I raise a brow when I look at him, and the man isn't smiling. Not even a little bit.

"You'll be thirty this summer. Time to start a family."

A family? Sure.

My dad's marriage is basically a sham. Arranged. And why shouldn't mine be, right? Because it would be a blast to live in a loveless marriage while my husband cheats on me with a different woman every month of the year. Miss January. Miss February. A bombshell blond for July because why not?

I don't know how my mom did it—hell, how she *still* does it. Maybe she has something on the side, too? If she does, she hides it a hell of a lot better than Dad.

"Do you have anything else you want to talk about? Maybe work related? The deal with Landon Enterprises has been finalized, and I was able to buy the property for under ten million." Hopefully I can shift his focus by talking about money. His one true love. Although twenty-year-olds with daddy issues are a close second.

"Good. And where are we on the Alexander & Sons deal?"

I shake my head. "No. I told you I'm not going to make a play for them. I'm friends with them, Dad. I sit on their charity board."

"And you can use your friendship to get us a better deal."

"Why are you so hell-bent on going after them?"

The Botox in his forehead is preventing him from showing any real emotion, but I can see the irritation in his eyes—his pupils expanding so large, engulfing the brown until his eyes look like frothy black jet fuel. "All that matters is that if you don't succeed, I'll have Cade take care of it. And he won't be as kind to your friends."

God, sometimes I really hate my job. We buy companies, rip them apart, and destroy lives all before an afternoon latte.

"And give Patrick another chance. That's not a request," he says over his shoulder before disappearing from my office.

The thought of letting Patrick anywhere near me again gives me the chills. But maybe my dad's right. There's a slight chance I overreacted to Patrick, but that's a microscopic maybe.

My stomach rumbles, and I realize I've forgotten to eat today. I touch my core and shut my eyes. Maybe it's not hunger pain. Maybe I'm just so sick and tired of this life that it's making me physically ill now.

What if I'd been born into another family? You know, had a normal childhood in a little house with a fence and a dog, with parents who were home for dinner at night. Got to choose my own boyfriends. Maybe my dad could've been cliché and threatened my date with a shotgun at the door on prom night.

Complaining about being rich—I know, I know. But I guess the grass really is always greener on the other side. Whoever came up with that slogan was dead-on.

Maybe Rachel's wrong—maybe the bitch in me died back in Athens last month.

3

GRACE

I SHOULD'VE BOUGHT A LOFT WITH AN ELEVATOR THAT OPENS right into the foyer. There are plenty of them in New York. What was I thinking when I got this place?

I drop my bag on the floor to search for my keys and glance over to see a pair of black loafers heading my way.

"You need help?"

There are two penthouses on my floor, and Evan owns the other one. The bastard is always hitting on me, even though he's married, and it makes me sick.

As I secure my keys, he touches my elbow and helps me rise to my feet. I need to make a quick retreat.

"I'm good." I smile at him, and he shoves his hands in his slacks pockets and angles his head.

I take note of the way he drags his gaze down my white blouse to my cream skirt, then back up again. Cheaters. Are all men lying cheats? Or just the men who have so much money they think they're God and can have whoever they please?

I should be numb to this shit by now. I'm definitely immune to the idea that true love exists—for me, at least.

"Good night. Tell your *wife*, Sarah, hello." Sarah's actually younger than me, even though Evan is pushing forty-five.

"Mm hm," he says while eyeing me once again. "Good night, Grace."

He nods and turns away after a moment, and I hastily shove my key in the lock and push the door open. I drop my purse on the table, lock up, and start down the hallway.

A splash of light shines beneath the door at the end of the hall. I swear I didn't leave anything on this morning.

I touch the knob, a slight tremble moving down my arm and to my hand as I think back to the hotel in Greece.

My stomach tightens and burns, and my pulse skates to a faster speed. I slowly twist the handle, but my mind is protesting, begging me to run. My body is stiff and my muscles taut.

Run!

I should've run that night in Athens. Why'd I open that door? Why am I opening this one?

I inhale a deep breath, holding it—and it's like the air in the room cocoons me and I can't exhale.

I'm expecting the worst. Athens, part two. Another incident.

But once the door is wide-open, I see a man crouched over a wooden beam on the floor, a tape measure in hand. The guy's shirtless. His tanned, muscled back has a slight sheen of sweat down his spine.

He's got to be part of the new remodel team I hired last weekend.

I bring a hand to my chest and try to calm down. To get my mind off Greece and back in New York.

"Who the hell are you?"

He's a carpenter, right? I just want confirmation.

My hand goes inside my purse, and I search for my phone just in case I need to call the cops.

The man releases his tape measure, and it retracts and snaps, falling with a thud to the floor. He slowly lifts his hands as if he can actually see me and I have a gun on him.

He rises to his feet. "Sorry. I work for Bella. She gave me the key." He turns toward me.

My lungs deflate as if they've been poked with a needle, and I'm losing oxygen fast. It's not because of Athens.

It's because it's…*him*.

Military Guy. Unless I'm wrong about him being military. I'm never wrong.

"You." His brows pull together, and his hands fall to his sides.

I remove my hand from my purse and drop the bag to the floor. I'm more comfortable now that I know the shirtless guy isn't some psychopath but in fact a construction worker.

But it's the hot guy from the bar, which is still pretty damn bad.

"You're Grace? I wasn't expecting—"

"And what were you expecting?" I fold my arms and remain standing just inside the living area. He's near the wall of windows overlooking the city on the other side of the room.

"I guess I pictured Grace as someone twice your age with a lot of cats." A sheepish grin sweeps across his face.

I open my palms and glance to the left then right. "Do you see any cats?"

His smile deepens.

"And does my name sound old?" Maybe it does. The hyphen doesn't help.

"Well, I don't think that anymore. Now looking at you—Grace fits."

I'm not sure what that's supposed to mean, and I don't bother to ask. I blink and try to figure out what the hell is going on.

"Are you stalking me?" I ask instead, though I know this must be crazy stupid luck that he's now remodeling my loft. Of the millions of people in the city…

He flashes me another quick smile, his white teeth a bright contrast to his sun-kissed skin. "No."

"So you work with Bella? But—well, why are you here at eight at night?"

I hired Bella Designs on Saturday after I spoke with Jessica last Friday, and Bella had managed to pull together beautiful plans within a few days. She must have had people in demoing during the week, but they'd kept it clean and tidy whenever they left. Props to Bella and her crew.

Or is he the crew? The only one doing all the work? He certainly looks strong enough to be.

"I'm surprised you'd so willingly give your key to a stranger. This is New York, after all."

I take a small step forward and hold out my hand. "Maybe I should have it back?" I cock my head, challenging him.

But Bella's a friend of Jessica's, and if Jessica says Bella is solid, then I trust her.

Shirtless guy, not so much.

"My sister said you wanted the job done ASAP, so I thought I'd put in some extra hours. I didn't think you were living here during the renovations."

"Sister? Bella's your sister?" I didn't see that one coming. They don't look anything alike. He's tall, crazy fit, with brownish-black hair and stunning deep blue eyes. His sister is five feet on a good day and a redhead.

"Yeah, she's my sister."

How is this happening? I've taken fantasizing to a whole new level this past week, and all my dirty thoughts have included this man now standing before me—because thinking about him is far better than remembering Greece.

And feeling scared and alone at night.

But I was never supposed to see him again. Dammit.

I steal a quick glimpse of the V starting above the top of his jeans. His body is carved in a way that can't be from only lifting weights. It's not bulky. It's, well…I don't have any word for it other than perfect.

There's a tattoo—or more like a collection of inked symbols near his left shoulder.

I clear my throat when he pats his hands on his jeans, wiping wood dust or dirt, whatever it may be, onto the faded denim. He's in front of me now, less than a foot away, and I can smell him. Pine, sweat, clean linen—it's not what I'm used to, and it's refreshing.

"I'm Noah." He extends his hand.

I look down at the strong forearm and slowly press my palm against his. He tightens his grip a little as he shakes my hand, then he lets go, and I turn away almost immediately and press my fingertips to the nape of my neck. My hair is in a bun at the back of my head, and it feels tight all of a sudden. I want to shake the mass free, but then he'd think I'm either practicing for an audition for a shampoo commercial or flirting.

"I appreciate your late hours, but maybe next time I could get some sort of warning that you'll be here." I face him again.

His eyes find mine, and I swallow. "Will do, ma'am. Should I go?"

"Um. Probably." I need to shower, and I'm not about to do that with him here.

He nods and goes to my couch, where he grabs a gray tee that's tossed over the back, and I can't help myself but watch, noting how his back muscles flex as he pulls on the shirt.

"How long have you been living here?" As he picks up the tape measure off the floor, my eyes trail along his backside.

When he faces me again, I feel heat in my cheeks as if he knows I'm guilty of having checked him out. He even cracks another smile.

Since when do I get embarrassed?

"Why do you ask?"

He approaches me again, which isn't a good idea because my reaction to his proximity is to take awkward steps away from him. What the hell is wrong with me?

He halts when I take my third backward step. "There aren't pictures on the walls or basically any signs of life here."

I look around the place. I saw potential when I bought it, but it's very nineties, with gold and brass everywhere. It at least has the wide, open-concept feel, but it needs some fresh white cabinets and some charm. "Well, that's why I hired your sister."

"Yeah, but I mean—the place is empty minus a few pieces of furniture."

"I have stuff crammed into the closets over there," I say, pointing toward the hall. "I moved in a year ago, but I work a lot. And I never eat at home, so…"

"Not even breakfast?"

I shake my head and regain some sense of brain functionality. "Wait, why am I explaining myself to you? It's late. You should get home."

"Whatever you say, boss." He winks and walks past me, brushing against my shoulder, and I know he does it on purpose.

I can't help myself—I need to know if I'm right, so I ask, "Are you military?"

He pauses but doesn't turn around. "I was."

"And you're not from New York, are you?"

There's a hint of Southern that drifts from his speech, but it's like a quick kiss caressing his words, rather than a deep love affair.

He faces me and smiles. "No, I'm definitely not from here."

I nod. "Okay." For some peculiar reason, I want to ask more, to know more about this man, but I stop myself. "So will you be here tomorrow?"

"Is that a problem?" He raises a brow.

"I have a date." I look at the semi-dirty hardwoods. "I don't know when I'll be home. But probably not too late. You can work until nine if you want. Anything to get the job done faster, I suppose."

I'm dreading the possibility of getting groped tomorrow for a second time by Sir Patrick, or whatever ridiculous name he goes by. I bet he has women call him Lord while they screw. Probably into the whole dominant-submissive thing. If I didn't hate the guy, I'd set him up with Rachel.

"The guy from the bar last week? He your boyfriend?"

So, Noah did pay attention to me even after he left me alone, huh?

When I look up, he's right in front of me, and I fight the urge to inhale, to breathe him in. "Mm. I think that's not your business."

But part of me wants to tell him no. Actually, I want to scream the word, then ask him to take me into the bedroom

33

and screw me until the sun comes up. But that's not the kind of thing a woman like me is supposed to think, let alone do. At least not with the guy who's fixing up my loft. Screwing the married man next door would be more acceptable in my social circle.

I need to look away, but I can't. His lips part, and I want to touch the stubble on his firm jaw or push away the dark lock that has fallen across his forehead. His hair is tapered on the sides, and a little longer on top—definitely not the quintessential military cut. I wonder how long he's been out of the military.

"Good night, Miss Par—"

"You can call me Grace." I don't want to hear my mouthful of a last name from him. I don't want to be that person to him. I'm not sure why, but I don't.

He nods. "Well, good night then, Grace."

Once I hear the front door close, I rush down the hall and bolt the locks, plus the new one I had installed last month. I only use that one when I'm home. I lean my back against the door and lower my head, trying to reel in my insanity.

It's been too long since I've had amazing sex. You know, sex with a guy who actually cares if I get off, and he's not just in it for himself. That has to be why I'm having such a strange, below-the-belly reaction to this man.

Most men I date are like racehorses. Quick in bed, always galloping toward the finish line, and to top it off, they aren't even Kentucky Derby one-hit wonders. They never get the G-spot, and they don't even try. Users. They take and don't give.

But Noah—that man looks like he gives…and a lot.

When I make my way back into the living room, I can still smell his cologne. Although I doubt he was wearing any. I think that's just him. All natural.

I suck in a deep breath and hold on to my desire for one more moment, knowing it can't last. One moment is all I have. The need to feel something deep, or even enjoyable, is off-limits for me.

4

NOAH

New York City. Truly the city that never sleeps.

I breeze past couples lingering on the streets outside bars. I take in the city lights that glow around me like some giant orb. And I give away the few bucks I have to some of the homeless I see as I walk.

When I first came to this city, I barely noticed a thing about it. I didn't want to pay attention or learn a damn thing. I never wanted this to be *my* city. But I'm beginning to realize I'm not going anywhere. If I don't try to embrace my new home, how the hell will I ever make it work for Lily?

And if I can survive the Middle East, I can surely grit my teeth and learn to live in a city so big that it almost feels small —as though it's closing in on me. I'm inside a pressure cooker, and I'm gonna pop. There are just so many people every place I turn that in some weird way I end up feeling alone because almost everyone's a stranger.

When I was a SEAL, I felt at home on the ship. I love being surrounded by water and nothing else. It's soothing. Peaceful. That's probably why I sold everything I owned and bought the boat. And when Bella told me our friend Jessica could rent me her dock slip on the Hudson for cheap, well, it was damn near perfect. A piece of home in the unknown city.

I shake my head as I wonder if Cindy is right about me. Did I put Cindy and Lily second when I was in the Navy? Did I not call enough? When we were together, did I not make it clear I loved them? Shouldn't they have felt like home to me? Lily always did, but Cindy…now I find myself questioning everything.

We were so wrong together, it kind of makes me sick that we spent thirteen years living a lie. But Lily is the saving grace of it all.

My mind drags up memories, and I flip through them like some old-school Rolodex.

Page by page of photos. And that's what so many of my memories are—pictures. Snapshots Cindy sent me. Birthday parties and such I couldn't be at.

Guilt stabs me in the chest. I want to blame Cindy and not feel this maddening pain, but every day that goes by that I'm alone makes me wonder if this is all my fault.

I drove Cindy into the arms of another man. I did that, didn't I?

I was always gone on assignments.

I clench my hand into a fist at my side as I continue down the street—finding myself heading toward my daughter's. It's late. She'll be asleep. But I can't seem to stop myself.

After I left Grace's loft, I had been halfway through my first beer at a nearby bar when I decided to go walk the city.

I weave around people on the crowded streets and dodge a group of tourists snapping photos of the Empire State building as Grace comes to mind. I never thought I'd see that woman again in my life, and now I'm remodeling her apartment to try to make enough money to rent a nice place.

Grace isn't just rich like I'd thought when I met her last

Thursday. The woman's a damn multimillionaire. But tonight, when we talked, she looked like another person who is lost and alone in this big city.

As alone as me.

New York becomes a blur as I continue to walk, and before I know it, I'm standing at Cindy's door. I tap a couple of times, not wanting to wake up Lily.

The door cracks open, and Cindy's eyes are blazing—anger simmering hot beneath her tan skin. "What are you doing here? Will is inside."

Maybe tonight's as good as any to finally look in the eyes the guy who stole my wife from me.

"I want to see Lily." I press my hand to the wall outside the door, and she shakes her head immediately.

"She's asleep," she hisses.

"I know. I just want to look at her. Kiss her good night." I step back and swipe my hand over my head.

"No. You need to leave."

"I'm her father. You're treating me like I'm some goddamn convict on parole." The anger in my voice is like a flare, running hot, and I hope I singe off what's left of her barely-there eyebrows.

She's had plastic surgery—a major breast enhancement, among other things. I had loved her for who she was, but the woman she's become in the last year—she's completely unrecognizable.

"When we're divorced, all of this 'Sunday only' bullshit ends. I've given you far more say about custody than I ever needed to, and that's only because I was still in the military at the start of all of this."

I have a bad feeling in my stomach, worried she's been playing me since I arrived in New York.

"She's not staying on that boat."

38

"That's temporary." Although I'll miss the thing. I need to be near water as much as I need air to breathe.

"The divorce is in a few weeks. We'll discuss this then. Please go." She starts to shut the door in my face, and my hand darts between it and the frame, stopping her. Her green eyes widen. "Go. I can smell booze on your breath. I don't want to mention that in court, but—"

My heart nearly stops, and I step back, my outstretched hand falling to my side. What the hell is she talking about? "I had a beer. Where're you going with this?"

I'm rattled now. I can feel it. Like a slow storm gathering, it's about to tear everything apart, leaving nothing in its wake. I remember the squalls on the ocean when we'd be out on the ship. The sky would grow dark. Everything so still. I loved that moment between the calm and the storm. I think I'm still living inside that moment now. Stuck. Cindy has me fucking trapped.

When she doesn't speak, I add, "And what is there to talk about in court? I thought we already agreed to everything."

She opens the door and joins me in the hall. Once the door is closed, she stands before me with crossed arms. "Noah, I think we need to change our custody terms. Joint custody is no longer a good idea."

My fingers bite into my palms as I replay what she just said to me in my head. I couldn't have possibly heard her right. "What the hell are you talking about?" I heave out a breath. "You cheated. Do you not remember that? You screwed up in the marriage. If anyone should get Lily—" I stop myself. I don't want to put my daughter in the middle of a fight.

I see a flicker of something in Cindy's eyes as she lifts her chin and finds my eyes. She knows that I'll do what I can to keep Lily safe. That's what I do. Well, what I did. I kept people safe. I fought the enemies so everyone else could sleep soundly.

"I moved here. I helped you get the court jurisdiction changed from Virginia to New York. I have been a fucking saint in all of this. And you're going to drop this on me?" I rasp. "What's the real reason you're doing this?"

"Things have changed." Cindy's hand dips down to her abdomen. "I'm pregnant. Will and I are getting married as soon as we can. We want to start our family the right way. He wants to adopt Lily. He wants her to have his name. This is your chance—go back into the Navy. Be the man you love. Let us go."

I can't even open my mouth.

My lips curl in disgust as I turn away and lower my forehead against my palm. I'm starting to sweat and struggling to keep cool. I can't give in to the anger slicing me open. I can't bleed all over this goddamn expensive carpet.

But the woman has cut me deeper than I thought possible.

"No." I face her, the blood in my veins going from hot to subzero temperatures. "Absolutely not."

"If you want to hurt Lily, then resist. But you'll lose. You don't have the kind of money you'll need to fight me in court. And once you've spent every dime you have you won't even have a boat to sleep on." She swallows, her face so tight I can't see emotion there.

"What happened to you? What did I do to make you hate me so much?" It can't just be the SEALs, can it? Or has this cold-hearted woman always lurked beneath the surface?

"*You*. I was chained to you. To your life. To the military." Her hand slips from her stomach to her heart, and she grits her teeth as she tips her chin up and finds my eyes. "I'm finally free. Will can give Lily an amazing life. Don't try to

SOMEONE LIKE YOU

screw up hers the way you ruined mine." She turns away and opens the door.

"Giving you Lily—was that how I ruined your life?"

She looks over her shoulder at me, her once-sparkling forest-green eyes now dull. "Lily is mine…I'll see you in court."

I'm damn near ready to explode, but I check my impulse to yell. "I'll see you Sunday, you mean."

She tucks herself back inside her home and starts to close the door. "No, you won't."

When she slams the door shut in my face, I raise my fist, prepared to pound the dark wood until she talks to me again.

I have to see my daughter. She's all I have. She's my light in this fucked up world, and I can't lose her. But when I picture her sweet little face and her big green eyes, the way she looks at me with such pride, I drop my arm.

I've got to think tactically. I've got to get Lily back using the best way I know how.

I don't want to do it, but Lily's my daughter, so I've got to go to war.

5

GRACE

I can't stop staring at his mouth.

Thin lips. Not kissable at all. A ski slope for a nose and eyes that are like cheap brandy. Every time he takes a tiny sip from his wine glass or takes small bites of his perfectly chopped salad with barely any dressing, I have the urge to throw my steak at him.

Normally I wouldn't pick apart someone's looks, but Patrick has me on edge. It probably has more to do with the fact that I can already see my father preparing our vows.

"So what do you think?"

"About what?" I raise a brow and reach for my wine glass, hoping to dull the boredom from this dinner with the Riesling.

"We were talking about my castle in London. Will you visit? There's even a dungeon."

"Ah, no." Wow, I must have dozed off somewhere between the explanation of his ancestral heritage and his love for cricket if I missed the castle conversation. "Does that get women to drop their, how do you say it, 'knickers' for you?"

I can't bite my freaking tongue tonight. It's as if my feisty grandmother has taken over my body and is possessing me.

God, I miss her. The only real person who ever lived in my family. That woman would tell it like it was. My dad says I'm just like his mom as if that's supposed to be an insult. But he hates her, so…

"Well, I'd love for you to drop yours for me—after dinner."

The douchebag winks at me. No damn joke. I'm not kidding. Then he sips his wine and motions for the check. Since when did it become okay for men to act like this?

I tip my head and set down my glass. "Do you want another knee to the groin?"

He clears his throat. "Maybe I like it rough."

Shit, I knew it. He's into floggers and spanking.

I press my palms onto the white linen tablecloth, trying to calm the sudden anger that's built up inside me after years of dealing with pricks.

But I can't stop myself. I can't reel in the fury. "Can we cut the bullshit? Let's stop pretending we're interested in each other and just tell our fathers to go to hell." Being set up with him doesn't make any sense, even if I was remotely attracted to him, which I'm not.

"You really think that's a good idea?" Patrick laughs—an annoyingly haughty one—and slides his hands to his lap as his eyes remain on mine. There's a hint of evil glinting in his dark irises. Maybe I was right to knee him that first night.

"The first date was a courtesy, and this one was a pity date. Consider it the last, though."

"I wouldn't be so sure about that," he says coolly as I rise to my feet.

I politely respond, "Have a nice flight back to London."

I leave before he has a chance to say anything else, and

43

when the warm night air sweeps across my face as I step outside, God, I feel on fire.

A real smile pulls at the edges of my mouth when my driver opens the back door for me at the curb. "Take me home, Frank. Please."

"How was your date?" He looks at me in the rearview mirror.

"Great, actually. Especially the end." I bite my lip and tip my head back, shutting my eyes and relishing in the small win I had tonight.

I, Grace Parker—screw the King—stood up for myself tonight. By turning down that asswipe, I stood up to my father. And God, it was amazing. Incredible. I kind of want to go bungee jumping, skydiving, or maybe have sex with a stranger.

Maybe Noah.

I touch my purse that's resting on my thighs. I'm waiting for the vibration of my phone—to hear from my father and get a lecture about my so-called behavior.

But no calls or messages yet.

Maybe Patrick's balls have shrunk to raisins, and he's packed them away for his flight home.

"Any weekend plans?" Frank asks me once we pull up in front of my building.

"A couple. You?"

"My granddaughter will be in town, so I'm hoping to see her when I get off work tomorrow."

I smile when he opens the door for me. "Frank, you should have asked me to take the weekend off." I shake my head at him. "Consider it off as of now."

"And how will you get around the city?"

"I do have a car. I'll be okay. Really."

Frank's eyes are still vibrant despite his late age. He's

always been sweet and kind to me—fatherly. He could offer my dad a few words of advice. "Thank you."

"Of course."

I nod goodbye, swipe my key fob at the side of the entrance, and smile at the security guard inside. I gave both a fob and key to Bella when I hired her company, and I can't help but wonder if Noah's still working.

The elevator doors start to close behind me, but a hand darts between them, and I almost drop my phone as I take a fast step back. My heart flutters, worry spreading through me, my body signaling danger…but I look up and find myself staring into the eyes of a man who can see inside me—to the hidden parts I never want anyone to see. Noah sees me, and it makes me want to bring my hands to my chest to protect my vulnerabilities.

"I didn't mean to startle you, sorry." He steps inside.

It's not until the doors close behind him that I remember to breathe. And when I do, I smell him. He smells like the ocean, a little salty with a touch of dark rum.

"Wh-what are you doing?"

He cocks his head to the side a little as his eyes dart to my lips, and I swallow. "I left my phone in your apartment. I was on my way out and realized I forgot it. I didn't expect you back this early."

He eyes the watch on his wrist. It's thick, black, and looks like something that could double as a compass if lost at sea.

Is he lost? He kind of looks out of place in this city. Rugged. Sexy. Like he belongs in a cabin in the mountains, chopping wood outside in the cold winters.

Heat floods my system as I imagine this gorgeous man making a fire, the sparks flickering before his face, casting a glow over his features.

We're on my floor already. When did that happen? And

he's standing between the parted elevator doors, allowing me exit. He walks alongside me down the hall, and I look at his strong forearm out of the corner of my eye as we approach my door.

"Your date has poor manners."

I face him as I dig inside my purse for my keys, but I notice he's already produced his and has it in the lock. I nod my thanks as he opens the door.

"The guy should've walked you to your door, don't you think? Or is that not a New York kind of thing to do?" His smile stretches. It's a beautiful smile. It reaches his eyes and even touches my heart.

My heart still works. I wasn't sure of that until now.

The beating is like a drum in my chest, and the pace quickens, finding my ears.

So loud.

What is it about this man? Maybe I'm embarrassed because I feel as though he knows my dirty little secret, that he can tell I've fantasized about him screwing me every which way.

"I think manners should be in style in any city." I shrug, hoping the gesture will also help me remove this weight from my shoulders, this burning intensity of desire that has taken me by storm since I first spoke with him at that bar. "But…I kind of ditched him at dinner."

I walk past Noah and continue down the hall, feeling his eyes on me. It feels good. I only wish I was in something sexier than black slacks and a red blouse. But I wasn't aiming for sexy on my date with Patrick. I flick on the lights and kick off my red heels once I'm in the living area and turn to face him.

"That bad, huh?"

My jaw tightens as I contemplate how much I want to

divulge. There's some compulsive need inside me to open up to this stranger. "That bad."

I drop my purse on the floor and wrap a hand around the back of my neck as he grabs his cell phone off the kitchen island. I need to schedule an appointment with my masseuse. I haven't seen her since I got back from Athens.

"I should get out of your hair, I guess." He shoves his phone in his back jeans pocket.

"You don't have to do that."

"Do what?" His brows draw together.

"Leave." The word floats from my mouth and through the air. It feels like it takes forever to reach him, for him to process that tiny word.

He raises a fist to his mouth and taps it once. "Okay. Uh, you have anything to drink?"

"I think I have beer in the fridge."

He nods, and once he turns away, I let out a small breath. I bow my head a little, trying to figure out what I'm doing right now.

Why did I ask him to stay?

I don't want to be alone. I hate being alone now. The memories and darkness wrap around my throat, strangling me, and I can't breathe.

I can breathe around him, though. Maybe a little too much, because I'm becoming light-headed. My attraction to him has taken me completely off guard.

"I didn't take you for a Corona kind of woman."

When I look up, he's popping off the tops with a pocket knife. I don't think I've ever dated a guy who carries around a mini blade.

I'm not dating him, though. Jesus…

And yet, I want those strong hands of his to cover every inch of my body.

Are my cheeks red right now? I need to cool off, to relieve this pressure building inside my stomach and teasing between my thighs.

"Why can't I drink beer?" I finally respond after what feels like an eternity of silence spearing the room.

"Well, you were drinking a martini the first night I met you."

I take the Corona and grasp the cold bottle, hoping that simply holding it will help lower my temperature a little. I actually don't like beer. It's only in my fridge because Rachel was here the other night and she likes the stuff. But I'm stubborn and don't want to tell him he's right about me.

He positions himself across from me, mimicking my stance by leaning against the other counter. He's maybe two feet away, and it becomes a challenge to not drink in the sight of him. His skin is bronzed, and I'm betting he didn't earn that color by lounging by pools or lying in a tanning booth.

He has a straight nose, great bone structure with a strong chin, and a beard coming in.

I think back to that tattoo of his—wanting to take off his shirt and study it.

A tingling heat wraps around my limbs as I watch his throat as he swallows.

Noah folds his arms across his chest, the bottle resting against his bicep, and I force my gaze to remain on his face instead of memorizing his sculpted arms.

Who am I kidding? I cataloged every inch of him the other night. His body is stored in a permanent file in my brain, and I have no intention of deleting it.

"So, you remember what I was drinking, huh?" I set down my beer and toy with the pearl strands on my neck.

He grins and taps his temple. "Steel trap. I remember everything."

I smile back but feel a tightness in my chest. Desire.

I push away from the counter and go to the wall of windows, stepping over the construction materials, careful not to hurt my bare feet. The place is a bit of a mess now, but it's starting to come together. He's building a bookshelf on one of the walls surrounding the fireplace. Plus, he's altering a few other things in the living area. Next, he'll be ripping apart the kitchen. I need something lighter—fresher.

My arms slide up and across my chest, a coldness emerging inside me as I gaze out at the city. "Where do you live?"

I've never had an issue with small talk before, but for some reason, I can't figure out what to say to this man. Maybe the memory of our first meeting is still in my mind—when he told me I wasn't his type. I mean, he's not allowed to be my type. And he's remodeling my house, so why his rejection bothers me is beyond me.

Noah is standing next to me now, and he touches the window with his index finger, pointing toward something. "I live on the Hudson."

"But homes there are expen—" I stop myself, not wanting to sound like a bitch.

"I live on a boat at the docks."

Goose bumps cover my arms at his words. "I hate the water," I say, without thinking first.

"Really?" He takes a swig of his beer as our eyes connect in the window. "Why?"

"Um." Why did I have to open my mouth? I don't tell people this about me. I always use excuses to back out of any plans that involve lakes, rivers, or oceans. I'm not supposed to have weaknesses. I'm a Parker-King.

"You're afraid of water or…?" He's giving me the chance

to finish, to share, but I hesitate and take a couple of steps back.

"I don't like the unknown," I say softly. "I hate not being able to see what lies beneath the surface."

It's the truth. A watered-down version of the truth.

"Hmm." His palm touches the window as his bottle rests against the side of his jeaned thigh. "Sometimes what's beneath the surface is worth getting to know."

I stare out the window and off into the distance. The moon falls like a soft glow over the city—and I'd almost swear the light finds him too.

"But sometimes what's beneath the surface is ugly," he adds in a deep voice, emotion threading his words.

It's hard for me to believe this tough guy has been hurt before, but there's a definite pain there, and I don't think it's from his time in the military.

"Do you think it's worth the risk, though?"

Noah takes a drink and turns to face me. "Sometimes."

He angles his head and closes the small gap between us.

I feel awkward. I don't know what to do with my hands or how to stand. These aren't feelings I'm accustomed to. I'm self-assured and confident.

Except that when my life flashed before my eyes in that hotel in Athens, I realized I don't have a damn clue who I am, only who I've been pretending to be for twenty-nine years.

"Were you a Marine?" I need to change the topic. I barely know this man, and somehow I think we just drifted into deep territory that neither of us was prepared for.

Noah scrubs a hand down his jaw. We're standing in front of each other like two teenagers waiting for the other to make the first move. But that's ridiculous, because we don't know each other, and whatever I'm feeling for this guy is purely physical. And maybe he doesn't even have any interest in me. Maybe he wasn't lying when he said I wasn't his type.

"I was a SEAL," he says at last.

"Really?" A grin sneaks up on me. "You guys are kind of badass, or so I hear."

His mouth broadens into a deep smile. "Only kind of?"

Part of me wants to slip my hands up his chest because that feels like the natural thing to do.

There's this tight band of tension between us, and I take a breath and release it as I wait for that tension to snap.

Is he going to kiss me?

His eyes are on my lips, and I instinctively wet them. The muscles in my stomach tighten as I find my gaze steadying on his mouth. The dark scruff around his lips—he has that sexy kind of dangerous look…but I can tell this man is only dangerous because he's forbidden.

I close my eyes and wait. I want to be someone else right now. Someone who is allowed to feel something real.

At the sound of Noah clearing his throat, my eyelids flutter open and my cheeks warm.

"Shit."

Not the word I was expecting.

"I'm supposed to be somewhere in an hour. I almost forgot." He looks down at his clothes. "I better go get cleaned up first."

I don't totally lose my mind and offer to let him shower here. But that'd be an amazing sight to see, right? This guy's rippled flesh as water glides over his muscles and down to between his hard thighs.

I blink the images from my mind and force a nod. "Okay. Well, I guess you'll be back on Monday?"

He glances around the apartment. "Yeah. I'll probably be able to start on the kitchen by Wednesday."

This is good. We're talking about the real reason why he's here. I need to get my head screwed back on straight.

"You've done a great job so far," I say when I look at the bookshelves, which he's hand-carved. "Impressive."

Maybe I'll even buy some books and start reading again. It's been years since I've read anything other than business journals or annual reports.

"Thanks. I mentioned to Bella you're living here during the remodel, but she was wondering if when we're almost done in a few weeks, you could spend a couple of nights out. She wants to do a big reveal with the decorations, but it's obviously up to you."

I smile. "Sure. I think I can handle that. Just let me know when you need to kick me out."

He nods and starts to swivel on his heel to turn, but he stops. "You want to come out? You're friends with Jessica and Luke Scott, right? They recommended my sis for the job, I think. Well, we're meeting up with them if you'd like to come."

I was planning on seeing them this weekend anyway, I rationalize. Wanting to go tonight has nothing to do with the fact I want to spend a little more time with Noah. And that I don't want to be alone.

"Sure. Where?"

He smiles. "My sister said she'll be texting me the address right before. She's being a little weird about it. I'm hoping she's not planning something for my birthday."

My mouth goes round in surprise. "Today is your birthday?"

"Yeah." He shrugs. "And this is the first birthday I'll have spent stateside in years, so I have a feeling Bella is up to something."

"Wow."

He waves dismissively. "It's no big deal. But, uh, if you want to stay with me—I just need to go shower and change, then we can go together." He smiles. "I promise I'm safe."

Yeah, I'll take my chances with a SEAL over being alone in New York any day.

My lip catches between my teeth as I find myself staring at him again. At his arms now. "Let me just throw on something a little more fun."

6

NOAH

THIS WAS SUPPOSED TO BE MY FIRST BIRTHDAY WITH LILY.

I've been home for one of hers and two of Cindy's since Lily was born. None of mine, though. And to be honest, I couldn't give a fuck about my birthday. It just means another year older. But it would have been nice to spend it with my daughter.

Thirty-two years on this planet. Almost half of them spent with a woman who is now getting married to a rich broker.

But if it weren't for Cindy, I wouldn't have Lily.

And now who knows what will happen since Cindy and I will be battling in court…I have to win, though. Any other option is unacceptable.

My phone vibrates, alerting me to a message. Bella's texted me the address, although she didn't mention the name of the place we're going to. If it's some crazy club like Cam dragged me to, that would be why she's leaving that info out.

I tap my thighs as I wait for Grace to come out of her bedroom. I have no idea what possessed me to invite her tonight. I'm not ready to date again. And even if I were, it wouldn't be with someone like her.

Okay, so I shouldn't hold it against her that she's insanely rich, but the idea of the two of us ever becoming anything is more than a stretch of the imagination.

There's tension, though. I've felt it since the moment I was drawn to her at the bar. She's gorgeous, no denying. And although we haven't spoken much, I can feel she's layered. And intense. There's a lot more to her than looks and money.

But I seriously doubt she's the kind of woman who'd let a man like me screw her and that's it. Because that's all I have to offer.

When I look up from the hardwood, Grace is standing in the doorway of her bedroom.

She's in nude heels, and my gaze glides up from her slender ankles, over her tan and toned legs, to the hem of her cream dress. It's sleek and classy and sexy as fuck. It's strapless, showcasing the curves of her breasts like a cherry perched on a sundae—she's utterly perfect.

Her hair is down now. It's like silk, brownish-blond and wavy, falling over her shoulders. She looks like she belongs at the beach—she just needs to lose that dress.

She's unbelievable.

And out of my fucking league.

I clear my throat and look away for a moment, hoping to still my sudden hard-on. I don't normally go balls-out, full-on crazy about a woman from just a glimpse of her in a dress.

She moves toward me, and when I drag my gaze back up, I find her eyes practically glowing. It's probably due to the touch of glittery eyeshadow she's now wearing, and it gives her an otherworldly look, like a princess from the fairy tale book I read Lily last week.

Lily.

My daughter—the number one reason I can't fuck up my

focus. She's all that matters. My cock needs to stay inside my pants and away from women right now.

"Is this okay? I didn't know how to dress since I don't know where we're going," she says softly, and she looks so much more fragile than before.

"I think you could wear anything and look perfect." I can't even lie to this woman. She's the kind of woman who can see through bullshit, so why not be honest? Why play games? I wasted too much of my life being with someone who was wearing a coat of lies—the truth is freeing.

"Thank you." A touch of red slips up to her cheeks and the innocence is captivating, especially on such a powerful woman. It makes me almost forget that we're from two different worlds.

Almost.

"I better hurry and get changed too. I got the address from Bella. I don't know the name of the place, but it's only a few blocks from my boat."

"Okay. Uh, you sure you don't mind me coming with you?"

"I wouldn't have asked if I did." I smile. "Let's go."

She's holding a small silver clutch, and I extend my arm, motioning for her to walk ahead. When we reach the street, I hail a taxi, and neither of us speaks until we're tucked inside.

"Have you always lived in New York?" I ask.

She peers out the window for a moment, then her eyes catch mine when she looks my way. "I spent most of my life at a boarding school in Switzerland."

"Are you shitting me?" I don't know why I find this hard to believe, but I can't imagine that parents really send their kids off to be taught by foreigners.

She tucks a strand of hair behind her right ear, and I see a large diamond stud there.

"That explains your lack of an accent." I wink at her.

"My accent?"

"You don't sound like a New Yorker." I press my palms to my jeans as my eyes focus on the edge of her dress, which has slipped higher since we're in the backseat of the taxi. I wonder if she's a runner.

"Well, of the two of us, you have the accent."

I should look her in the eyes now. "I guess even being overseas the last decade didn't kill the Southern in me."

"Does that go for all things?" She turns to fully face me, her shoulder brushing mine as she does so.

"Which would be?"

She wets her lips. "Being a gentleman. Having manners. Country music. Sweet tea and kindness…"

I grin. "Oh? Stereotypes?"

"Mm. So those things aren't true? Damn."

This woman is night-and-day different from when I met her at that stuffy bar. Maybe she was on edge that night. Maybe this is who she really is—or maybe I'm getting played again. I'm too out of practice, and I'm not exactly trusting of the opposite sex after Cindy.

But what does it matter? I work for this woman. End of story. Period.

"I do listen to country, but I don't drink sweet tea. And although I have a sailor's mouth, I try my best to be polite," I finally answer.

"Do you have a cowboy hat and boots?"

I shake my head. "I'm from Tennessee, not the Wild West."

Her mouth opens, and a gorgeous smile sweeps across her face. She lowers her head a little, looking up at me from hooded eyes. Does she have any idea how damn sexy she looks right now? For a moment, I almost think we're two strangers sharing a cab ride. Two normal people who don't come with pasts. Although I don't know what hers is, I'm betting it's interesting.

"What?" I'm smiling now. It's contagious.

She takes a deep breath, and I watch as her chest rises, the swell of her flesh moving as she releases a lungful of air. Then she looks down at her lap as if embarrassed. "Nothing."

"Oh, come on. It's my birthday. You can't leave a man hanging like this."

We roll up to the curb near the entrance to the docks, and she looks over her shoulder at me as she reaches for the door handle. "I just think the cowboy thing is too bad."

Her smooth voice has the hairs on the back of my neck on end. "Let me. I gotta keep up with the rep of a Southern gentleman and all." I grin and get out of the car.

I offer her my hand once I've opened the door, and her face is radiant as she looks up at me when rising out of the car. Maybe it's the way the light from the street lamp is pouring over us, enveloping her as though she's beneath the spotlight on a runway—but to me, she looks like an angel. A beautiful and perfect creature, and it takes my fucking breath away.

I press a fist to my mouth and fake a cough, stepping back from her on the sidewalk.

I can take down a target with a sniper rifle—no problem.

I can choke out a group of terrorists from a cell in under two minutes.

But talk to a woman like Grace?

Well, shit, I'm in uncharted territory. And she thought I was playing some game at the bar that night. Yeah, sure.

I take note of how her eyes have settled over my shoulder, observing the Hudson. There's a tepidness to her now and in the way she stands; her shoulders have dropped into a sloping line. "You okay to walk on the dock?"

"As long as you don't go throwing me in the water, I'll be okay," she says, but her voice falters a little.

Bringing her here might have been a mistake. "Here."

I'm probably nuts, but I hold my hand out, offering it to her. She looks at my open palm as if unsure, then she finally allows me to tighten my hand over hers. We don't lace fingers —this isn't meant to be romantic—yet as I walk her to my boat, I can't help but feel some strange pull of emotions travel up my arm and splinter throughout my body.

"This is me," I say once we reach my boat.

"It's nice."

She's probably being polite. The speed boat is small, and not only is it not, in fact, speedy, it barely moves. I had to have someone deliver it to the docks. The navy-blue paint is chipping, the color faded…some of the wood is rotting.

I shouldn't have bought it, but I guess living on a boat reminded me of being a SEAL.

"Who's Madeline?" She points at the name in white cursive on the side of the boat.

"The previous owner's late wife. He wanted the boat to go to a good home, and I promised I'd fix it up, but now—" I stop myself.

"Now what?" She looks at me.

I glance at our clasped hands, realizing I'm still holding on to her as if it's the natural thing to do. I should let go, but I can't seem to bring myself to do it.

"I need to sell it soon so I can rent an apartment."

"If you love living by the water, why move?"

"I—"

She shakes her head. "Sorry. Not my business."

I clear my throat. "Okay. Well, you ready to come on board?"

Her hand leaves mine, and she steps back, folding her arms across her chest. Her clutch presses tightly against her breasts. Her lower lip has the slightest tremble, something most people wouldn't notice, but I've been trained to notice any little change in people. I've interrogated some of the sickest fucks in the world. I can practically see the tick of her pulse in her neck climbing up, and even if my eyes were closed, I'd hear the change in her breathing.

"I'm so sorry." I rest my hands on both her forearms to calm her down.

Startled, she tips her chin up and looks me in the eyes.

"I should have never brought you near the water, but I also don't want to leave you on the docks while I jump in the shower, so—maybe I'll just go out smelling like sweat and remain covered in dust."

A small smile slips across her face. "No, I think the man of the hour should at least show up to his own party clean." She chuckles a little, and the sound fills my ears and makes my heartbeat bump up a notch.

My hands move up her biceps, and I'm so close to her that my body is almost flush against her chest. "What if you go below deck?" I have to look down at her to see her eyes, to get a read on her level of comfort. "Would you feel better if you didn't see the water?"

Do I sound like some creepy psychopath inviting her into a basement? Jesus.

"I think I can do that." She nods, and I release her and step back.

"Take my hand."

"Mind if I keep my eyes closed and you guide me? I—" She swallows. "I guess I can trust you since you offered to lay your life down for this country as a SEAL. I think what you guys do is amazing."

Her brows pinch together, and I swallow as I note the subtle change in her. She's focused on me now, not the water. If it's easier for her to come on board, then she can picture me naked if she'd like. Hey, whatever helps.

"Well, I don't serve anymore, so—" My jaw tightens, my body tensing a little.

"Once military, always military, right?"

I bow my head and look at her free hand. "Yeah, I guess."

I hold my palm up, then she closes her eyes and her shoulders relax, as I guide her onto the boat.

"Two more steps to the stairs," I say while watching her navigate the deck in her heels, relying only on my hand and the sound of my voice.

She opens her eyes once we reach the tiny downstairs of the boat, and I flick on the sole light in the room. "You're a good leader. I didn't even trip once."

The way she's looking at me has my dick standing on alert. Her eyes are laser-focused on mine, and we're standing in the small space at the base of the short set of stairs, so close together that I can almost hear her heart beating.

Then she takes a step back, breaking her hold, and looks around the cabin. There's not much to see. A stove, fridge, and well, the bed occupies most of the space.

She glances at the plaid bedspread, which looks like something from the eighties. Her gaze falls back on my face a moment later, and she nods at the door off to the side of the steps. "Bathroom?"

"Yeah, let me just grab some clothes, and I'll be in and out fast. Make yourself comfortable."

And there goes my dick again as I watch her sit on the edge of my bed, her dress sliding up to show her toned thighs.

I bet she could wrap herself around my hips and hold herself there just with the strength of those killer legs.

I clear my throat, grab some black slacks and a tee, and go into the bathroom. I don't normally wear anything other than jeans, but I'll be going out with Grace at my side. I guess I need to upgrade my wardrobe somewhat for the evening.

I strip out of my clothes and toss them on the floor in the bathroom then turn on the water. My hand darts up to the wall to hold up my weight as I lower my head, the cool water crashing over me.

After five minutes and an attempt to get dressed and ready quickly in the tight space, my large frame bumping against the walls as I pull on my slacks, I exit the bathroom and find Grace standing in front of the bed. All I want to do is pin her down and see how good she tastes. I'd press my mouth to the inside of her thigh and work my way up.

No, scratch that. I'd start on the inside of her calves and take my time. She's the kind of woman who deserves every ounce of a man's attention.

"You clean up nice." A smile lights up her face.

If I were in the desert, I'd swear the woman was a mirage. "Thanks."

"You like jazz?" She's holding one of my vintage vinyl as she glances at the record player on my small kitchen table. It basically occupies the entire table, but it's too important to me to store.

"My mother was a singer when she was younger. Jazz. Blues. All that good stuff. She got me into the music." I grab my loafers from under the bed, my makeshift shoe storage. My sister made me buy them last weekend for such occasions because my flip-flops, sneakers, and boots weren't cutting it. Cam ratted on me after our trip to Club Y, and I decided I'd rather buy some shoes than get another earful from Bella.

"Miles Davis is great. 'Blue in Green' is one of my favorites."

My brows pull together in surprise as she removes the record from its sleeve.

"Do you mind if I put it on?"

I nod like a fool, unable to do much else as I watch her lift the needle. The notes from the piano drift to me, through me, all around me. I get sucked in as Grace closes her eyes, her fingers sweeping across the base of her throat, taunting me. It's another place I suddenly want to kiss.

Her hips sway. "This is a little bit of heaven, isn't it?"

"That's one of my mom's favorites. Mine too." I clear my throat. "I'm surprised you like it."

Her eyes open, and she angles her head. "Why?"

I shrug. Cindy hated my collection of vinyl. "I don't know."

"I studied music in college."

Her words catch me off guard. "Really?"

"Well, I did for a year until my father said it was a waste of time."

"A waste?" I cross my arms. When she remains quiet, I ask, "Sing? Write?"

A smile tugs at the edges of her mouth, and she shakes her head. "No to singing, and any songs I tried writing sounded more like Dr. Seuss books."

I laugh. "I doubt that." My shoulder presses against the fridge, and she's wedged between the bed and table, maybe two feet away from me.

"I played instruments, though."

I straighten and cock my head a little, studying her. "Which ones?"

"Piano. The cello. Even the guitar."

"The guitar?" Warmth wraps around my body at images of Grace strumming strings.

"What? You sound surprised." She lifts the needle and stops the record then slides the vinyl back into its sleeve.

"I'm a country boy, remember? So the idea of you playing a guitar is pretty damn hot."

She squints a little at me and crosses her arms. "Maybe I used to jam out to Led Zeppelin on an electric."

"Either way," I say while smiling, trying to picture her headbanging to rock, "it's sexy."

Our eyes meet again, and it's as if I'm seeing this woman almost for the first time. The hard exterior Grace sported when we first met has dissolved into a puddle at her feet, and right now she's this beautiful, exposed woman. No walls. No bullshit.

"We should get going." And her shield claws and scrapes its way back up, protecting her. She quickly brushes past me, heading out of the cabin, killing the moment.

But there can't be any moments between us, I remind myself and follow her. But I don't get far. She's standing at the entrance to the deck, frozen in place.

"You okay?" Shit, I shouldn't have let her up here alone. "Here. Let me help you off." I touch her back and guide her with my hand on her hip.

"It's a stupid fear." But she's shaking. An obvious tremble moves through her as I help her off the boat.

"Let me lock up." I hop back on board, lock the cabin, then meet her on the dock. "You good?"

Her gaze flashes over my shoulder to the water, but she nods.

"Come on, let's get you away from here."

"Sorry you had to see me like that," she says in a soft,

almost delicate voice once we're farther from the water and closing in on the bar.

"You know it's okay to be scared of some things. It's called being human."

"Yeah, well, um, I think I see Jessica." She's escaping whatever possible depth of a conversation we could have potentially slipped into. That's probably for the best.

I follow her gaze and notice Jessica entering a little brick building that has a green flashing sign hanging outside, which says P&D.

I brush off the weird desire to hold Grace's hand as we walk in silence the last few hundred feet to the bar. I step back and open the door for her, and when we enter the bar, I see a ton of familiar faces. They look my way and smile, raising their beers.

"You know them, I take it?" Grace asks.

"Yeah. Mostly military guys."

"I was expecting them to at least yell 'surprise.'"

I glance around the room, noting my sister is heading our way. "Well, it's not usually the best idea to jump out and scream at a sailor." And I assume she catches my drift because as my eyes land back on hers she nods.

"The look on your face is priceless!" Bella is in front of us now, but she's quickly averted her gaze to the gorgeous woman at my side. "Oh. Hi, Grace. Wh-what are you doing here?"

"Noah invited me," Grace says, hesitation in her voice.

I feel my sister's gaze burning through me, but I can't look away from Grace. My heart is skidding around, and the brakes don't seem to be working.

"Ahem." At the sound of a voice approaching, I finally pull my eyes away from Grace. It's Luke.

"Hey, man." I give him a quick one-arm hug. "Good to see you."

"Yeah, you too," Luke says.

"How'd you pull this off?" I ask Bella.

She wraps an arm around Luke's then nudges his side a little. "Luke, Jessica, and a few others helped me. Everyone's here. Well, everyone who isn't currently overseas on duty."

A lot of my old SEAL buddies are now civilians, but many of them are lifers. They'll serve until they're booted.

"Noah!" Owen hollers and comes up next to Luke. We served on different teams but our paths crossed enough that we became good friends.

I'm still standing near the entrance, and I notice Grace has gone farther inside and is talking to Jessica. At least she won't feel totally out of place in a room full of a bunch of SEALs.

But what the hell am I so worried about Grace for? She's not exactly some meek and shy woman. And she's not mine to worry about.

"Been too long, brother." Owen grips my shoulder. He's about my height and build, but with lighter hair and hazel eyes. "At least you haven't let yourself go to shit." He laughs as he taps me in the arm with a right hook.

"Like you," I say. "You staying out of trouble?"

"Hell no. Why would I go and do that?" Owen brushes a hand through his dirty-blond hair, which he's let grow longer since I saw him last.

"You know Owen." Luke flashes a smile. "The offer still stands if you want to come and work with us." He rubs his hands together. "Like good old times."

He's been asking me to join Scott & Scott Securities since my feet touched the ground after my last deployment. "As tempting as that sounds—"

"Hell no," Bella interrupts. "I need him for *my* business. You have almost all the guys working for you. Don't go stealing him on me."

She chuckles, but I know she's not kidding.

Owen claps his hands together. "So let's get this party started. There are a lot of fuckers here who want to see you!"

God, I need this. I really do. To be around friends who know how it feels to be swimming in the dark. Trying to adjust to a new life, one that doesn't involve a rifle.

When I move through the crowd of people gathered here to see me, I can't help but look at Grace. She's talking to one of my buddies now. Her eyes find mine across the room, and I swear the music and the loud chatting dims at that moment.

She takes a sip of a cocktail and looks away.

I think my heart skips three beats, but I know my body is just reacting to a hot woman. I haven't had sex since those random hookups I barely even remember months ago—God, I need to, though.

I need to get this woman out of my system.

I notice the subtle breath she takes before bringing her drink back to her lips. She wants me too.

But I'm the so-called safe one in my group of friends— the "good guy." I wasn't cheating or screwing around on Cindy. I wasn't jerking off to *Playboy* magazines like most of my team. I loved my family. And now—now I kind of don't want to be the good ol' boy, the one who worries about everyone else first.

My body heats and my muscles tighten at the thought of abandoning my principles. But hell, I know I won't do it. I won't act on impulse.

I'm a father. I can't be reckless. So, no matter how much I want to have a one-night stand with Grace, I know I won't use her because that's just not who I am.

"You still good with brunch Sunday?" Bella asks Jessica, who is now at her side.

I wonder if Bella's already told Luke and Jessica why we're meeting tomorrow. She's been asking me for months to hit them up for an investment…now I have no choice. If we don't make more money, I may not be able to win against Cindy in court.

"Yeah. And are we on for dinner tomorrow night?" Jessica directs her question to Grace.

"Definitely," Grace answers.

It's strange how we're all connected. Then again, maybe not. If it weren't for Jessica's friendship with Bella and her friendship with Grace, my sister wouldn't have landed the gig that brought us all together.

"I never asked, but how do you know Jessica and Luke?" I look at Grace.

"We met when their office outfitted my company with the best cyber protection known to man," she explains.

"You still working cyber security gigs, too?" I ask in surprise. Last I heard they were mostly dealing with bodyguard jobs and such. "I thought—"

"No, we're not working many cyber jobs these days," Jessica cuts me off. "Been busy with, uh, other stuff lately."

"And I assume you and Luke met in the military?"

I nod.

"You've been out for, what, two or three years?" Grace asks Luke once he joins us.

"A little over two," Luke says.

"And thank God he's out because my business would just be Scott Securities. Adding that extra Scott just spices it up so much," Jessica jokes.

"It's so damn pretentious, don't you think? Like we're

68

lawyers or some bullshit." Luke shakes his head and drinks his beer.

"You would've done fine without him. You're a genius," Grace notes. "Wish I'd had you guys in Athens with me, though."

"Like Athens, Georgia? Or *the* Athens?" I ask.

"Greece." Grace touches her stomach and looks down into her now-empty glass. Her dark lashes splay across her smooth, golden skin, and I can sense the pain inside her. It makes me curious as to what's upsetting her, even if I have no business knowing.

"What happened?" I prod.

"Nothing." The word came from her lips so fast, I nearly missed it.

Jessica clears her throat in a not-so-subtle way to notify me that this conversation is off-limits. "Come on, this is a party. We should dance." She grabs Bella's arm.

There isn't a dance floor, but that doesn't seem to stop her.

"Oh, I'm not really—" Grace shakes her head, but Jessica snatches her glass and sets it down then reaches for her arm.

The guys step back so the women can dance. There's a hip-hop song playing, and Grace begins to move her hips to the music. She's laughing at something Jessica says to her.

I fold my arms and lean back against the bar, continuing to observe them as a slow smile creeps up on me. Grace holds the hem of her dress and mimics Jessica's moves, then she begins to run her fingers down her chest as she dances. Grace looks up and shrugs at me, and my mouth broadens into a deeper smile.

"This place is a sausage fest. The few women here are mostly taken." My cousin Cam slaps me on the shoulder. "Happy birthday, man."

"Thanks, but don't feel obligated to stay since there aren't many women for you to hit on."

"Shit. She looks familiar." Cam's eyeing Grace.

How could he ever forget her? The moment I saw her in the bar that night, her face became permanently etched in my memory. You don't forget a woman like her.

"Bella and I are remodeling her place."

"But…" Cam faces me, looking a little speechless.

"Ironically, she's the same woman you struck out with the night we went out."

He laughs. "So did you. But here she is now. You think I can take another shot?"

"No." I didn't mean to say it so fast, but the idea of Cam going near Grace isn't something I'm comfortable with.

"Oh." Cam rubs his hands together, a grin touching his face. "Ohh. I see." He nods, curls his hand into a fist, and bumps my chest. "Finally back in the saddle. Good job, buddy."

"No, I'm not."

"Uh-huh. Sure. Well, I gotta get out of here and to a place where the ratio of women to men is much higher. Later, man."

"Stay out of trouble," I say, but I'm already looking at Grace.

"Now watching a bunch of hot women dance is an unexpected birthday present, I bet."

I look over my shoulder at Owen, who's now at my side. "Watch it. One of them is my married sister."

"How are you holding up?" Owen asks a few moments later, and I know he's referring to both Cindy and my adaptation to civilian life.

"I'm surviving," I say, looking away from the women.

"That's the best we can really do, right? Survive," he says in a low voice.

I want to say yes, but is it stupid of me to want a little more than that from life?

My gaze slides back to Grace as she moves freely now, forgetting where she's at and maybe who she is. And I realize I know what I want.

I want...*everything*.

7

GRACE

HE LOOKS JUST LIKE HIM. THE SAME DARK EYES, THE PINCH
to his brow, and the harsh lines in his face. Midnight-black
hair that sweeps over to the side, slicked down with gel.

It can't be him. He's in Greece, right? God, I hope so.

A slow tightness in my chest builds into an intense pain,
and I move a few steps back, bumping into Jessica.

I stop dancing. I can't take my eyes off this man. He's
stealing the feeling of safety from me.

I need to get out of here—even though I know in my gut
it's not the same guy. My rational brain says there's no reason
to be afraid, but the walls are closing in on me and I need air.
I need to breathe.

"I'll be back," I mutter to Jessica, but I don't think she
can hear me.

I take in my options to make a quick escape. There has to
be a side or back entrance.

A glimmer of relief finds me when I see a neon red exit
sign in the back not too far away. I rush toward the door as
fast as I can in my heels, dodging well-built former SEALs.
I'm probably safer inside than alone on the street, but there's

a strangling hold on me. A vise on my throat. I can't think straight.

Once outside, I bend over and press my hands to my thighs. Oxygen fills my lungs, and I take in slow breaths, trying to calm myself.

Is this a panic attack?

"Hey, you okay?" A hand touches my back.

I snap upright and turn, raising my fists in defense.

Noah places his palms between us and takes a step back. "Just me."

I look at the dark starless sky and nod. I must look like a psycho. "I'm, um, fine." My body's still shivering as if it's thirty degrees outside even though it's warm and humid.

His arms relax at his sides as he studies me. "What's going on? When I looked at you in the bar…well, you looked scared, and then you ran out of the place, so I—"

"I'm okay. Really." I have no idea what to tell him.

And I think he's not exactly sure what to say either. His hand darts through his thick hair, and he musses it up while he probably tries to gather the right words.

"You should go back inside. It's your birthday, and I'm pretty sure they're about to make a big deal out of you and sing. Plus, I'm betting there's some delicious cake." My heart isn't beating quite as fast all of a sudden, and the nausea is fading.

This is good. I'm starting to feel normal again, thank God.

"I'll go in when you're ready."

His blue eyes find mine, and the sweetness of his words and the way he places his hand on my shoulder, squeezing it a little, lets me know everything will be okay—and I almost break apart into tiny pieces. I've been holding myself together for so long, trying to be the woman I have to be,

73

instead of the person I want to be. And full disclosure, I'm not even sure who I want to be.

Right now, I want to fall into this man's arms and find comfort. I want the memories of last month gone. I want the fear to disappear. But he can't help in the long run. Only I can patch myself together and be me again.

I glance down at the road between us.

But what if I don't want to be her? Grace Parker-Fucking-King.

"Grace?" A dark brow arches as he angles his head, then his hand dips beneath my chin and he's urging my face back up. His eyes seize mine. He takes no prisoners with that gaze. It's powerful and demanding. So intense that I wonder if the ground could swallow my feet and I wouldn't even notice.

I don't want to look away.

"Yeah?" I murmur in response to the beautiful caress of my name on his tongue.

His hand shifts to my cheek, and he brushes the side of my face with the pad of his thumb. I want to shut my eyes and just be…

"What do you need from me? What can I do for you?"

His questions have me stiffening, my spine bowing forward a little. He's so straightforward, with zero bullshit coating his words.

I'm not used to this. A directness that bleeds kindness. He's a real man. A good man.

I wet my lips and swallow. "I need you to kiss me," I whisper.

His brows pull together, and his focus cuts to my mouth for a moment before returning to my eyes.

And then both his hands are on my face as he steps closer, taking me by surprise.

His lips touch mine gently at first. Then he groans a little against my mouth. His hands fall from my face to my hips, and I gasp as he lifts me. I follow without thought and wrap my legs tightly around him as my back goes against the brick building behind me.

Without much effort, he holds me as his tongue parts my lips, and he takes my mouth. And I mean he takes it. He fucks my mouth with his tongue in a way that no man has ever done. It's so deep, slow, and sensual.

My fingertips bite into his back while my other hand travels to his head, threading into his thick hair like I've fantasized about doing since we met. His hard chest is against mine, and I can feel the material of my dress shifting, my strapless bra slipping.

He may be sweet and kind, but the man knows how to make a woman feel good. And right now, all I can think about is him filling me deep.

And then, just like that, he breaks our kiss and pulls back a little. I open my eyes, finding a tortured look in his—pain. Or sadness. I'm not sure what happened, but he releases a breath and slowly guides my legs back to the earth. His eyes flicker to my chest, and he clears his throat and reaches for me, covering a partially exposed breast.

My cheeks grow warm and embarrassment floods me as I take over fixing my dress.

He lowers his forehead against his palm then swipes his hand down his face. "Grace, there's something I should tell you."

My heart stops. My body, slightly damp from dancing earlier, cools at the sound of regret lacing his words.

I don't want this man to betray the image I've developed of him in my head. I need him to be different from the pricks like Patrick.

Noah's arm falls to his side as his eyes steady on mine. "I'm married."

I stumble back, almost falling, but the building behind me keeps me upright.

God, no. No. No. No!

Not this man.

I read him so wrong. I don't understand—

"Wait, it's not what you think." His hand stretches between us, his eyes narrowing. "My wife and I are getting a divorce. We've been separated for almost a year. But I like you, Grace. I respect you, and I wouldn't want you to think that I'm—"

My body shivers and goose bumps quickly scatter across my skin. "You don't have to explain."

"I do." He nods and grips the nape of his neck. "I have a daughter. And I guess I'm sort of in a custody battle now. I don't want to mislead you. I just can't be with anyone. I need to focus on getting my daughter. Hell…" His large hand drops, slapping against his outer thigh, and he kicks at the road between us. "I don't know if you even want something, but I'm not the kind of guy to lead someone on or play games."

My words are gone. They've been stolen.

I don't even know how to react to a man who tells the truth. That's crazy, right? Lies and manipulation are things I know how to handle. Men who like to brag about their castles and their portfolios.

I don't know what to say to a man who's not only *not* a cowardly cheater, but someone who wants to put his daughter before his own desires. So no, I don't have any words because I've never been in this situation. This gorgeous, strong, and sexy former SEAL is making me lose my mind right now.

"Um, well." That's the brilliance I come up with.

I take a step toward him, and he cocks his head and studies me with hooded eyes. So damn sexy I can barely stand it.

But I think what makes him even more attractive is his honesty.

"I hope I didn't screw up the job. We really need this gig." He shrugs and thrusts his hands into his slacks pockets.

After a moment passes, I say, "Of course not. Thank you for not making me a rebound." Although I don't know if I'd mind that much. To be his in any capacity sounds pretty spectacular.

A slow smile pulls at his lips as he shakes his head a little. "I highly doubt you'd ever be any man's rebound."

I blush. "This is my fault. I asked you to kiss me. I had too much to drink in there. This isn't like me." Partial truth, although he deserves more. But how can I tell him that although I've never done this kind of thing, it's definitely not because I drank too much?

"Of course." He gives me a curt nod, then holds his arm out toward the door. "You ready to go in?"

"Um." I can't go back in there. If I see that man again, I'll have another panic attack, and I'm now fairly certain that's what it was.

Noah's studying me. He's trying to get a read on me, I can feel it. And I'm so damn scared he'll be able to figure me out.

"Yeah, let's go sing 'Happy Birthday.'" I force my lips into a smile and start past him toward the door, but his fingers wrapping around my forearm stop me as my other arm grasps the handle.

I glance over my shoulder as he releases his grip. "Could you do me a favor?"

"Anything," I say without a second thought, but I

continue to hold the handle as though it's a lifeline. I need something to keep me from falling. Too many foreign feelings are swelling beneath the surface.

"Would you mind not telling Jessica or Bella about my custody issues? I haven't told anyone." His voice is practically raw, stripped down. I can't begin to imagine how he must feel.

My heart breaks for him.

He's a man who'd make a daughter proud.

"I'd never talk about anything you and I discuss in private."

He takes a shallow breath, and I see a flash of relief etched in the lines of his face. "Thank you."

I'm not good with these kinds of conversations, so I smile again before heading back into the fray.

"There you are!" Bella comes rushing up to us, her eyes darting between Noah and me. "We've been looking for the birthday boy."

Noah looks over his shoulder at me as if he's asking permission to leave my side, or maybe he wants to check to see if I'm truly okay. So, I give him another fake but reassuring smile—flash a little teeth to make it look real—and he allows Bella to yank him toward the bar, where a cake glows with so many lit candles, I wonder if it'll set off the smoke alarms.

As he walks away, I can't help but wonder what happened to his marriage and how any woman could ever lose a man like him.

* * *

I HAD JESSICA TAKE ME HOME AN HOUR AFTER THE CAKE. THE creepy-looking guy was gone when I came back inside after

78

Noah and I kissed. He must have realized the bar had been rented out for the party. Thank God.

But I was still acting like an awkward teen, and Noah and I didn't exchange but a few words for the rest of the evening. What could I possibly say? Tell him what happened in Athens? That I'm a coward who can barely sleep at night?

Ugh...

As I lock my front door, the sounds of the bolts sliding into place make me think back to Noah's words about me being too trusting, giving a stranger a key to my place.

After what happened to me, how could I have been so careless? I know I never would have done it if Jessica didn't one hundred percent vouch for Bella, but still...I need to be smarter.

I flick on the lights and start down the hall. I can still smell a faint hint of Noah.

The man is everywhere. When I look around, I can't help but think about that gorgeous smile of his, and the kiss. Holy hell, the kiss.

And I was on his boat tonight. I haven't been that close to water since I was eight.

My phone rings, which is strange. Who would be calling me this late?

I grab it out of my clutch and look at the unknown number. "Hello?"

"Hi. It's Noah. I got your number from Bella."

"Oh, hi. Everything okay?"

"Yeah, I wanted to make sure you got home okay. I know Jessica drove you, and that woman is a hellfire on wheels."

I laugh. "That she is."

I hold the phone to my ear as I move through the living room toward my bedroom. My palm goes to the frame of the door, and I have to take a breath as I turn on the light.

No one is in here, I tell myself.

"You could have sent a text."

"I've never been much of a texter," he says.

"No?"

"I prefer direct communication."

Of course… "Are you back on the boat?" I look around my walk-in closet, checking for any intruders—not that I have a way to defend myself if some creep is lurking behind my dresses.

"Yeah."

I picture Noah tucked inside the cabin of his boat, lounging casually on his bed, shirtless. I stop in front of the long mirror above my dual sinks and study my reflection. My hair is tangled and eyeliner a little smudged. I don't look like my typical, put-together self. "Is there anything else?"

My fingertips brush across my collarbone as I look into my eyes, and staring back at me is a girl. Not the woman I am today, but the person I once wanted to be. I can almost see her watching me, wondering how I let myself become who I vowed never to be.

I did have dreams, didn't I?

"No. Nothing else. Eh, have a good night."

"Wait." *Shit.* "I'm sorry." My shoulders slump forward, and I turn away from the mirror. I can barely face myself. "I don't know what to say to you. I'm not normally like this."

"Like what?"

"At a loss for words." I press the speakerphone button and set the phone down so I can unzip my dress.

"And why do you think that is?" His deep voice crawls through the phone and glides across my skin, giving me chills.

I look at myself in the mirror again, standing only in my

strapless nude bra and matching panties. "Because you're different."

"Not rich?" There's a hint of a joke in his voice, but also a tease of the serious.

"You're real," I say without a second thought.

"Mm. I would hope so." I can tell he's smiling based on the slight change in his voice. "I shouldn't be on the phone with you. I probably should have texted." His voice is gravelly now. Frustrated, maybe?

I grab my phone off the counter and go back into the bedroom so I can get into some pajamas. I choose a pair of silk pink shorts and a matching camisole as if Noah can actually see me and it matters what I'm wearing.

"And why shouldn't we talk?" I'm walking a dangerous, fine line.

A soft hiss comes through the phone. "Because I enjoy hearing the sound of your voice."

My nipples harden at his words as I take off my bra. "Oh."

I sink onto my bed and press a palm against my thigh as I clutch the phone with the other hand. He's still on speakerphone, and I hold the phone before me, staring at it as if I can see his blue eyes.

"Good night, Grace."

Before I can say anything, he's already gone.

He's got his reasons for staying away from me. He's smart enough to know he's playing with fire, and I'm the flame. I don't want to burn him, though. He's a good man. And a genuine, honest man is hard to come by, so I hate letting him slip through my fingers, but I don't have much of a choice.

What more could we ever be to each other than sex? A quick screw? A wham-bam and cliché "thanks, ma'am."

I chuck my phone onto the bed before getting beneath the cream covers. I love the feel of silk against my body, but I tense at the thought of something I'd like to feel much more —Noah.

My eyes flutter shut as I draw up the images of him I've stored safely in my mind. I bite my lip as my hand slides down my panties, unable to stop myself from the need to get off—this desire for him is out of control, and I need to end it.

8

GRACE

"Are you following me? How'd you know I'm out with Jessica?"

"A friend saw you guys together," Cade says through the phone. "I'll swap places with you. I'll have dinner with her, and you come—"

"Stay away from Jessica." He had a bit of a reputation with women before his engagement, so I try to keep him away from my friends. "You're engaged, remember?"

"Drop it," he snaps, and I know I've hit a nerve. The dreaded marriage he doesn't want to happen.

I glance over my shoulder at Luke and Jessica eating at the table in the restaurant. I had to excuse myself to take Cade's call after his fifth attempt. I was worried something might have happened to Corbin. Usually Cade only calls me outside of work hours when our brother is in trouble. We had to discreetly bail him out of jail a week ago when he got into a bar fight. He was protecting a woman from some grabby guy, or so Corbin had said.

Despite how different he is from Cade, my father refuses

to let Corbin be free, to be the man he wants to be and not the guy in the suit that my father demands him to be.

I'm as trapped as Corbin, though. We've both joked about running away some day.

Maybe we will.

"This isn't a good time."

"Wait," Cade demands.

I shake my head and look at the tiled floor. "What?"

"I was serious about trading places. I arranged for you to have drinks with James Alexander. And it's right now, but he'll only meet with you."

"No. What the hell? I'm at dinner right now. And I already told Dad their company is off-limits."

"We need this deal. It's not up for discussion," he bites out.

Need? We've never needed anything. My stomach rolls. Is our company in danger? My father doesn't let me anywhere near the financials. Only Cade has access. I'm a VP, but I feel so in the dark. I've always wondered if he's keeping something from me. Who the hell knows why, but I don't like it.

"What's going on?"

"Just come for drinks, and we can talk details later."

"Sorry, but no." I hang up before he can rebut.

Cade tends to be broody, bossy, and annoying as hell, especially when it comes to the business. My father made him that way.

Once I'm back at the table, Jessica asks, "You okay?"

Last month, I would've put the business first. I would have been a good little soldier and followed his orders, but when your life flashes before your eyes, your perspective changes. "My family is just driving me nuts. Nothing new."

Luke's light brows pinch together.

I take a quick drink of my wine to steel my nerves.

"What's really going on?" he asks as my gaze meets his blue eyes.

"My father's trying to get me to broker some sort of deal even though I've made it clear to him the company isn't for sale."

I don't want to say too much because they know the Alexander family, and if word gets out that a potential hostile takeover is heading their way…but maybe I should warn them? Maybe if the news came from Luke or Jessica, I could avoid my father's wrath?

"Which company?" Luke asks.

I have to make a decision. Family or friends? Right or wrong? Sometimes it's not so easy, not so black and white.

"The Alexanders," I finally say.

Jessica's gaze sweeps over to mine, her blue eyes sparkling like always. She and her brother both have blond hair, blue eyes, and strong cheekbones to match their tough-as-nails personalities. But they have to be sharp in their business, especially when Luke puts his life on the line to protect other people.

"Who's trying to take them over? I haven't heard they were in any trouble." Jessica clears her throat and glances at her clutch on the table as if she's ready to reach for her cell and call them up.

"I don't think they're in trouble, but if someone is positioning themselves in hopes of a takeover of some kind, something must be up," I say. "James Alexander is with my brother right now."

James is getting older, and I know his sons are slowly taking over, but it worries me that Cade might try to take advantage of an old man. Maybe I should have gone for drinks, if anything, to protect James.

"Which brother?" Luke asks, his eyes darkening like storm clouds. He doesn't exactly get along with Cade. Two alpha, dominant personalities. When they're together, the tension always fills the room and it's like waiting for lightning to strike.

"Cade," I say.

His chest expands, filling with air.

"We should warn them. I'll look into things on my end," Jessica says, and I assume she'll be putting her cyber genius skills to work. I should be relieved, but I know there'll be hell to pay when shit hits the fan.

"Thanks." I stare at my barely eaten food, my stomach a tight ball of nerves.

"So Luke leaves for Nashville tomorrow night. Why don't we ditch this restaurant and go out dancing?" Jessica suggests.

"We danced last night. Maybe we could just go for a drink?" I'm not much of a dancer, even though it did feel good to let loose a little.

Jessica leans back in her seat and eyes me suspiciously, laying a hand on her heart. "What's with you and Noah?"

"What do you mean?" I nearly choke on my words, my mouth going slack.

"You guys looked pretty friendly last night, and he did invite you to his birthday party. When I recommended them for remodeling, I didn't know you'd end up having a thing for him. I mean, I don't blame you, the guy is ridiculously gorgeous. He's got the body, the brains, and the heart."

"I, uh, don't have a thing for him." I glare at Jessica. "And you know I could never be with someone like—" I stop myself, but it's too late. The damage is done. I might as well have said the words.

"Like what?" Luke straightens in his seat, his broad shoulders suddenly arching back in defense mode.

Jessica pushes her long hair to her back and tucks her hands into her lap. I look at her blue eyes instead of focusing on Luke, but I'm not sure which is a safer bet. She looks pissed too.

"Noah's a good guy," Jessica says.

"I know he is." I fidget with my fork, rolling it between my fingers, focusing on the metal instead of the heated stares I can feel burning my flesh. "I would kill to be with someone so amazing." And that's the truth. "But you know my father will never let me be with anyone he doesn't approve of, and remember, my father's an ass."

I look up, and this time I don't see anger in their eyes. Pity, maybe.

"And you're an adult. You can't let your parents make decisions about your life anymore," Jessica says.

She's right, but following her advice is easier said than done. And I don't know if I'll ever have the courage to do it.

"Don't start now, not with Noah," Luke says, his voice low, deep, and intense.

"What?" I have no intention of doing anything with Noah, but I can't help but want more information.

Luke's shoulders relax a bit as he reaches for his wine glass. "He's been through a lot. And I don't want anyone else screwing with his head. He deserves better."

I lean back in my chair, digesting his words. Noah's getting a divorce and fighting for his daughter. A lot of men I know would happily give up custody but not Noah.

"He's a good guy. A better man than I could ever be. Don't let him be your guinea pig in whatever game you might play to thwart your father's wishes." Luke finishes his drink, his eyes on me, then stands and tosses some cash on the table. "I need some air."

What the hell was that all about? Guinea pig? Really?

I bite my tongue out of respect for Jessica, and I wait for him to be out of sight before I blow out a breath.

"I'm sorry. Luke's angry about Noah's ex and what she did to him."

What did Noah's ex do? I can't help but wonder.

"Luke is just looking out for him. Friend to friend. SEAL to SEAL." Jessica clears her throat and presses her hand to her chest. "He's super protective of his military buddies. They might as well share the same blood."

"I understand. Besides, Luke has always been a little standoffish with me." I wet my lips as I try to think of the right words to say. Jessica and I instantly clicked when we first met, but I've only spent time with Luke on his visits.

"It's nothing personal. War can change people."

Had it changed Noah?

My mind drifts to the record player on his boat. I still can't believe I went on a boat. But with him at my side, I knew I was safe. And when I played that record, I was nineteen again, a freshman in college. I was untouchable during those months. Living how I wanted—being who I wanted.

"Grace?" Jessica waves her hand in front of my face, which makes me blink, then her hand covers mine and my gaze sweeps over it, focusing on her diamond tennis bracelet. "It doesn't have to be. You can be happy too. Stand up to your father. You may have been born into this life, but that doesn't mean you have to let it control your future."

"I don't know." I pull my hand free of hers and drop it to my lap.

"You came back from Athens different. And although I'm

so sorry about what happened to you there, at least you're okay. And maybe one good thing has come from it."

How could anything good come from Athens? I look back up.

"Maybe now you have the strength to be who you really want to be." She tilts her head and studies me. "You just need to figure out who that person is."

But I know who that person is. I felt her waking up last night, but I'm pretty sure I have to bury her again.

Jessica scoots away from the table. "We'll go out another time. Good night." She squeezes my shoulder and leaves.

The server comes to my side. "Ma'am, would you like anything else to drink?"

"Yeah. I'll have a vodka and cranberry. Light on the cranberry," I say as I watch Jessica head toward the exit.

Guinea pig.

I can't get that out of my head. I would never use Noah to spite my father. Never…

Okay, so I attempted to date some guys in the past to try to get some sort of rise out of my dad—to see he still had a pulse—but they were always assholes.

No one came close to being like Noah.

So real. So honest.

So…out of my reach.

9

NOAH

THE NIGHT IS SO DAMN HOT, BUT I CAN'T RESIST SITTING
outside instead of being pressed up against a bunch of people
inside the bar.

"Hi."

I set my can on the table, pressing it between my palms
when I glance at the woman standing at my side. She's pretty.
Long, pin-straight blond hair, hunter-green eyes, boobs that
spill out of her tank top, and a nice smile. A little too Cindy-
like.

"Hi," I say back.

"Is this seat taken?" she asks while motioning to the bar
stool opposite me.

I contemplate her question, deciding whether or not this is
a good idea. A woman hitting on a guy instead of the other
way around is a nice change, and if I don't do something
about my blue balls soon, they might fall off.

"Sure," I decide.

She sits down and crosses her legs off to the side, making
sure I can see them. "I'm Lisa."

"Noah." I nod and take a long swig of my soda.

"Nice night." She attempts to hold my gaze, but I'm not feeling it, so I glance at my drink.

What the hell is wrong with me?

"You must work out," she says after an awkward moment.

Jesus. Really? And I thought I was out of practice. "Sure."

"I'm a yoga instructor, so I can always spot a guy who takes good care of his body."

Yoga? So, she's flexible. And I really need to get laid.

But there's nothing. Not even the slightest twitch of my cock. And it's not because of Cindy. I don't seem to have this problem when I'm around Grace.

"What kind of workouts do you do?" she continues as if I seem interested.

I finally look back up at her, not wanting to be an asshole. "A little of everything."

She wets her lips and threads her fingers through her hair. She's probably barely twenty-one. And since I'm thirty-two now, I think anyone under twenty-five should be off-limits.

My phone begins to vibrate in my pocket, alerting me to a text.

"So I—"

"Excuse me a sec." I retrieve my cell, and my mouth opens in surprise. "Uh, I have to go. Sorry."

I don't wait for the girl to respond. I hop off my seat and start for the back exit. My boat is only down the street, so I shove my phone into my pocket and sprint toward the docks.

My heart is throbbing, my pulse pricking in my neck when I arrive at my boat.

Cindy stands up on the deck. I step onto the boat, anger lashing inside of me, tiny pops of pain branding my body.

"Why are you here? Unless you've changed your mind about custody?" I haven't gotten any papers about it.

My fingertips bury into my jeans, trying to ease the tension.

Cindy shakes her head and looks at the deck. "No. And please don't come tomorrow. We won't be home. We're leaving in the morning for Denver for a week."

"What's in Denver?"

"Will's father."

I step closer to her, breathing in the smell of her sharp, bitter perfume. Overwhelming as always. "You can't just take her across the country without even talking to me about it first."

"I'm here, aren't I—telling you?" She fakes a laugh. "But really…does it matter? You were gone almost her entire life. I got used to making decisions without you."

I can't find it in me to respond. It's the same recycled line she's been spewing since I came to New York.

"Well, we're going." She shrugs. "So now you know."

"I'm not even sure I believe you." Maybe she's just trying to keep me away.

She digs into her large Prada bag and grabs her phone. "See." She shoves it in my face, and there's an email of her airline itinerary.

"I don't like this." But can I stop her? "I want phone calls every day. I want updates."

"Fuck you," she says as casually as if she's asking me to pass her the salt at Thanksgiving dinner. She stows her phone back in her purse. "I used to travel all of the time while you were at sea. Sometimes we didn't hear from you for weeks. Weeks, Noah!"

"I can't believe you're throwing that in my face. I was taking down terrorists. Are you serious right now?" I turn away and shove my hands in my hair, unable to handle her craziness.

"I didn't come here to do this," she grumbles.

"Do what? Argue?" I spin back around to face her, my body burning with hate, with anger that's sort of torn me apart for years, but I've kept it buried.

Every time she made me feel guilty for being gone.

Every time she made decisions about our daughter without me.

And when she'd go on long trips to Charlotte to see her mom and not even tell me about them—and was apparently screwing Will.

When she'd buy things we couldn't possibly afford and get money from her parents.

When she wouldn't ever dance with me.

When she stopped laughing.

Stopped loving me—our family.

I've been angry for a while, but I either didn't realize it, or I took my stress out on terrorist scumbags to compensate.

"Noah, I want to make sure you won't do anything stupid and spend all of your money on a lawyer to fight me in court."

Her words are like a smack in the face, but it also wakes me up. "Oh, I see why you're here. You're worried I'm going to delay your wedding by tying you up in court."

She blinks a few times, but there's something in her eyes —something that tells me that's only part of the truth.

"I won't give up Lily. So, if you haven't changed your mind then I'll see you after you get back from Denver."

"Noah." She sighs.

Is this conversation really something that warrants a motherfucking sigh? I don't think so.

"Noah, we were together forever, so there's still some part of me that loves you—"

"Bullshit," I can't help but say. I've lost all sense of calm since this woman cut my heart out of my chest nearly a year ago.

"I truly don't want to see you get hurt by fighting a battle you can't win." Her green eyes move over my shoulder and out to the river.

"You're a walking contradiction. Please don't pretend to give a damn about me or our marriage. You fucking stepped all over our wedding vows—so you don't get to give a shit." I step back. I need space.

I need an entire ocean of space.

"Move on—don't make this messy. Start a new life," she says in a soft voice as if she's some fragile being, but she's not. She's stone cold. Heartless.

She places her hand on my forearm, and my brows snap together as our eyes meet. I don't move. I don't fucking flinch. I hold her eyes for a moment, time seems to still, and I finally break contact and place my hands between us.

"Get out of here," I grit out, my chest aching fiercely as if I've been shot, and I'm bleeding out.

"Take this." Cindy produces a small envelope from that big bag of hers.

"What is it? The petition for custody?" Doesn't that need to be served by someone else, though?

She shoves it in my hand and turns away, folding her arms. "You've been doing your homework?"

"Damn straight I have. And the courts won't rule in your favor." I've been scouring the Internet, looking into every possibility. I should feel relieved that she doesn't seem to stand a chance at sole custody, but she's so damn confident, I can't help but be worried.

My countdown until D-Day—our divorce…is now on pause. Who the hell knows how long it will take, but Cindy is out of her mind if she thinks I'll throw in the towel. Doesn't she even know me at all? Obviously not.

"Just open the envelope before we meet with the lawyers."

I toss it on the couch as little flashes of light appear before my eyes, my nerves twisting with frustration. I go to the edge of the deck and grip the railing, hanging my head low as Cindy's words and what she did to our marriage wrap around my neck, suffocating me.

"I understand you're angry about everything, but in time, you'll realize this really is for the best."

My body heats, the vein at the side of my neck pulsing.

"Good night, Noah."

I wait until she's gone, snatch the damn envelope, and toss it in the trash bin before unlocking the door to my cabin. My hand balls into a fist and I lose control, punching the door to the bathroom.

I press my palms against it and bow my forehead, trying to breathe. To think.

The space is too tight down here, and I'm losing oxygen. I need to walk, to get out of here.

I go to the drawer by my bed, grab a small box, and head back up to the deck. I snap the blue box open and look at my wedding band inside. I shake my head, close my eyes, then toss it into the water before heading back into the New York night.

The city is a blur. Lights. People. The noise.

My hands are tucked in my pockets as I move in a total state of numbness. I have no idea where I'm going, but I need to keep moving.

After an hour of wandering the city, I slow when I realize where I am. I look up at the tall glass building, wondering if Grace is home.

Thinking about her and the kiss last night is the distraction I need right now. Anything to lessen the pain in my chest. It's as if a tight knot's inside, right by my heart, and two people are on each side of it, playing tug-of-war. At some point, the rope will snap.

I cup my jaw as I step back and sit on a bench near the bus stop a couple feet from Grace's home. My palms go to my thighs, and I rub them, trying to absorb the shock, to reel in my emotions so I can calm the hell down.

"Noah?"

I glance up as Grace's eyes find mine. She's just stepped out of a cab.

Her forehead pinches in surprise, and she moves toward me. "Is something wrong?"

The woman is simply stunning. A white sleeveless dress stops above her knees, and tall black heels show off her killer legs.

I think my body brought me here on auto pilot. I needed to see someone good after being around Cindy. I stand, scratching the side of my head as I try to drag up some lame excuse for my presence. "I was on a walk, and I ended up here."

"Oh. Um, you want to come up?" There's hesitation in her voice, but I could be off my game of reading people right now.

"Sure." This isn't what I should be doing. But what the hell do I know anymore?

She smiles, and I follow her inside. I say hi to the security guard I've gotten to know a little these past few days. He's a good guy. A vet. Served in Nam.

Once we're in the elevator, I take a breath, and with it, her perfume drifts into my nose. It's not like Cindy's. It's light and sweet, like vanilla. Everything about this woman is refreshing.

But I'm a fool when it comes to women apparently. None of my buddies ever liked Cindy. They didn't tell me while we were together, but damn, the truth came out after they heard of our separation. They fucking hated her. They could see what I couldn't, I guess. Love is supposedly blind. Like justice. Sure…

"How was your dinner with Luke and Jessica?"

"Oh." Her cheeks develop a soft blush, and she looks up and our eyes meet. "It was okay."

Maybe my radar isn't off because I can tell she's had her own shitty night. "What's wrong?"

Her eyes narrow. "How do you know something's wrong?"

I step closer to her as the elevator ascends. "You wear your emotions on your sleeves." I smile as I look at her bare, toned arms. "Well, your arms."

When she returns my smile, her eyes light up. Like a bolt of lightning, the energy shifts inside me, and my anger calms.

"I never did before," she says as the doors open.

"Before what?"

She doesn't answer because a man is standing on the opposite side.

"Hi, Evan." She nods while getting out of the elevator.

The man's eyes rake over every inch of her body. He's fucking her in his head. It's obvious. I notice the flash of gold on his ring finger. Figures.

"Good evening." He looks my way, assessing me as if I'm competition before finally walking past me and into the elevator.

"Nice guy," I note with an obvious sarcasm as we walk.

"Yeah, but his wife probably disagrees," she says as she retrieves the key from her bag.

We go inside her place, and I follow her down the hall into the living area. My supplies are all over the space, and I'm sure she's anxious for me to be done.

"So." I fold my arms and lean against the wall facing the kitchen as she goes to the fridge and grabs two beers. "You going to tell me what happened tonight?"

She pops both tops and guzzles her beer, which has me straightening in surprise. She lowers the bottle and coughs a little while blinking. "Nothing we need to talk about." She swipes her lips with the back of her hand.

I hesitantly take the beer she's offering. I didn't notice it when we were on the streets, but her eyes are a little red. Either she's been crying or drinking. I'm guessing the latter. This is my cue to back up and leave, because in my current state, I may not make the best decisions. Clearly, she may not either.

My mouth is dry, though, so I take a sip and ignore my brain. "Did someone say something to upset you tonight?" I'm pushing, and I don't know why.

She sets her bottle on the counter and bends forward, her cleavage on display as she unbuckles the little straps by her ankles. I can't tear my eyes away, and my body stirs. Unlike the woman at the bar tonight, who didn't evoke any feelings inside me, Grace can make me hard with a simple look.

She stands back up and catches my eyes on her, and I can't look away or feel bad about it. All I can think about is how her body felt against mine last night and how her mouth tasted. Sweet as sin.

She unties her hair, releasing the mass, and it hangs straight down just above her breasts.

"I've had a bad night. I should probably go." It took every ounce of strength inside me to string those words together.

I set my bottle down as Grace's fingers sweep across her collarbone and travel up to her throat. Her hand remains there as her eyes hold mine. "I'm supposed to stay away from you."

Is she saying that because of what I told her?

But she takes a small step closer and her mouth parts. "But if I'm being honest—like you do with me—I'm glad I saw you outside my place tonight. I don't think I've ever been so glad to see someone. I don't know what that means."

And I can't stop myself.

I reach for her hand and tug her against me. Her palms land on my chest, and I know she can feel my heart racing as she looks into my eyes. I stare at her for a moment, trying to convince myself not to kiss her. But I fail.

I slowly lower my mouth over hers, and a soft mewl escapes her lips, which has me deepening the kiss. She stumbles back against the counter, and I lift her onto it.

I brace my hands on each side of her, and she leans forward, cupping the back of my neck, pulling me closer—taking over, her tongue finding the inside of my mouth, and it's me who's damn near growling this time.

My hand shifts to the strap of her dress, and I slip it off as I kiss her neck now, working my way down to her shoulder. Her head tips back as my other hand goes to her thigh, sliding up her smooth leg. I stop just shy of her panties, refraining from my desire to rip them off and stroke her clit.

"Touch me." Her mouth is at my ear, her breath warm. Her hands land on my jeans, and she's working at the button as my mouth claims hers again.

But I don't touch her where she wants—she's been drinking, and I can't take advantage of her.

I gather all my strength and finally take her wrist, stopping her before she unzips my pants. I don't have *that* much restraint. I step back and find her eyes. "We can't."

I watch her chest rise and fall with shallow breaths. Her cheeks blossom crimson as she bows her head, and I feel like such an asshole.

"I want you, trust me, but—"

"But it's too soon for you," she finishes as our eyes meet again.

"Because you've been drinking." If it weren't for the alcohol, I don't think I'd be able to stop myself from taking every piece of her—making her lose her mind, orgasm after orgasm.

"I'm not drunk."

I rush a hand through my hair, trying to keep my hands off her.

"But this shouldn't happen anyway, I guess." She scoots off the counter, her feet finding the floor, and I fix my pants and button them. She grabs her beer and takes a drink as she fiddles with her strap, securing it in place.

I turn, ready to leave, but she says, "Don't go. I don't want to be alone."

I want to ask her why. What happened to make such a strong, successful woman scared? But I bite my tongue and control my thoughts.

"You barely know me, but I like that. I like that you don't already have some idea about me, that you don't know the me before—" She turns away.

"Do you want to talk about whatever it is that's bothering you? I'm a good listener." I touch the small of her back, and her shoulders relax.

"Could we do something else instead?" Her voice is barely above a whisper.

"Well, uh, the one something else I have in mind is off-limits, so…" I say with a bit of a smile.

"Do you like movies? We could eat popcorn and watch a movie." She shakes her head. "Shit, I don't have popcorn, and I guess the living room is a mess to watch a movie in, which leaves the bedroom. There's a TV in there. A couch too. Not just the bed."

"The couch in your room works."

"Okay, good. What do you like? Are you a Stallone fan? I have the collection of *Rocky* movies."

"You like *Rocky*?" I ask, totally surprised. The woman is throwing me a curve ball here, and I might just fall in love right now.

"Looks can be deceiving." She flicks her wrist, motioning for me to come to her bedroom—a place I know I should stay the hell out of.

But I follow her. I wonder if I could follow this woman anywhere.

When we go into her room, it's barely decorated, like the rest of her place, which shouldn't surprise me. There's a massive four-poster bed in the center and a seating area with a couch and large flat screen TV near the windows that overlook the city.

"I'm going to change. The movies are in the cabinet beneath the TV."

"Grace?"

She glances over her shoulder at me. "Yeah?"

"Mind wearing something not too sexy?"

She chuckles. "Define sexy."

I smile. "Anything."

"So nothing it is." She winks then disappears behind the closed door.

I shake my head, still smiling. I crouch in front of her TV

stand and look over the titles. Her taste in action movies is spot-on with mine, and it makes her all the sexier.

I find her remote, start up *Rocky IV*—the best, in my opinion—and settle down on the brown leather couch and rub my palms against my thighs.

When the door opens, I almost half expect to see Grace standing there naked, her glorious body on display. But she's wearing silk pajama pants and a white tank top, and thank God, a bra. Not that I wouldn't like to study her nipples in greater detail.

"Is this okay?" She comes toward me while braiding her long hair at the side and resting it on her shoulder.

Fuck me. She's like a fantasy come true. Why the hell do I have to be a good guy?

I look at her as she stands before me, and I want to reach for her hips and pull her onto my lap, to have her grind against my cock as my tongue darts over her breasts and teases her flesh.

"This is my favorite *Rocky* too," she says after I've pulled my head out of the gutter and pressed play.

She glances at my lap as she sits down, and I swallow, my cock stiffening. It's obvious I'm hard, and I swear she's torturing me on purpose as she pulls her lip between her teeth.

"Movie," I nearly grunt as I tip my head toward the screen.

She laughs a little and positions herself to face the TV instead of me, and I try to relax. I try to think of my mom, my grandmother, something to reduce this erection.

And then Cindy comes to mind, and the heat in my body and the pain between my legs dies. In its place is a pain in my chest.

My daughter…

I'm barely paying attention to the movie now. My thoughts go dark as I bounce around ideas of how Cindy plans to stab me in the back and make me bleed even more than I already have.

I feel Grace leaning against my shoulder, which pulls me back to the moment, but when I look at her, she's asleep. Her chest lifts and falls slowly and her dark lashes are splayed against her skin, her pouty lips as kissable as ever.

I exhale, still a little surprised I put myself in this position, then I gently shift her so she's resting her head on the cushion of the couch so I can stand. I turn down her comforter before lifting her into my arms.

She feels good here.

I sling her arms around my neck, and she latches on as if it's the most natural thing in the world. After I set her down on the bed and cover her up, I decide I should stay since she didn't want to be alone.

Once the lights and movie are off, I remove my shoes and lie on the couch. My arms cross over my chest, and I squeeze my eyes tight, allowing my mind to drift to life before New York. To when I was a SEAL and everything made sense. I was the team leader. Confident in my choices, never doubting my decisions.

Civilian life is so much more complicated. But I can't go back to the military, can I? I can't run away from this life because it's fucking hard. I can't leave Lily.

But my stomach tightens. So much more shit is heading my way, and for the first time in my life, I don't know if I'm prepared to deal with it.

* * *

I JERK UPRIGHT AT THE SOUND OF MOANING. NO, IT'S MORE

like a cry. It takes me a minute to remember where I am, but when I do, I rush over to Grace's bed, where she's tossing and turning. Her fingertips are biting into the bed, clawing at it as if she's being attacked.

Jesus, what the hell is she dreaming about?

I don't want to startle her awake, but I hate seeing her like this.

So, I do what I think is best. Hope so, at least.

The weight of my body sinks into the bed, and I wrap my arms around her, hugging her tight against me. "Shh…" I whisper in her ear, hoping she won't wake.

Her shoulders jerk a little more, but she slowly stills and relaxes against me. And I hold her like that until I wake a few hours later to the feel of the sunlight peeking through the partially open blinds.

I'm groggy. I'm normally up before the sun rises, so I feel off-balance. Plus, my arms are wrapped around Grace, and she's got my one arm pinned. I'm afraid if I move, she'll wake up and freak out.

I need to do this slowly, to prepare her to the fact that I'm in bed with her.

"Grace." I lift my top arm off of her and edge back a little. "Grace. It's me, Noah."

She stirs and her back lands against my chest, molding into me as if she belongs there. And I still have my morning wood. Great.

Her firm ass presses against me, and my body doesn't need any further encouragement. I'm reared up to go.

"Grace," I say again, needing to get my dick away from her. I doubt she'd want to wake to that.

"Yeah?"

Oh, good. "Grace."

She slowly rolls over, and I slip my arm free and prop my head up as she focuses on me, blinking a little.

She sits upright, clutching the sheet to her chest as if she's naked. "Did we…?"

"No. I was on the couch, and you were having a nightmare. I tried to calm you down, so I held you. Sorry." I get out of the bed and scratch the back of my head and arch my shoulders back, stretching. I'm not used to sleeping on such a soft mattress. So soft I think my back actually hurts.

"You stayed." Her fingers brush across her lips as she finds my eyes.

"You asked me to."

"True." She drops the sheet, probably realizing she's still dressed. "Thank you. That was the best sleep I've had in a while."

"Really?" My brows snap together. "With that nightmare, I would have assumed it was a rough night."

She scoots to the edge of the bed, and her legs drop down. Her pajama bottoms are a little twisted, so she touches the waistband and fixes them before tugging down her tank top that had risen.

And I want to push it right back up, to kiss her there and all the way to her mouth.

Her sleepy morning look is turning me on. I need some black coffee to pull myself together. Or my morning run.

Probably both.

"Normally I wake up after the nightmare, and I don't go back to sleep." She looks at the floor as she stands, and I wonder why she doesn't want to look me in the eyes.

"*The* nightmare? Same one?" I ask, concern flickering through me.

She waves. "Never mind that. You want some coffee? I

don't have food, but I have a machine that can whip us up a good cup."

"A woman after my own heart." I smile, and she seems to relax with the subject changed.

"Let me brush my teeth first."

"You have any mouthwash or a spare I could use?"

"Sure. Follow me."

Her bathroom is probably triple the size of my boat's cabin. The shower occupies half the bathroom, a glass wall offering a partial view. There are three—yes, three—shower heads. Two rain ones on top and another hand-held one attached to the wall.

Jesus, the woman gets wet.

And there goes my dick again.

I raise a fist to my mouth, faking a cough as she studies me in the reflection of the mirror as if she knows what I was thinking.

"Here." She hands me an unopened toothbrush.

We go about brushing our teeth side by side as if she's my wife and this is our normal ritual.

I watch her out of the corner of my eye as she rinses, and I can't help but feel good. I miss having someone next to me. I always appreciated the little moments when I wasn't overseas, like being able to get ready next to Cindy in the morning. Although she rarely got up when I did. But that also meant our early riser daughter and I had more time to hang out just the two of us.

My chest constricts. I need to let the memories go. For now at least. I'll get Lily back. I will. I won't let Cindy steal her from me.

But I wonder if I'll ever marry again. If I can ever find someone who wants to share their mornings with me. If I can ever trust again…

"You okay?" Grace turns off the water and rests her hip against the counter, looking at me.

I toss the toothbrush I used in her trash and nod. "I was going to ask you the same thing. You shouldn't be having nightmares. Not like that, at least."

Her eyes flash shut for a moment, and I can see the tension rising back up inside her as her shoulders slouch. She's fighting something. I just have no idea what it is.

"Let's get coffee." She brushes past me in a hurry.

I hang my head for a moment, trying to let go of my own problems, then I meet her in the kitchen.

"So you really think this will all be done and decorated in the next week or two?" She turns on the single server brewer and faces me as the water heats in the machine.

Part of me wants to drag this job out longer because I know once I'm done, I'll probably never see her again, but that'd be ridiculous. "I think so."

"Well, there's something I'd like to show you today if you're up for it."

"Sure. What is it?" Before she can answer, it dawns on me that I'm supposed to meet Bella today. "Shit," I mutter. "I can't."

"Oh, right. Brunch." Her shoulders sag, disappointment flashing in her eyes. "Another time."

"Sure." But I hate disappointing her. "I guess I should head back to my place and clean up. We're having breakfast at some place near Central Park. I still don't know my way around this city. I can navigate the hills of Afghanistan better than the streets of Manhattan."

She chuckles. "Well, you still want coffee, at least?"

I want to say yes, but if I stay with her much longer, I'll probably ditch the meeting. "I should get going."

Her forehead creases as she nods. "Okay."

Something hurts in my gut—something is off. "But if you want to talk about that nightmare…" I leave my sentence hanging, waiting to see how she'll respond.

"I'm fine. Really. It's not a big deal."

I come toward her, and she startles a little and steps back. "You don't have to do that."

"Do what?"

"Be so afraid of letting someone in." I want to kiss her again. To take away whatever pain is eating at her and let this woman breathe—make her feel good. I can't handle seeing anyone hurting.

"How could I let you in? You're practically a stranger." Her fingers press against her lips as if she's remembering our kiss, and I stop in front of her when she's back up against the counter where we were last night.

"Sometimes it's easier to open up to someone who doesn't know you well." I'm staring at her mouth, at her fingers there. Her nails have cream polish on them, so light I can barely see the color. "I could be that someone for you if you need me to be."

I see her tense and her hand falls from her mouth, brushing against my chest. I angle my head and study her, unable to control the impulse to just absorb every part of her into my mind. I've never felt this way before. I've never been so drawn to someone. I don't remember ever feeling this way about Cindy, and it's confusing.

"Why do you want to be?"

I'd almost swear there was a crack in her voice. Raw, visceral pain curves around her words as she says them. I touch her arm, wrapping my hand around her bicep, and she looks down for a moment before catching my eyes again. "I think you could use a friend."

"I have friends." Her lips draw tight.

"A friend who hasn't had a chance to see the you that you've been pretending to be for however long."

"What makes you think I've been pretending?"

I squint one eye at her. "I'm a human lie detector. I was always good at reading people in the military." I just couldn't read my wife.

She smiles a little. "What about your plans?"

She's giving in to the idea of me. It's what I want, but I'm also worried. I don't want to add any more pain to this woman since I can't ever be the kind of man she'll need.

"Bella can go. She can fill me in on the details of their meeting."

"Details?"

I release my hand from her arm and step back. "We need an investment in the business so we can keep it running, and I need to be able to afford a lawyer to go to bat with my ex." The truth pours from my mouth so fast and easy with her. Maybe I'm right. Maybe it's easier to talk to a stranger. A stranger I've had my mouth on.

"Oh." She turns away and presses her palms to the counter as if she's trying to decide what to do.

Before I change my mind, I pull my phone from my pocket and scroll to the last text I got from Bella.

I can't make it. Make the deal without me. You've got this. I'll be in touch later. And don't take more than we need.

I re-read my text then send it. "What'd you want to show me? My day is officially free." Although originally the day was meant for Lily…

Grace looks over her shoulder at me as I tuck my phone back into my pocket and ignore the vibration from a text.

"Are you sure?"

"On one condition." I smile. "Since I'll be going in my

109

clothes from last night—without a shave and a shower—you go as is too."

She chuckles. "In my PJs?"

I tilt my head and glance at the silk bottoms, and there's another stir in my pants at the thought of peeling them down and pressing my mouth to her center.

"Ahem." She chuckles.

I raise a brow as I find her eyes again. "Fine. You can change. But where are we going?"

A smile lights her cheek. "It's a surprise."

GRACE

"You have a Bugatti. A two-toned Bugatti. It looks like a demon race car from hell."

"You say it as if I don't know." I laugh. "My dad got it for me when he promoted me to vice president two years ago. This isn't exactly me."

"Huh." He fastens his seat belt. "Nice gift, though."

Noah eyes me as I attempt to back out of my parking space. I probably look like a teen taking her first driver's ed course. I suck at driving. It's pathetic. I've barely ever had to drive.

The odometer reads less than three hundred miles, and I think those miles are from when Corbin test-drove it around town one wild Saturday night. Another night he ended up in jail.

"You want me to drive?"

I put the brake on and switch to park. "That'd be great. You know how?"

"It's like driving a Toyota." He smirks and hops out of the passenger side, wasting no time.

Once we've swapped seats, his hands stretch across the

leather wheel before gripping it. "Always wanted to drive one of these." He reaches for the stick. "You buckled?" He shoots me a teasing smile.

"Don't go speeding in this bad boy. My brother Cade might have a lot of judges up his sleeves to get you out of a ticket, but I can't save us if we wrap around a pole."

He laughs a little, but I'm not kidding.

"Trust me, I can handle her."

"Her? You've decided it's a her?"

He shifts into reverse. "Oh, hell yeah."

My head jerks back against the seat as he tears around a corner, winding through the parking garage, then he slows down a little and steals a glimpse of me. I'm bracing against my thighs, hanging on for dear life.

The car slows even more. "Just testing her out. Seeing what she can do. I'll be good."

I relax when he pulls out into traffic. "We have a bit of a drive. Is that okay?"

"We can drive all day." He smiles and shifts gears, changing lanes with ease as though he was made to drive this car.

"Okay. Well, we're going to the Hamptons."

He peers over at me. "What's in the Hamptons?"

I relax, memories floating to my mind…times from my childhood when I wasn't abroad at school. "My home."

"You have another place?"

"Yeah, but I rarely go there. But I'd like you to see it."

He fiddles with the music while driving and puts on the XM radio. "What would you like to listen to?"

I reach for the controls to help, and his fingers caress my hand as he pulls back. It's like a tiny zap, the cliché electric buzz passing between us—the moment when you know somewhere deep inside yourself that you feel something unexplainable.

This is the first time I've experienced *the* moment.

And I notice his shoulders arching back against the seat. He swallows while focusing on the road, his hand resting on the stick. He's uncomfortable, isn't he? Not with the car, but because I think he feels something too, and he doesn't want to, or he's afraid to.

He doesn't want me to be a rebound. Jesus, he said those words to me the other night, but it feels like forever ago.

My phone rings and I dig inside my purse. "I could have sworn I turned that thing off." I roll my eyes at Patrick's number. The man's persistent, I'll give him that much.

"Not going to answer?"

"No." This time I do power off my phone and toss it into my bag on the floor by my feet, then I turn on the EDM station. I'm not sure if he likes electronic dance music, and I wonder if I should switch to country. I have the feeling Noah's not the kind of guy who would want someone doing something for his benefit, though.

But I reach again for the controls and switch it to something I know we both like. Bluesy jazz music filters through the speakers, through my blood, and warms my body almost instantly.

"Can't go wrong with this," he says after a few moments and taps his hand against the wheel in time with the bass.

"Figured it could be our common ground. I'm not a country fan, and I don't take you for a techno kind of guy."

"I don't discriminate against good music."

"Good to know." I smile.

"You ever think about playing again? Or…do you still jam out? Maybe at night and in your underwear?"

My cheeks warm at his words, and I notice his hand tightening around the wheel.

"I only play naked," I lie. The only thing that's gone near my instruments is dust.

Noah glances at me, and his blue eyes deepen as his pupils expand. I want to shut my eyes and remember the feel of his hands on my body last night, the touch of his tongue in my mouth.

He stayed with me when I was afraid.

And he's here with me now.

"How long were you in the military?" I have a sudden desire, a burning need to know more about him.

"Twelve years. I was supposed to be in for four."

"Why only four?"

He drags in a slow breath—and I want to be that breath. I want to be so close to his mouth. I'm losing my mind because I'm jealous of air.

"I didn't have the money to go to school, and the military can assist with that."

"Oh." I'm being nosy, but I press for more. "And what'd you want to go to school for?"

"Architecture." He clears his throat. "My father was a carpenter. I was sort of his apprentice when I was a kid, absorbing everything he could teach me. I was his shadow."

I can picture him as a kid, working with his hands, wanting to be like his father. I was always in my father's shadow, hidden by it—and its vortex. Never alongside him.

"What made you stay in the service longer?"

He shifts gears as we head toward the Long Island Expressway, and we pick up speed. "I got addicted to it. Became a SEAL, and once I was in that deep, there was no turning back."

"Until now?"

He swipes a hand down his jaw. I'm curious if he'll keep up with whatever dose of truth serum he seems to have in him when he's around me. Or maybe he's always like this—strictly honest to the core.

"Your ex?" I prompt, hating myself for pushing but unable to stop myself.

"I was torn over whether or not to re-enlist when she dropped the bombshell on me that we were getting a divorce and she was moving to New York." His words are weighted down by gravity, but not quite as heavy as I'd expect.

Is he truly over her, or does he still have feelings for her?

I shouldn't care. I shouldn't worry about this. "I'm sorry."

He briefly catches my eyes, and his brows pull together. "I'm not. Not anymore. I don't think we were ever right for each other. We'd been together since high school, so…" He looks away. "But having my daughter in the middle of all this—that's what's rough. I thought we were being civil, but I guess not."

I can't imagine, so I don't say anything. What can I possibly say? This man, who served our country for twelve years in one of the most lethal jobs on the planet, has a tender heart like none other I've witnessed.

"Was your sister already here in New York?" Since he's not speaking and I'm completely clueless as to what to say about his daughter, I decide to do what's natural—change the subject.

"Yeah, luckily for me, and she was starting up her design business."

"She's got a real eye. So do you. Did you ever finish school?"

"No."

"Do you still want to?" I look back at him.

"Maybe. But I'm happy with what I'm doing right now. And my job brought me to you."

I blink a few times as if I didn't hear him right, but he doesn't look my way. I wonder if he doesn't even realize he said it, so I let it go. His words fall down the annoying cracks between the gear shift and the seat where things go to die, never to be found again.

Minutes pass.

"So you have brothers. You said something about your brother and a judge. How many do you have?"

I straighten in my seat, my shoulders tensing at the mere thought of Cade. His words from our call last night echo in my head. "A younger brother, Corbin. And an older brother, Cade. Cade's engaged, but Corbin will probably never settle down. Well, not until my father forces his hand like I think he's trying to do with me."

"With you?"

Shit, I didn't mean to… "He kind of looks at marriage like a business deal. What would be the most profitable for our family and what would help propel us further socially."

"And how do you feel about that?" he asks.

"It's like my music. It's a waste for me to try to think about anything that makes me happy. I don't control my fate. He does."

And we both stay quiet again.

The silence wraps us up in some sort of bubble where I can barely hear the falsetto of the singer on the radio. Then Noah's hand moves from the stick shift to my bare thigh, and my breath catches at his touch.

"Nobody controls you but you." His voice is so firm, so resolute; it's almost as if I can believe him, embrace his words as the gospel truth.

"I guess you caught me in a lie, huh?"

"What do you mean?"

I look at him, but his eyes are on the road. "When you asked me that night we met at the bar if I had everything I wanted in life…well, I don't."

Not even close.

* * *

"For someone afraid of the water, why do you have a home on the ocean?"

I lean against the side of my car and look beyond the house at the beach. My own private beach. "It was my grandmother's place. She left it to me when she passed away eight years ago."

I take in a lungful of salty air and close my eyes. Memories from the stories she'd tell me by the campfire dance to my mind. Cade never wanted to come here. He wasn't close to her; their personalities clashed.

Hell, none of my family really liked her, which is why they basically kept her out at this house and away from the city in her later years. But Corbin and I adored her. She was truth bottled up into one tiny woman. An amazing spirit and nothing like my father.

"This is the reason I brought you here." I push off the car and approach him. He's looking at the Cape home, observing the structure, probably noting the work it needs. "My apartment was a test run." I spread my palms open. "This is the real job. I want it fixed up."

"To sell?" He turns and faces me.

"God, no."

"But the water…" He comes in front of me, his face tight with concern.

"Just because I don't plan on going swimming doesn't

117

mean I can't lie on the beach and get a tan." I chuckle. "I have a fear, but it's not that bad. I won't start shaking or something." I slap his chest. God, it's so hard, like pure steel carved beneath his T-shirt.

"Are you serious about the job?" He looks back at the home, the color of blue cotton candy. It probably needs an exterior face lift as well.

"Of course. It'll probably take a lot of time and work, though. Is that okay?"

More time with him. I try to convince myself this was always the plan, to hire someone for my apartment then have them work here, but honestly, until Noah, I didn't know when I'd come back here again.

"Bella should come."

I clasp my hands, and we walk side by side down the path toward the front door. I hang back inside the kitchen and allow Noah to get the lay of the house.

"I have someone take care of the place for me, which is why it doesn't look like a haunted mansion," I call as he comes down the main staircase at the center of the house.

"It's big. Depending on what you want, it could definitely take months." He scratches his jaw, the dark stubble there. "Six bedrooms, seven bathrooms—the main living room and kitchen alone are a lot of work."

"But you're up for it?" I pop onto a bar stool at the kitchen island, which doubles as a breakfast bar.

"You shitting me? Bella is going to flip."

"Should we talk money?"

He waves. "You can work that out with Bella. I'm just the hard labor. Although we might need to take on an actual crew for this project." His eyes light up as his gaze sweeps across the room.

"It needs updating like my apartment. I'd like a French

country look. Maybe even some Southern charm. And that wall needs to be taken out to join the living room and kitchen together for a more open concept."

He nods. "It has great bones, though." He reaches into his pocket and pulls out his phone. "Should I call her?" Then he shakes his head and sets his phone on the counter. "Maybe later."

I shrug. "Sure. You want a snack? Water? I think there might be some stuff here." We popped through a drive-through on our way here for a bagel and coffee, but that probably wasn't enough for him.

"I'm good, but maybe we could get some fresh air? It's a perfect day."

Low seventies in May with a slight breeze from the ocean —a walk would be nice.

"Sure."

We go out the sliding glass doors and head beyond the deck. We have the ocean to ourselves. Noah slips off his shoes and walks barefoot in the sand, and I follow suit.

"How close is too close?"

"Hmm?" I'm staring at the ocean, watching the waves rise and crash, and a slow sense of panic builds within me. I flinch and step back, my throat growing thick, but then Noah touches my elbow. "I—"

His fingers glide down my forearm and thread with my own, and suddenly the pounding in my chest dulls to a regular beat, and the fear dries up beneath the sun rays.

"I almost drowned when I was eight. Got sucked out in a rip current—on this very beach." My eyes close as I drag up images from when I was a kid. "I thought I was going to die." I shake my head. "I remember doing what I'm not supposed to do—swim against the current. It's a losing battle."

"What happened?" He squeezes my hand, which has me

opening my eyes, and I find him looking at me. He's standing before me, still holding my hand—holding my heart at the moment.

"Cade was on a jet ski. Just as I was about to give up, to quit the fight and slip under, he saw me." I owe both my brothers my life now. "I haven't gone near water ever since. Not even rivers or lakes. Pools. I can handle pools." I force a slight, probably crooked smile. "And here you are, a man who lived on the water—still do."

"What if you start small?"

"What do you mean?"

He tips his head toward the water. "We step in. Just one small step. That's it."

I look at the water as it rolls over the sand and glides back out. "One step." I hold up my free index finger, and he nods.

"One step."

"You must think I'm such a wuss to develop a crazy fear of water because of what happened."

"I would never think that about you."

And I believe him.

I glance at the water. The waves don't look tough today. Like a slow trickle of movement softly flowing in over the sand.

My jaw clenches, but I allow him to walk me out farther. Facing my fears.

I close my eyes and wait for the moment when the water will touch me. It's quick and cold, splashing me. But I don't step back.

Shit. I'm such a damn coward. Noah was facing terrorists in the Middle East, and I get hot and sweaty and nervous at the touch of the ocean on my feet. What the hell is wrong with me?

I suck in a deep breath, pull my hand free of Noah's, and walk deeper into the water.

"What are you doing?" he calls.

I can do this. It's just water. My fear is absurd, and if I can overcome this, then maybe there's hope for other parts of my life. Maybe I can move on after what happened in Greece.

I continue to move with my eyes closed. Soft waves crash against me—little bits of pressure on my legs. Chills rush through me, but the warm sun touches my head, and I push forward even though it's getting colder now that the water is to my knees.

"Grace."

His hand goes to my arm, but I pull away. I don't want to be stopped. I need to do this, to know that I can. A larger wave splashes me, but I hop up with it to keep myself from getting totally doused. The waves—they're what scare me the most. The power of them. The damn current...

When the water is up to my hips, the bitter cold sinking into my bones, I stop and open my eyes.

"You took a lot more than one step," he says as he comes in front of me, and I realize his jeans are soaked. The bottom of his shirt floats at the top of the water, and I look down at my own black tee as another wave hits me.

I'm so damn cold, my teeth start to chatter.

"I think that was good enough for one day." He grins, and I see pride in his eyes.

Or maybe that's how I'm feeling about myself. Proud.

He holds my elbow as if he's afraid he might lose me to the ocean, and he guides me back to the sand. "You're shaking."

And my teeth just keep jamming up and down in time with the rapid beating of my heart.

"Let's get you warm."

We dash inside the house, and Noah starts for the fireplace. With a flip of the switch, the flames roar to life.

I'm anxious and so alive right now.

I did that. I went into the water. Me.

Maybe it's the high—or the cold—but I peel off my shorts without thinking, needing to get the heavy wetness off me. Then my top too.

Noah must be freezing as well. I think Corbin has clothes here he can wear.

But the man's not even shaking. Not even a flinch from the wet or the cold. The strength and power beneath his clothes, the compassion inside him…he's so sexy right now. Suddenly I forget about the cold, and I think I'm shivering for another reason.

"That should help. Plus, you might want to change—" He's facing me now, and his brows slant inward. His eyes start at my chest and go down, taking me in, and I want him to.

I'm in a bra and underwear—sheer, at that, so I'm basically nude—and his eyes on me feel incredible. But his hands and mouth would be better.

I watch his Adam's apple move when our eyes finally meet again. "Grace."

"I was cold," I say, almost in a daze, as I look at his strong, corded forearms. God, he's such a man. A real man. Not those fake men in suits who care only about money and status.

He glances at a blue throw blanket on the couch by the fire and starts to go for it.

"I don't need that."

He pauses mid-step and stands erect, squaring his shoulders. His hands turn to tight knots at his sides, pressing against his outer thighs as if he's wrestling with a decision to make.

And I want to make it for him. I want to cross that red line that has been carved, practically in blood—by the blood of my family—and I want to be with a man I know can make me feel so much more. I reach around behind my back and start for the clasp, still holding onto his gaze.

"Grace." It's a warning, I know.

"Sex," I say in a rush. "It can just be sex." I remove the straps and drop my wet bra to the floor. My nipples are hard not only from the cold but from the heat of his stare.

I've never done something like this before. Maybe Rachel's right; maybe I do need a little naughty in my life. Even though this doesn't feel wrong to me.

For the first time, something in my life feels right.

Noah cups a hand over his mouth, and I greedily take in the sight of his body. His partially wet shirt sticks to the muscles of his stomach, and his cock is hard, straining against his jeans.

I slip my fingers down my abs and to the top of my panties.

"I can't offer more than that," he says in a throaty voice.

"Me neither," I whisper, afraid if I speak too loud, my voice will shake. "So we use each other for sex. No strings."

He edges a little closer, but he's fighting this, and I know why—he doesn't want to hurt me. And I respect that, but dammit, if he doesn't take me into his arms soon, I might lose my mind.

"This is what you really want?"

I don't hesitate—I just nod and shove off my underwear. I'm standing buck naked in front of this man with the sunlight pouring in through the windows as if I'm under a spotlight.

"Fuck." His eyes darken. He comes toward me in two quick strides and immediately lifts me as if I'm weightless. His mouth crashes over my lips, and his tongue twines with mine as he carries me into the living room.

My hands go to the back of his head, and I push my fingers up through his thick, dark hair, which is a slightly rougher texture than silk.

I'm nearly panting when he drops me onto the couch and sinks to his knees before me. His eyes follow the path his fingers are burning across my skin as his hands work up my legs, then he gradually wedges my knees apart. I tilt my head back as he kisses my inner thighs.

I've thought about this so many times since we met, but nothing can compare to the real thing.

One hand wraps around my ass, and he squeezes as his mouth covers my sensitive flesh. I buck my hips up and gasp in pleasure. He's giving me what I need, building the intensity and the pressure with his tongue and fingers at the same time. Then his hand goes up to my breast, and he pinches my nipple.

"I don't want to come yet." I want the first time to be with him inside me.

"Shh…"

He has me crying out as he strokes me again with his tongue. He's hitting every chord in perfect harmony, and I'm about to peak. My shoulders arch back, straining, pressing into the couch as my eyes roll back. Tremors rip through my body, and I can't stop.

He holds my hips in place and it's almost torturous, but he doesn't stop. I press my hands to his shoulders, not sure if I can take any more pleasure without losing consciousness.

"Noah…" My voice breaks.

His lips move back to my thighs, and I relax as he trails

kisses down to my calves and begins kneading my flesh, giving me a massage.

Is this man for real?

"Do you have any protection here?" he asks once he's upright and on his knees.

Suddenly I feel so naked and exposed with him fully clothed. I'm trying to use my brain—to formulate coherent thoughts, but it's hard. "I, uh, my brother uses this place from time to time. Maybe the bedrooms have some."

He stands then takes my hand, helping me.

I angle my head toward the stairs. "This way."

Noah catches me off guard by slapping my butt on our way up the steps, and it turns me on. When we get to the top of the stairs, I can see that this man is coming undone with need. And I love that I'm the one doing it to him.

My back ends up against the wall as he pins my hands above my head and kisses me. I can taste myself on him, and I try to let go and live in the moment. He palms my breast with his free hand then reaches between my thighs again, parting them, demanding entrance, and I obey without question.

"Which way?" His voice is like velvet on my skin, soft and smooth. I could listen to him speak all day. It's not just the Southern accent; it's the way he speaks with authority but also with passion—like every damn word he says is meaningful and goes straight to my bones, starting a fire inside me.

He slowly lowers my arms, and I point down the hall in a daze. I'm cold from his wet jeans and shirt, and I want his naked body to cover mine and warm me.

I allow him to take my hand, and he follows me. I flip on the switch in the guest room and head toward the white painted end table by the bed. Thank God. Inside the drawer is a string of purple foil packs, and I have to squeeze my eyes for a second and remind myself that the woman taking care of the house has washed the sheets since my brother has been here.

But maybe we should go to another room…

Before I can voice my idea, Noah has me falling backward onto the bed, and my hair fans out behind me. I stare at him as the condoms drop from my hand.

He's looking at me, that dark, almost pensive expression in his eyes as he peels off his wet tee. His hard, golden chest moves up and down slightly, and I follow his hands to where he works at the button of his jeans.

When he's standing in only his navy boxers, his cock stretching out the wet fabric, I have to bite my lip and force myself to clutch the plush comforter instead of touching myself—missing his hands on me.

"Wait for me."

He must notice my hands are twitchy with need. My back arches off the bed, my breasts jutting in the air as I wait—like painfully slow ticks on a clock when you're desperate for something and time stands still.

He's making me physically hurt for him to be inside me.

And damn, I can't even begin to describe the intense pain between my thighs as he removes his boxers, exposing his hardened length. I have to look away from his muscular thighs and the V above his hip bones—but when his eyes capture mine, it's worse. The intensity of his gaze has my stomach muscles clenching, and I can't help myself. My hand slips to my breast and my other hand slides down to my center, but Noah shakes his head and comes down on top of me, moving my hands away.

"Only my touch," he rasps before flipping me onto my

stomach in a quick move that reminds me of this man's powerful strength. "I'm not nearly done with you yet."

I dig my fingertips into the pink rose petal bedspread as he shifts my hair away from my ear and trails kisses down the side of my neck. His mouth moves down my spine to the small of my back before touching the curve of my ass, and I want to bite something to stop from screaming.

I've never felt like this before. No man has ever brought me to the edge with a touch, with a kiss. I feel him spread me apart, and I inhale at the feel of his tongue back between my thighs, then he's hitting my sensitive spot again, but from this position, it's making me unable to see straight. White dots dance before my eyes, so I close them tight and ride this unbelievable wave of pleasure.

"Please." I'm begging again. But this time I'm begging for release because I can't take it anymore.

Within moments, I'm already peaking again, unable to hold back, then he grips my ass with both hands, squeezing tight as I jerk and buck against his face, losing all sense of control.

And then he flips me over, and he's looking down at me, bracing his hands on each side of me as I pant like a damn crazy person in heat.

"Are you ready for me?"

I want to return the favor, I want to give him everything he gave me, but I can barely move. My legs are like jelly.

He pushes up, grabs the string of condoms I dropped, opens one, and slides a rubber over his cock, the veins prominent there. My body is already tightening, greedy for him. He lowers himself over me and brushes his knuckles across my cheek. His lips part a little as he stares into my eyes.

"I'm ready," I whisper before he positions his tip at my

center. When he eases himself inside me, my head goes back, and my body shifts up to slam against his, wanting—no, needing—to take all of him.

"Jesus," he says under his breath, and I almost miss the word.

He moves in and out, slowly at first, stretching me. I'm so tight, and then his thrusts go so deep inside me that I wonder if we'll ever come apart. I don't want him to. It feels so right. Like he belongs inside me.

"Look at me."

His demand is throaty, and I can tell he's hanging on the edge the way I was moments before. Hell, the way I still am. I'm so sensitive that even the slightest pressure will make me snap.

My eyes are closed because I'm afraid to see the man I'll have to give up.

"Grace…"

The moment I force myself to give in to his wishes, I find release, my body shaking as he climaxes with me, all the while keeping eye contact.

"Wow," I say after a minute, and he gradually slides out and lies beside me.

I turn my head and look at him. His eyes are closed now, his head tilted toward the ceiling, and I'm wondering what he's thinking. Does he regret crossing the line?

Then I catch sight of his tattoo—the artwork there. I shift to my side as my fingers skate over his shoulder. "Does the tattoo have any significance?"

"Tattoos," he says without opening his eyes, but the muscles in his stomach tighten.

There are different symbols all blended inside what looks like a giant circle. An anchor, fox, tiger, and more.

"They represent the people I lost," he says after a moment. "Nicknames and such of the guys."

I immediately drop my hand from his body and lower back to the bed, the air from my lungs deflating. "There are a lot," I whisper, not meaning to say the words out loud.

"Are you okay?" I ask when he doesn't speak.

The warmth of his hand covering mine takes me by surprise, and the heat of his touch spreads throughout my body.

I take a shaky breath as he shifts my way, his eyes now open, and he palms my cheek with his free hand. "Right now, here with you, I'm more than okay," he says and then presses his mouth to mine.

11

GRACE

My body is sore. Deliciously sore. And yet, as Noah drives us back to the city, all I can think about is him pulling over so we can have sex again. Too bad I don't have an SUV.

If we're really going to have a no-strings-attached kind of relationship, I know it won't last long, and I want to get as much of my fill of him as humanly possible.

"Tell me what happened in Athens."

I blink a few times, and his words kill my sudden desire to slip my hand between his thighs while he's driving.

"Why?" My heart is pounding in my ears now, but the extra beats aren't doing anything to help warm my suddenly chilled body.

Noah grips the wheel tighter as he shifts gears with the other hand. "I want to know what happened. I don't deserve to know, but I need to know how to help you."

"I don't need help," I barely squeak out. I'm lying, and it's really hard to lie to this man, especially after he spent the day studying every inch of my body. Why does he want to help me? "Just because we had sex doesn't give you the right to know more about me."

He glances at me out of the corner of his eye but looks back at the road. "Fine."

A quick word can hit you harder than a mouthful of anger every day of the week, even on Sunday.

"Shit, I didn't mean…" I cross my arms and lean back in my seat. I've already opened up to him about my stupid water fears. Why does he need more from me? Why can't the sex be enough? "You understand this thing between us is just—"

"Sex?"

It's not a statement. He's making sure we're on the same page. Is this some kind of test? Does he want to make sure I'm not all hearts and rainbows like most women might become? You know, the ones who promise no strings to get the guy while harboring secret hopes of him falling madly in love. That's not me.

"If this really is going to be just sex, then you shouldn't be afraid to talk to me. If you think opening up to me is going to make this more than it is, more than it can be, then we shouldn't do this again."

This? Sex?

His attitude has thrown me for a complete one-eighty. What happened to Mr. Nice Guy? Maybe this is some sort of defense mechanism? He's building a wall around his heart and wants to make sure I don't have a big enough sledgehammer to knock it down?

Well, I don't. I'm a coward.

"I was almost killed." I let the words fall from my mouth so fast that I know my admission is out of anger, but at the same time, it's a little freeing. Only my family and Jessica know what happened in Athens.

Noah's eyes are on me, but I gently punch his shoulder, demanding he looks back at the road, so we don't crash.

"What the hell happened?" His voice is gritty, like sandpaper.

I don't want to do this. I don't want to tell my story, but if this man is going to be a prickly pain in my ass about it—or worse, withhold sex from me when I need that more than anything—then I'll share if that's what he wants.

"Do you really need to know?"

"Yes," he bites back.

I tense, and my quad muscles lock up as my mind takes me back to that night in Athens. "Some guy was targeting wealthy female travelers in Greece. He would stalk them first and then attack. The police said he kidnaps them from their hotel rooms. And before killing them, he has the woman transfer a large sum of money to an untraceable bank account."

"Jesus."

Noah's looking at me again, and it's hard for me to say more with his eyes on me. I need to discuss this as though it's some story on the news and not related to me. I wait for him to focus on the highway, and my fingernails bite into my thighs as I shut my eyes. "I was in Athens working out a business deal for two weeks."

My hand darts to my core as I remember everything.

The dark hotel room.

The hand covering my mouth after I entered.

My heart slamming into my chest, a bitter pain like nails clawing into my flesh.

Maybe they were nails—his nails piercing my skin.

The knife nicking my throat.

My fingers sweep up to the side of my neck where the man had positioned the blade.

"I, um…" *I can do this.* "Well, I was walking back to my hotel room after a business dinner, and I had just said good night to my brother Corbin, who was traveling with me. Our rooms were on different floors. I heard something behind the door when I was searching for the key in my purse."

My eyes flash open at the feel of Noah's hand covering mine. I stare at our hands, trying to find the strength to continue.

I'm alive. The bastard didn't get me. I have to keep reminding myself of this.

"I shouldn't have ignored the weird feeling I got in my gut. I shouldn't have opened that door, but I did. And the guy was waiting for me when I got in." I nod a little as I process my thoughts, trying to sort through my recent nightmares and what really happened. They've become jumbled at this point.

"I tried to fight, but he pinned me to the floor. He was so big. And we—we struggled, and he muffled my screams. And then I heard a knock at the door." I capture a lungful of air and let it out, needing a second. "My brother had forgotten to tell me something, and I wasn't answering my phone. It felt like minutes had passed since I'd walked into my room, but it was probably less than sixty seconds. My brother heard the noise outside my door, and he had the second key to my room—thank God. I have a habit of losing mine, so when we travel together, I give him the spare."

"What happened?"

I pull my hand from Noah's and press both of mine to my chest, trying not to have a panic attack. But my chest grows tight with one coming on.

"You're okay, Grace."

His voice brings me back to the car and out of that hotel room, and I take a minute to try to steel my nerves, to calm my pulse. "My brother fought him, but the son of a bitch got away."

"Shit. Thank God your brother was there. I can't even begin to imagine—"

"The guy had killed three women the police knew of before he attacked me." My hands form tight fists in my lap, and I stare at them.

"Please tell me they found him."

"Not yet." He could still be out there—murdering…

"I don't even know what to say. I'm so fucking sorry."

"So now you know." I look out the window, unable to face him.

"The nightmares are about this?"

When I finally look at him, my eyes are coated by a thin film—I try not to cry, not to crack, but when Noah veers off the highway and parks the car, I nod.

And I break.

I cry so damn hard that my chest burns. I don't know when he unbuckled himself and my own seat belt, but he's stretched across the stick, his arms wrapped around me as I sob against his chest. Noah combs his fingers through my hair and presses his forehead against mine when I finally come up for air.

"I don't know where that came from." I swipe at my face. There's no mascara there since we showered earlier, but I still feel like a mess. I shift back and press a palm to my face. "I get scared when I'm alone at night. I remember Athens every time I close my eyes."

I see the tension in the few lines in his forehead and the slight crinkles by his eyes. It's not age—it's experience. Experience with death, with probably having to kill and witness his friends killed…

"You have PTSD," he says.

I squint at him.

"Are you talking to anyone about what happened?"

I shake my head. "Do *you* have PTSD?" My voice is soft. I've always struggled with talking to my veteran friends about this issue. I've never even broached the subject with Luke.

Noah rubs his jaw with one hand, then he presses his palm to his thigh. "Sometimes I wonder if I'm messed up because I don't."

"What do you mean?"

He shrugs. "I miss the life. I've never had regrets or struggled with the decisions I had to make in the service. I've killed people—bad fucking people. I've had to choose whether someone lives or dies, and I've never doubted my choices." He looks at me. "I miss the friends I lost. I think about them. But hell, I don't shake; I don't get angry or have nightmares. I'm just me. And shit, there must be something wrong with me if I don't feel messed up, right?"

"A lot of people struggle when they come back, but that doesn't mean you have to be one of them."

He swallows and takes a breath. "And there's no reason why you should feel bad about it either. What you went through...well, I can't imagine. If that happened to my sister, I'd probably cross the ocean and kill the motherfu—" He cuts himself off as if swearing around me is offensive, even though he's been doing it regularly. His so-called sailor's mouth isn't as bad as some of the others I've heard, and I'm not exactly a saint either.

"You're a good brother."

"Sounds like you have a good one too."

"One, at least. The other is a bit intense." I force a small laugh.

"Aren't brothers supposed to be?" He takes my hand

again. "I really think you should see someone." His tone is more serious. "You need to talk about what happened."

I pull my hand from his as if I'm guilty of feeling more than I should.

"That's okay. That's what locks are for, right?" I fake a smile and push a hand through my hair and relax back into my seat and buckle up. "We should get back to the city. It's late."

"Grace."

"I'll talk to someone." I look at the New York skyline in the distance. "This doesn't change anything between us, okay? You know what happened to me, but I don't want you to pull back because of it."

He repositions himself behind the wheel.

"I want to make this work, this whole sex without those damn strings thing. Just don't let my past be the strings— don't cut me out of your life yet. I need this. What we did today—it's exactly what I need."

Noah looks at me, his brows knitted, and although the sky's becoming a dark navy as the sunlight disappears, I can still see the emotion in his eyes as his pupils expand. "You're sure?"

God, I need the sex, but can I really be with someone like him and not fall?

"Yes," I say, not sure if I'm lying.

CADE'S THIS FORCE OF POWER, LIKE A TORNADO THAT COMES in and wrecks everything. He's tall, broad-shouldered, and intimidating as hell to most men. He fills the room with his presence and his arrogance. He's strong like Noah, but he's a total asshole. I don't know how we're related.

"Did you talk to Jessica?" He tosses his suit jacket on my couch and tugs at his burgundy tie, loosening it as if it has a stranglehold on his neck. "Did you tell her we were making a play for Alexander & Sons?"

I lift my fingers from my computer keys and lean back, studying him as he stands before my desk. His focus shifts to his sleeves now, and he rolls them up to his elbows, exposing some of the ink on the inside of his arm. He must not be in the right state of mind because he never lets *anyone* at work see his tattoos.

But right now, he's ready for a fight. I'm prepared to throw down with him, to stand up for what I believe in even if I have to suffer his wrath. Clearly Jessica spoke to one of the Alexander sons.

"Drinks didn't go so well on Saturday night, I take it?" I stand, wanting to be on an even playing field, but he still has several inches on me.

Where's Corbin when I need him? Someone to run interference between us. Cade and I both have fiery personalities.

He glances at the closed door and releases a breath. "We're in trouble." He tilts his head back, looking at the ceiling for a moment before his eyes meet mine again.

"What do you mean?"

"Come over here." He flicks his wrist toward the wall of windows as if he's afraid someone is somehow eavesdropping through the door. I cross the room as his palm presses against the window. "Dad made some shit decisions this past year, and it's put us in trouble. He's planning a merger, but the company we were going to unite with was only willing to join if the deal with Alexander & Sons was on the table."

Is he kidding? But Cade doesn't joke about anything. And

although he's not thrilled about marrying the daughter of the governor simply because Dad thinks it's a smart business decision to have someone political in our family's pocket, Cade doesn't mess around when it comes to work.

I cross my arms, struggling to believe I could be kept in the dark for so long about a merger. I knew about a few bad deals, but since I never see the overall financials, I had no clue things were this bad. "What are you saying?"

"I'm saying that without that deal, which is officially off the table now that the Alexanders' know we were coming for them, thanks to you, Dad can only come up with one other way we can get out of this mess."

The blood rushes from my face, and my stomach tightens. Oh, God, no. I swivel on my heel and turn away from the window, needing to think, to figure a way out of this. I can't be next. I can't be the next one Dad tries to marry off for the sake of business.

"Patrick," I whisper, too afraid to say it too loud. "We're merging with our competitor?"

"I'm sorry," he says in a low voice, sounding almost sympathetic. I want to believe he truly cares, but if he did, why would he put me in the same position that's making him so unhappy?

"Why does a merger with Taylor Enterprises have to involve me? This isn't the 1850s."

"Dad has had this in the works for weeks as a backup plan if the Alexander deal didn't work out. Richard Taylor feels better about the deal if our families are connected through blood."

"So *you* marry him! Screw the governor's daughter. You don't love her anyway," I rasp, anger flaring through me.

I've always known my family would try to twist my arm and force me to marry someone I don't want to, but part of me has been holding onto a tiny bit of hope that I could marry for love.

You know, someone like Noah. A real man who loves with his heart and not his wallet. A man who makes my body thrum with excitement from a simple touch or look.

My body instantly stirs when I think about him.

I need sex. Pure, unadulterated, crazy wild sex.

I need to lose myself and pretend this insanity doesn't exist. That I'm not the daughter of someone who would put the business ahead of his child's future and happiness.

"Grace?"

"Yeah?" My eyes have basically glossed over, and I can't think straight. "I have to go. I can't have this conversation right now."

I grab my purse and start for the door, not caring that I was in the middle of an urgent email—I need to get the hell out of here.

"This discussion isn't over," he says.

I glance over my shoulder at him as I open the door. His lips are in a tight line, and his jaw strains as he shoves his hands into his pockets.

"Maybe you could protect me the way Corbin did. You ever think about that?"

My own words surprise me, and his brows slant as he absorbs what I said. I don't mean to hurt him. I'm just angry that he's letting this happen to me and he's actually trying to broker a marriage deal between that asshole Patrick and me.

I know how he feels about what happened in Athens. Even though he doesn't show much emotion, I know it shredded him, and it's why he insists I have a bodyguard when I travel internationally now, but still—I was in Athens because he needed me to fill in for him. He blames himself.

He bows his head and grips the bridge of his nose. "That's not fair."

"You're my brother. That should come before money." I don't wait for him to look up. I slip out of the room and leave before the walls close in on me.

1 2

NOAH

"It doesn't work. The speed setting and arm are broken."

I lift the arm and examine the cartridge. If I replace it with a magnetic one, it should be good. And I can fix the speed setting. "It's still in decent condition. I think I can get it to work." I nod at the man and slide the money over the counter.

"It's all yours then," he says as his bushy white brows pull together.

I close the box of the antique record player and carry it under my arm out of the pawn shop. I'd been walking by the store and nearly stopped dead in my tracks at the sight of it displayed in the window. Like striking gold—a find like this.

The vibration of my phone in my pocket has me slowing on the street, and I grab it without dropping the record player.

It better be Cindy. I've been trying to reach her to make sure everything is going okay for Lily in Denver. So far all she's managed to send me is one little "we're fine" text.

But it's not her. Of course not. But it is Jessica—someone else I really need to talk to.

141

"Sorry I missed your call earlier. I was in a meeting," she says.

"And I'm sorry I couldn't make it to eat yesterday. I, uh, got tied up." Memories of yesterday with Grace plow through my mind, and my body tenses at the thought of having Grace's body beneath mine.

"I'm sure it was important, but we worked out the details with Bella, so I think we're good. And please don't stress about paying the investment back anytime soon. When you get to it, you get to it."

"I was actually calling for a different reason." I blow out a breath and pause in front of a shoe store. I stare at my reflection in the glass. I can't believe my life has come to this. "I need a lawyer."

"For?"

"I have a lawyer for the divorce, but he's not good enough now. I need the best if I'm going to get custody. Well, joint custody." My voice drops with each of my words as the gravity of what I've said slices me open and weighs me down. I might as well be standing in wet cement. It's as if the earth is swallowing me.

"Wait…I thought you guys already had this worked out? What the fuck!" Jessica doesn't normally swear, but we're on the same page right now. "Tell me that bit—" She clears her throat. "Tell me that Cindy isn't suddenly trying to get full custody."

I nod as if Jessica can see me. "She's pregnant, and her fiancé wants to legally adopt Lily." The words are bitter on my tongue, and my stomach swirls. "Please tell me you know someone amazing who won't cost me a fortune."

"Don't worry about the money. I know a lot of lawyers. Some are clients. I've got your back. Give me a day or two."

"Bella doesn't know, so…" I look away from my

reflection, hating that I'm keeping this from my family, but I don't want them worrying.

"Cindy won't win." She pauses. "What makes her think she can pull this off? It's freaking insane."

"I don't know, but I've got a bad feeling. I can't lose my daughter."

The line crackles from a huff. "We're not going to let that happen, you hear me? I'm in your corner, and there's no damn way I'll let her do this to you. I'll make some calls. You going to be okay?"

I start walking again, moving through the crowd of strangers. I was planning on heading back to Grace's, but I'm not sure what she's expecting from me. How does a no-strings kind of relationship really work?

"I'll be okay. Just call me when you've got a name."

"You're going to get through this. I promise," she says softly then hangs up.

I put away my phone and head to the docks, but when I get to my boat, all I can think about is that damn envelope.

I set the record player on my bed and head to the trash for it.

I still can't bring myself to open the thing—it's as if I'm worried there will be a personal invitation to hell from the devil himself.

I open my safe and put the envelope inside, take a quick shower, then I head back into the city, back to Grace. It's confusing, and it's messy, this thing with her, but it feels good. For the first time since I've been out of the SEALs, something feels right. I shouldn't be screwing around, but I also need to stay sane. And the way her body responds to me, the way her face lights up when we talk—I need that.

"Forget something?" Grace's security guard asks when I enter her building twenty-five minutes later.

I nod. "Yeah. Is Grace home?"

"Got in ten minutes ago." He winks as if he knows there's something going on between us.

"Thanks."

When I get off the elevator, I come face to face with her neighbor, the man who couldn't take his eyes off Grace even though he's married. He's with a woman—I assume his wife. She's a tall brunette and pretty, but she's no Grace. Hell, no one is or ever could be. Grace is a rare beauty whose presence fills the space around her and takes your breath away.

"The carpenter, right? I've seen you coming and going," the woman says and drags her gaze up and down my body. How has she seen me around but I haven't noticed her?

Her husband grabs her elbow and nudges her along. I tip my head and smile at them, not sure what the social etiquette is in this situation.

"Good night," she says, but I don't look back. I don't feel like dealing with a jealous, hypocritical husband.

I hit the buzzer then stuff my hands in my jeans pockets and wait. After a minute, I hear all of her locks unclicking. I wonder if she added extras after Greece. God, I can't even think about what could have happened to her in Athens without a serious ache in my chest. It makes my palms twitchy with the need to grab a rifle and take justice into my own hands.

Once the door opens, I raise a brow and smile. "You checked the peephole, right?"

"Of course." She steps back, but I don't walk in yet. She's still in her work dress, but she's taken off her shoes. "What are you doing here?"

"Since you never have food, I thought you might be hungry."

Her lips are a soft pink as if the lipstick she had on has

worn off. She glances at my hands as I remove them from my pockets. "I don't see any food."

I press a palm outside the door, and her eyes drift to my forearm. "I was thinking we could order in." My cock stirs in my pants because all I want to eat is her, every damn inch of her.

"Oh really?" She holds her hand out and swipes it through the air. "Then by all means, come in."

I don't have patience. Before yesterday, I did; I was able to resist the urge to take her into my arms. But now that I've had her, I can't help myself—I step into her place, push the door shut, and take her face in my hands and kiss her. She relaxes against me, her lips opening, inviting my tongue's entrance. When she moans, my hand falls to her hip and around to her perfect ass, squeezing.

She pulls away, breathless, and brings her hands to my chest. "I've been waiting all day for this. I was hoping you'd be here when I got home, and now—"

My mouth drops back over hers, stealing her words because I can't control myself. I need her. Plain and simple. I wrap a hand around the nape of her neck and slide my fingers through her hair, feeling the silky locks as my cock hardens and throbs.

She undoes my jeans' button, then the zipper, before stepping back and lowering herself to her knees, shoving my jeans down as she goes. My back goes to the wall. She takes my shaft into her hand and pumps slowly before her mouth goes around my tip, and I groan.

"Fuck," I growl when she moves faster, and she looks up at me, our eyes connecting. I'm not going to last long. She's going to shred me so damn fast. I don't want to stop looking at her, but I don't want to blow my load so soon.

"I want to come while I'm inside you," I say, my voice

gravelly and deep as I hang on the cliff—about to fall. My hand turns to a fist, and I tap the wall to my side as my jaw strains, trying to resist the urge to lose it.

And then I do.

My body jerks, and I come, and she takes it all.

When I open my eyes, she's standing in front of me. She goes for the zipper at the side of her dress, and I swallow a lump in my throat as I watch the material fall to the floor. She's only in a white lacy bra, her nipples poking through the material, her full breasts swelling.

"No underwear?" I rasp as I stare at her smooth center and reach between her legs. She's soaking.

"I took them off when I got home. I was about to get in bed and get myself off because I was so damn horny thinking about you, and then you knocked—"

I slide a finger inside her, and she bucks against my hand. "You teasing me, or…?"

"Mm. Guess you'll never know," she says in a seductively soft voice as she tightens her thighs around my hand. "But since you're here now, maybe we can beat our record yesterday. You think you can?"

I tug her lip between my teeth for a moment then pull back a little so our eyes can lock. "Challenge accepted."

I'M NOT SURE IF I'M SUPPOSED TO GO. IT'S NEARLY ONE IN the morning, and Grace has finally fallen asleep. Her head is on my chest, and her arm is slung over my stomach. I hate the idea of leaving her alone, especially if she might have a nightmare, but I also don't want to blur the lines we've set.

I lift her arm, position her head on her pillow, and slide out of bed. Her eyelashes flutter a little, but I don't wake her.

I don't know if I'm being an ass for leaving or not, but I've got to set some sort of boundaries and stick with them. I can't fall for this woman. The last woman I fell for was Cindy, and look where I am now.

I tug on my shirt and find my jeans and shoes. When I look back at her, stabbing guilt rips at my chest, but I'm making the right move. I can't open myself up to this woman when I need to focus on Lily.

Sex is sex. If I allow myself to feel something beyond that, what if that somehow jeopardizes my chances at getting Lily back?

I can smell Grace on me when I get back to the boat. It's late, and I should get some sleep before I get up in a few hours, but I can't stop thinking about her. How her body fits so perfectly with mine, and the way she lets loose when we have sex. Her cries and moans, even yelling my name the last time she came—it's such a damn turn-on to see this normally controlled woman come to pieces with me inside her.

I peel off my jeans and fling them in the laundry basket by the bed. I'm already hard again, in need of her. I can't help but wonder if Grace and I had met at a different time, could she have been the one for me? I'm a father, and she's Manhattan royalty—but what if we'd been from the same world? Could it have worked?

I didn't realize I'd even fallen asleep until I dart upright in my bed, my fingertips buried in the bedspread on each side of me. My forehead and chest are damp with sweat as I try to catch my breath.

Grace was attacked in my dream.

I watched it happen, unable to help. My arm outstretched —and I couldn't get to her. My body stuck in quicksand.

My mind replays the nightmare.

I close my eyes and fight back the anger that sears my

insides. Knowing what she went through and that this guy is still alive kills me. My fingers twitch, and I ball my hands. My mind goes back to my last mission in Iran.

My hand trembles now, and I open my eyes and rest it in my lap. This feeling, this desire to find that scumbag in Athens and murder him—what does that make me?

Am I just as bad—a killer?

Maybe I was wrong when I told Grace I'm okay.

13

NOAH

"Still no word from Cindy?"

I look at Bella. She's examining my work, walking around the room like an inspector. I feel as if I'm in basic training again, when they'd check my bed, my gun, my everything to see if it's perfect.

"She texted me earlier with another vague 'everything is fine, stop bothering me,' text," I grumble. At least she responded. She didn't answer my calls or texts yesterday.

"I'm so sorry." Bella's shoulders sag. "But, um, this place is really coming together. Better than I imagined." Bella's hand glides over one of the cabinets in the kitchen before she reaches for her iPad.

"You should be able to decorate by the end of next week. I already told Grace she'll need to stay somewhere else for the big reveal." I cross my arms and lean against the counter.

"Perfect." She tightens her grip on her tablet and taps it against her stomach as she squints at me.

"What?" I cock my head, waiting for some sort of blow. I know my sis well enough to know something is coming.

"What's going on between you and her?" Her voice is

softer than normal, as though she's worried I'll snap or react poorly to her words.

I got a text from Grace this morning, which surprised me. She didn't mention my disappearing act last night, but she did invite me to dinner tomorrow. She has a business meeting tonight, which kind of bums me out since I'm already anxious to be with her again, but it's probably best not to see her every night. But I wonder if a formal dinner is crossing the line. I said yes, though. I can't seem to get myself to say no to her, even if I should have when she first proposed being friends with benefits.

"Noah?"

Shit, I guess I have to say something. "Nothing is going on. In fact, I have good news." I grab my phone and flip to my pictures. I'd been waiting to share the news about the Hamptons home—waiting for a moment like this. "I got us a huge job."

Bella sets her tablet on the counter and swipes through my images. "Wow. This place is amazing—and huge. Whose place? Where is it?" She looks at me with her Bambi eyes.

"It's Grace's home in the Hamptons. Right on the beach. I guess this gig was a test run and she's happy, so she wants us to remodel the entire house."

Her mouth drops open, and I swear she stares at me for a solid minute straight without speaking.

I look her in the eyes, smiling. "You, uh, gonna say something?"

"Maybe we won't even need that investment from Jessica and Luke." Her eyes widen. "This is great news. You were there in person? You saw the place?"

I bring a fist to my mouth and look away. If she sees my eyes, she'll be able to read me. "Grace asked me to come see it on Sunday, which is why I had to bail on you. She wanted it to be a surprise." Not too much of a stretch.

"You two went to her beach house together? Alone?" She forces her way in front of me.

Dammit. I drag my gaze up to meet hers. "What's the big deal?"

She holds her hands up between us. "No! Are you two sleeping together?"

I shrug, not sure what the hell to say, because I know if I lie, she'll see it on my face. "If you're concerned about the job, don't be."

"Are you kidding?" She gives back my phone as her hand darts to her collarbone. "I'm worried about you. You'll get hurt. This is too soon after what Cindy did to you, and Grace is, well…"

"It's been almost a year. It's not like I haven't been with anyone since Cindy. Grace isn't the first."

"I didn't need to hear that." She looks away and braces against the island with both hands. "But, Noah, Grace is—"

"Grace is what?" I want her to say it. Maybe I need to hear it from her and remind myself as many times as possible that under no circumstances am I allowed to fall for her.

"She's not the best rebound option."

"That's not what you were going to say," I bite out. I'm the one coming around in front of her this time.

"She's rich. She's this classy businesswoman, and you're—"

"Not good enough?" I rub a hand down my jaw, the stubble pricking my fingers. I need to shave, especially before dinner tomorrow.

"It's not that." Bella lets out a breath and finally looks at me. "You're the best guy I know, but Cindy screwed you over. The last thing I want is another woman hurting you."

I almost laugh. But hell, she might be right. I trusted Cindy, and she cheated on me. And now she's trying to break me by stealing my daughter. Maybe I'm good at reading terrorists, but with women, I don't have a clue.

"End it now."

"I'm a big boy. I can take care of myself."

"Fine." She huffs, snatches her tablet, and starts for the hall that leads to the front door.

"Bella, wait." I don't want my sister pissed at me.

She halts but doesn't turn around. "The last thing I want is to ever have to say 'I told you so.' But I warned you about Cindy in high school, and I'm doing it now. It's not that Grace is too good for you. You're probably too good for her."

Bella leaves, and I let her. She's my sister, and she's only got my best interest at heart, but I know Grace better than she does. I don't think Grace is anything like Cindy, but that doesn't change the fact that nothing can ever happen between us.

My chest feels heavy, and I've lost my desire to continue working. I check the time, and it's nearly five. I might as well call it a day. On my way out, I get a call from Jessica.

"Tell me you have good news," I answer once I lock up Grace's apartment.

"I have a friend who'll meet with you. She's booked during the day tomorrow, but she can fit you in at dinner time."

A small bit of relief hits me. "Thank you."

"I'll text you her information, and you guys can work out the details. And she's doing this case *pro bono*."

"What? Are you sure?" I step inside the elevator.

"Yeah. She owes me a favor, so this squares us."

"Wow. Thanks, Jessica."

"All I want is a play date with Lily once you've won in court," Jessica says, and I can almost see her smile.

Thank God for good friends. "Deal." I end the call as I realize I was supposed to have dinner with Grace tomorrow.

Can we postpone dinner to Thursday? I can't meet up tomorrow.

I send the text, and one pops up a few minutes later.

I'll have to get back to you.

Having to wait to see her sucks. And the fact that I'm disappointed is a bad sign.

Maybe Bella is right.

Maybe I'm in way over my damn head.

* * *

MY NEW LAWYER, SARAH, LOOKS OVER HER SHOULDER AT ME as we walk toward the docks. We just wrapped up dinner at a nearby place. "I really don't believe she has a shot at custody."

"Then why the hell did she file?"

Sarah checked the records before we met for dinner tonight, confirming my suspicions that the petition for custody must be inside that envelope in my safe. The court docket was marked around the same time she showed up on my boat.

This is all insane.

I don't want to open the envelope, though—why bother now? I know what's inside. I don't need to see more of her betrayal, her selfishness, in print.

The divorce I accept. No questions. I don't contest that.

But custody? This could become one of the biggest battles of my life—because I'll be fighting for my daughter.

I stuff my hands in my pockets and look at the sliver of the moon in the sky.

"Well, I think this is a slam dunk case. You were a Navy SEAL with an impeccable record. You have more medals than God and were even invited to the White House to be honored. Hell, we'll make the president a character witness if we have to." She chuckles a little, probably trying to lighten the mood. "So I honestly feel really confident. But maybe we won't even need to take it that far."

She's hoping Cindy is anxious to get married and won't want to delay the divorce much longer.

I hail her a cab. She flicks her long black hair off her shoulder and smiles at me. She seems too young to be one of the most reputable attorneys in New York, but I did my due diligence and researched her last night. She's the real deal.

She reaches out and wraps a hand over my shoulder and looks me in the eyes. "We're going to get your girl back."

And I believe her.

I have to.

I nod and close the door after she's in the cab. My eyes follow the taxi before switching to the docks on my right—to Grace.

I never heard back from her after her text last night, so seeing her approaching in jeans and a graphic tee—not her norm—throws me off guard. My body tenses at the mere sight of her, and I start toward her, closing the gap of a hundred yards or so.

"What are you doing here? You shouldn't be at the docks at night." My mind races to thoughts of her attacker, to my nightmare the other night.

"I'm not stalking you, I swear." She laughs a little, but it's a nervous one. "I was out with Rachel. She's my assistant. Well, more like my friend. But we were at a bar not too far away, and I thought maybe you'd be around. I know you were busy for dinner, but I was hoping that maybe…" She looks at the ground. "Stupid idea."

I tip her chin up. "I'm glad you're here."

She swallows and is quiet for a moment. "I, uh, didn't know we were seeing other people while we were having sex. I mean, it's okay, but—"

"Are you kidding?" My hand slides down to her forearm, and I tug her close, her chest pressing against mine. "You're the only one I want to be with."

She stumbles back a step, and I'm not sure if she doesn't believe me or if my words sound a little too heavy for this casual sex stuff.

I need to clarify probably. "I have zero intentions of sleeping with anyone else."

"Me neither."

"Good, because I was hoping I'd wear you out enough that you wouldn't need to get off when I'm not around." I still have no idea if she was kidding the other night when I showed up and she was without underwear. I wonder if she's wearing any now.

Jesus, I'm already hard.

"Mm. I was alone last night, so—" She wets her lips, turning me on even more.

"Then we'd better not go that long without being around each other." I swallow the lump in my throat. "Do you want to go on my boat? Not sure if I have the patience to wait until we can get back to your place."

She looks over my shoulder at the water then back at me again. "Yes, please."

I take her hand and our fingers lace, but as we walk down the docks, I feel the need to offer her more of an explanation. I know our sort of relationship doesn't necessarily require one, but after what Cindy did to me, screwing with my head, I don't want Grace to have to question my intentions.

"I had to cancel because I was having dinner with my new lawyer." I tip my head over my shoulder while we walk as if the lawyer is behind us.

"Oh." Grace suddenly tightens her grasp.

"She thinks I can get joint custody." It's strange that Grace knows this but not my parents or Bella. But it's kind of nice having someone to share this with. Sure, I told Jessica, but that was only because I needed her help.

"That's great news."

I stop in front of my boat. This gorgeous woman is looking at me as if I'm the damn sun or something. Maybe even the moon. It's an odd feeling, and a good one.

"So maybe we should have some wine to celebrate." She flashes me a smile as the back of her hand goes over my smooth cheek. I finally shaved the three-day-old stubble-slash-beard.

She looks over at the water, and I notice her flinch a little.

"We'll stay down in the cabin."

She nods, and I take her hand and guide her on board. I unlock the door, and we go beneath.

"Mind if I play some music?" she asks while I search for a wine opener, hoping I even have one. I've got a bottle of wine a client gave me after I finished a job last month, I think.

"Please do." I search through the few drawers and find a bottle opener, but I also realize I don't have wine glasses. "You good with red cups?"

She laughs. "Never had wine out of a red cup before."

"I figured as much." I tip up my shoulders. "Always a first time."

"And I like that it'll be with you." She immediately looks

away as her brows pinch together, and I can tell she regrets her words.

I never knew how hard it could be to try to maintain a relationship based on sex and no emotions. Is that even possible? I'm willing to find out. I've only had a taste of her…

I pour the wine as Frank Sinatra begins crooning "My Lady."

She fakes a curtsy when I hand her a red cup. I watch her raise it to her mouth, realizing I would rather be tasting her instead. Why not skip to the good stuff?

"Mm. It's, well—"

"Horrible?"

"I've had worse." She laughs and sets the cup on the table, near the record player, and I follow suit, not giving a damn about the wine.

"Well?" She raises a brow.

I take that as my cue and close the short gap between us in one stride. I lift her, and she chuckles as I toss her onto my bed.

"Well," I say while unbuckling my pants, "I'd like to know if you're wearing any panties tonight."

Her hand darts to the hem of her jeans, and she holds my eyes as she slowly unzips. "Why don't you come find out?"

14

GRACE

S EX.

It was once a three-letter word to me, but God—I swipe a hand through my hair, closing my eyes as I think about Noah on his boat last night. Being with him is like taking a vacation to an adult amusement park where it's all about a woman's pleasure.

Yes, sex—S.E.X. All caps with cheerleaders shaking their pom-poms. It's that good with him. And knowing he's in my apartment right now, working up a sweat while sawing or sanding or whatever it is that he does, makes me want to leave the office and attack him. I've become a sex addict since we started this up on Sunday.

Hell, who am I kidding? I became a crazy horny woman when I met him at the bar two weeks ago.

Never has a man done this to me.

"You're glowing. Like hardcore glowing. And last night —you lied to me, didn't you?"

I open my eyes. Rachel's sitting on the edge of my desk, staring at me with pursed lips.

"I didn't lie."

"Yeah, okay." She rolls her eyes and shakes her mass of hair to her back. "You're having sex. Don't even try to tell me no this time. You're either pregnant"—she draws some sort of circle in the air with her finger—"or you're banging someone. A lot."

"And you're an expert?" I close my laptop and practically squirm in my seat, anxious to get out of the confines of my office. It feels like a prison now, especially after the wonderful heart-to-heart Cade and I had in here.

"I'm an expert. I'm, like, the queen of sex." She hops off my desk. "Speak, woman. I demand it." She coils her hair into a bun at the top of her head and ties it with a rubber band.

Maybe I'm becoming the sex expert now. I almost laugh, but Rachel wouldn't get the joke. "It's with the guy remodeling my apartment."

I clear my throat as if that will diffuse the tension. I wanted this thing between Noah and me to stay between us. Not that it's forbidden, but well…who am I kidding? It kind of is.

Her eyes bulge. "You're screwing a construction worker? Are you friggin' kidding me?" Her face lights up, and she slaps her hands together. "Oh, he must be so hot. Does he spank you with his tape measure?" She waggles her brows.

She's crazy, but I love her.

"Oh yeah," I joke.

"I knew it. I knew you had some naughty in you waiting to come out." She comes around next to me. "How about a threesome? If this guy is good enough for you, he's got to be unbelievable in bed."

"Now you've lost your mind." I stand and massage the small of my back, a little sore from Noah's bed. It's not all that comfortable, and I shouldn't have stayed the night.

"You guys aren't serious, though, right? I mean," she says while setting her hands on her hips, "he's a handyman."

I pause to think about her words. "What are you trying to say?"

I don't need her to spell it out for me, but I'm giving her a chance to back out of the shit pile she just stepped in. I expect this kind of attitude from my family, maybe even some of my colleagues, but not from Rachel. She scratches the back of her neck and her forehead pinches as she studies me, eyeing me as if I'm a scared animal about to jump and run the other way. I'm considering sharpening my claws and going straight for the jugular actually.

"Oh my God. It's not just sex." She shakes her head. "When your family finds out you're falling for this guy, you'll be in so much trouble with them." She covers her mouth and steps back, her eyes widening.

"Falling for who?" My brother's words sail through the room, and the deep timbre of his voice has the hairs on my arms standing.

Rachel shoots me an apologetic grimace, a little too late. "See ya, babe. We'll pick this up later."

"Yeah, how about never?" I gripe as she smiles at Cade and makes a beeline for the door.

"I guess you didn't take our talk the other day all that seriously."

I don't want to turn and face him. I don't want to deal with him right now. I want to go back into Noah's arms and lose myself. I want to be nineteen and in college, majoring in music and enjoying my life. That's how Noah makes me feel. Free.

"Why is Dad sending you to do his dirty work?" I cross my arms and finally turn to confront him.

He's pouring himself a glass of bourbon at the bar on the

other side of the room. When he approaches with the drink, his pupils dilate a little as he takes a sip. "He's in London with Richard Taylor."

"Great, is Dad writing the prenuptial agreement?" I half-joke, my stomach becoming even more knotted by the moment.

"Yes." The muscles in his face are taut, and I can barely read any emotion there—he's become such a cold, icy person. "Who was Rachel talking about? Is there something I need to know?" There's a slight pull around his eyes, finally displaying concern. Of course this subject makes him uneasy.

I sit back down.

Cade's brows pull together as he sets his drink before him. "Please tell me your neighbor's suspicions aren't right."

My head drops forward a little. "Say what?"

"You're not screwing the guy remodeling your apartment, are you?" He can't even look at me. It's as if he's accusing me of doing something repulsive—like committing murder.

My family thinks they walk on water and have the ability to part the seas. I've tried to fit inside the hard mold they've created for me, but this desire to break out has cracked the case. It's crumbling, and I don't know whether I should fight to keep up the walls or just let them down. But what will I do with my life if I don't do what my family tells me anymore?

"Grace?" Cade drags in a deep breath before letting it go. "Jesus Christ, don't tell me you actually care about this guy you're—" He waves as if shooing a fly.

"Don't."

"You and Corbin are going to give me a heart attack." He rolls his eyes as I stand and approach him.

"At least Corbin knows how to live his life." *Unlike me.* "Dad ruined you. You weren't always like this."

His eyes darken, and he steps back, bumping into the

chair. "Do you love this guy? This man you're running around with?"

What the hell did Evan tell him? Does he spy on me or something? He only saw Noah and me that one time, right? It's creepy.

"Why don't you focus on your own life and tell Dad to come talk to me himself? Don't let him make you the bad guy." I turn away, my hand darting to my chest as I try to stay strong.

"No good can come from being with someone he doesn't approve of."

When I finally get up the nerve to face him, he's gone. But the tension has left some sort of shadow in the room, and it's like a stranglehold.

I settle back in my chair and wave away one of my admins when he appears in the doorway a moment later. He tucks himself back out of sight, and I look at my phone. I want to do the one thing my brother doesn't want me to do—I want to see Noah.

But the thing is, I don't even feel like having sex right now. I just want to see him because being around him makes me feel so much better. And that scares me to death.

15

GRACE

THIS DAY HAS TURNED OUT BETTER THAN I COULD HAVE expected, and I don't want it to end. I want it to bleed into Sunday. When my father comes back from London on Monday, I'll have to face reality—so right now, I just need a piece of heaven, and part of that involves a delicious piece of pizza.

"You're right. Brooklyn does have the best pizza." Noah swipes at the sauce on his cheek with his napkin before taking another bite of his deep-dish pepperoni.

After the nightmare confrontation with my brother yesterday, I decided I needed to clear my head and have a little fun. And of course, spending time with Noah came to mind.

"I still can't believe you've lived in New York almost your entire life and have never been to the Statue of Liberty or the top of the Empire State Building." Noah smiles.

I slide my plate to the side, my stomach protesting—any more food and I won't be able to walk out of here. "A lot of people here don't do the touristy things. But since you're new, I thought you might like to go."

He finishes his last bite and tosses his napkin on his plate. "Well, it was cool going to those places with another first-timer."

"And I'm totally exhausted now. I suck as a tourist."

"Maybe you need to start working out with me to build up your stamina."

I stand up fast, lean across the table, and slap his chest. "I'm in damn good shape!"

He catches my wrist and presses a quick kiss to my lips. I pause in front of his face, his eyes holding mine, then I slowly shift back and onto my seat. He clears his throat, and I swallow, trying not to decipher whatever odd moment just happened between us. A simple kiss shouldn't feel so strange, but it does. Maybe it's because we're in the open, or maybe it's because it felt like a "couple" thing. I don't know, but I'm struggling with what to say next to break the sudden tension.

"I never thought I'd like living here," he says while tucking his hands in his lap, leaning back.

"And now?" My heart is beating erratically as if I'm going back and forth between a slow-paced jog and an Olympic-style sprint with hurdles. A lot of hurdles...

"It's growing on me." His lips go tight, and his eyes flash to his plate. "It'll be better when I can see my daughter on a regular basis."

His daughter—we haven't talked much about her, and I haven't wanted to bring her up. I never know how to broach the subject of his ex. I mean, he's still officially married, which always makes this feel a tad on the iffy side.

I work up the nerve to ask, "Do you have a photo?"

He nods and pulls out his wallet. He opens the black leather and hands me a small picture.

She must take after her mother because she's got light

hair and green eyes, the total opposite of Noah. "She's beautiful. What does she like to do?"

I hand him back the photo, and he studies it for a moment, as if in a daze. I can't imagine what he must be thinking right now. It must hurt to be so close to someone you love and not have access to them whenever you want.

He stuffs his wallet back into his jeans pocket and scratches the nape of his neck. "I was gone more than I was home, and that's the life she knew—but when I was home, I spent every minute with her. I had no problems dressing up like whatever she wanted and drinking tea if that made her happy. Of course, the fact that she likes sports was a plus. We'd throw the ball around."

He's speaking in past tense, and it breaks my heart. I hope to God the judge sees what an incredible man he is when he goes to court.

"She starts elementary school in September. I have no idea where the time went." He snaps his fingers. "I blinked and bam! She's almost six."

"I doubt if I'll ever have kids." I don't know why I said that, and I want to take the words back right away.

"No?" His eyes narrow, and he's clearly waiting for me to elaborate.

"Truth?"

"That's been our thing, right?"

A slow smile sweeps across his face, and it gives me pause. He's so gorgeous. Inside and out. How'd I get so lucky to meet this man? Then I remember Luke's warning—don't hurt Noah.

Maybe I'm the one who's going to get hurt.

"I don't want my kids becoming like me," I say.

"And what's so bad about you?"

I take a sip of my drink to stall. I almost want to tell him about the shit situation I'm in now, to have a shoulder to cry on, but he has his own problems, and he doesn't need mine. He's already held my hand to face my fears of the water and listened to the nightmare of what happened in Greece. Why add more to the mix?

My drink is empty and my stomach too full to eat more, so I have nothing to do now but speak. My shoulders sag as tension wraps around my spine at the thought of having to talk to my dad in a day and a half.

"I mentioned my family is overbearing, but they're so intense that it's like I can't breathe half the time. After what happened in—" I take a quick breath. "Greece…"

I just can't say more. I don't want the negativity to ruin the happiness I feel when I'm with him.

Noah's hands go to the tabletop, and he clasps them tight, as if he's hesitant to reach for me, but wants to.

The situation is confusing.

"They must have done something right. I've never met anyone like you before." His voice is deep and gravelly, and there's emotion there. Sincerity. He isn't some guy trying to get into my pants—he's already been there—this is something more.

I wave a dismissive hand and force a smile. "You've just been hanging out with too many guys in the SEALs is all. Limited contact with women." His wife. Shit. "And you were married." *Is* married. Damn the details.

Noah doesn't look away from me as I expect him to with the mention of his wife. Instead, it's as if his focus on my eyes intensifies, as though he's trying to solve the puzzle of me. Ha. Good luck with that. I'm clueless in that department.

"She cheated on me." His back meets the booth again as my lips part in surprise.

"Ohh."

His Adam's apple moves and his breathing becomes a little deeper as his chest inflates. There's anger beneath the surface, and I don't blame him.

"Being in the military can be hard on spouses, but Cindy—my ex—well, we were never right for each other. She wanted different things in life, things I could never give her."

"Like what?" I didn't mean to ask, but I'm honestly shocked that someone could be with Noah and find herself ever wanting more. I'm almost envious of this woman for being married to him. She had him all to herself. Who would ever want to risk losing a man like him?

"Money." The word is almost a whisper as if it's a dirty thing to him. It's become something dirty to me, given what my family is trying to put me through.

Neither of us talks for a minute.

"What were your parents like?" I finally deflect, but I'm genuinely curious what life was like for someone like him, someone who wasn't raised in a damn ivory tower and forced to eat from a metaphorical golden spoon. Is the grass really always greener…? I've had the pressing desire to know this for a while now.

His shoulders relax, and he smiles. "They were high school sweethearts. My mom stayed at home and took care of Bella and me while my dad worked. We didn't have much in life, but we didn't need it."

A pebble of jealousy flickers through my stomach like a stone skipping on a pond.

"They loved to dance to my mom's jazz music. I'd watch them dance around the living room, laughing and so damn happy."

I can imagine a young Noah, and it makes me chuckle a little.

"They still live in the house I grew up in outside of

Nashville. Someday I'd like to build them a new house, but every time I mention it, they insist they're happy as is."

"Wow," is all I can muster. "I've only seen my parents dance at stuffy black tie fundraisers, and they've only done it to keep up pretenses, never because they wanted to."

I'm not sure how this happened, how we're sitting at a little pizza place on the other side of the river, talking about our families when this was supposed to be only about sex, and yet I wouldn't trade this moment, this dinner, for anything.

"I have something for you. I was going to wait for Bella's big reveal, but—"

My cheeks warm. "A surprise? Where is it?" I slide out of the booth, feeling like a kid at Christmas. I sling my purse strap over my shoulder and wring my fingers together as I wait for him to get up.

"Oh, so you want it now, I take it?" He points down and squints an eye. "Like right now?"

I slap his chest for the second time tonight, but this time I leave my hand there—feeling his heartbeat beneath my palm. A slow and steady beat. His eyes drop to mine, and he opens his mouth to speak, but he stops himself for some reason.

"Right now," I whisper, and I'm pretty sure he's picked up on the double meaning.

I turn, anxious to leave, but he whispers from behind me, his breath at the shell of my ear, "It's at your place."

I stop and his hands go to my hips, bracing me. "I have a surprise hiding at my own place?"

He nuzzles the back of my head again, his mouth near my neck, and goose bumps spread across my skin beneath my T-shirt and jeans.

"Yes, but I also don't know if I can wait until we get to Manhattan to have you."

I nearly groan, but I catch sight of a family in a nearby booth and resist the compulsion to turn around in a pizzeria and press my mouth to his. I peek back at him over my shoulder. "I'm worth the wait."

* * *

"You want some wine?" I ask.

"I'm good," he says.

"Not much of a drinker, huh?" I switch to the music app on my phone, and a Calvin Harris song plays. "I'd put on the entertainment system, but it's not connected."

I set the phone on the couch still covered by a blanket and glance at Noah as he bends over and picks up a few materials from the construction job. He moves them to the other side of the room, clearing out a space near the bay window.

"I have a different idea." He swipes his palms over his jeaned thighs, leaving wood dust behind.

"Sure you don't hate the music?" I smile as he takes two long strides, nearly closing the gap between us. I hold my breath, wondering what he'll do once he's within arm's reach.

"This music is fine, but I thought you wanted your surprise." He raises his brows and cocks his head, studying me.

Damn him, he's still standing too far for me to touch him. I know I can move, I can go to him, but the anticipation has built up so much from our trip back from Brooklyn that I'm worried I might trip over myself going to him.

I'm not acting like an almost thirty-year-old woman. No, right now, I'm like an awkward teen from a nineties sitcom. I just need a hair scrunchy, leg warmers, and some sparkly gloss.

We've been playing different music stations every time

169

we make—shit, I stop my thoughts when the L-word dangles in my brain.

No, making love is for people who are committed, who are in relationships. For people who have known each other for months. Years, even.

I pause the music on my phone. "I do want it. Now."

I bite my lip, hold out my palms, and close my eyes. My body tingles with nervous anticipation, loving that I have no idea what he's going to give me—this excitement and energy pushes out any negative thoughts about my family business issues. It's just him and me right now.

"Give me a minute. And stay like that." He's moved because his voice sounds farther away.

It feels like forever as I wait.

"Okay," he finally says. "Open your eyes."

"I don't feel anything in my hands." I fake a pout, eyes still closed.

"It's too big."

I can tell he's smiling just by the way he spoke.

My eyes slowly open. Noah's by the window, standing next to a black table I've never seen before. Bella must have bought it with the shopping budget I gave her. But what's on it is what matters, and I slowly move toward him, my hand coming to my chest.

"It's an antique. I was passing by a store when I saw it in the window. It needed some fixing up, but I managed to find the right parts." He positions the needle over the vinyl.

I stop in front of the table, mesmerized by the gift. "I don't know what to say." I look into his blue eyes. There's so much heart and soul there.

"Do you like it?" He smiles. "After seeing your response to mine on the boat, I thought maybe you'd like your own."

My tongue rolls over my teeth as I steal another minute to

think, to contemplate the right answer, but a heavy weight is pressing down on my chest.

"You okay?" His hand goes to my shoulder.

I almost shut my eyes as the music of Miles Davis fills my home. The same song we listened to on his boat the night of his birthday. "I, um…I think it's the best present anyone has ever given me."

He laughs a little. "Now you're pulling my leg."

"No, really." I reach for his hand and lace my fingers with his. "Will you dance with me?"

I want to take the words back the second he steps away, and his facial muscles grow tight, his jaw clenching a little. My hand falls at the obvious rejection.

His eyes go to the floor, and his hands turn to fists before he unfurls them, and his gaze finds mine again. "I think I should go. I'm so sorry."

What just happened?

"Maybe this was a bad idea." He starts past me almost immediately.

I want more than anything to turn and call out to him, to beg him to stay, to cross the line with me.

I don't turn, though. I don't try to stop him. I remain staring at the record player, my insides burning—pain ripping through me. I've only known him for a few weeks, so why do I feel like this?

This might be the end of the road.

The line in the sand has become a trench, and things will get too messy if we even try to get to each other…

And we can't try, can we?

I lift the arm of the record player, stopping the music.

"Grace."

I startle at the sound of his voice. His hands rest on my shoulders, and I flinch as chills move through me.

"I'm sorry," he says.

I look down, too afraid to meet his gaze in the window's reflection, but also afraid to see myself. "Why are you apologizing?"

He removes his hands, and when I shift my attention back up and to the window his eyes find mine.

"I miss my daughter," he says slowly. "It's not you. Even though my ex never wanted to dance to the records, Lily loved to." He taps a fist against his mouth for a moment. He shrugs as if the emotion will fall away.

"Ohh."

"I don't have a clue what I'm doing right now in this new life. Being a SEAL made sense." He tosses his hands up as if frustrated. "I knew what needed to be done and how to go about it. But as a father, it's scary and unpredictable. And what's worse is I could lose the one person who cares about me."

"You won't lose her."

He folds one arm under the other and grips his forehead, his eyes masked beneath his large hand.

I suck at this. I've been working on the cold-hearted bitch thing for so long that I've forgotten how to be me, how to be there for someone and support them when they need it. I lack empathy or something. I'm a mess. But all I want is to be here for this man right now.

"There's not a judge in the world that would ever take someone like you away from her." And I believe it. I have to, because my faith in life and justice will be gone if Noah loses her.

"I'm not that great of a guy."

I reach for his arms, forcing them down so I can look into his eyes. I need to say this before I lose the nerve, before the words die inside me in that place where all my hopes and dreams have gone to die over the years.

"There's more than one person who cares about you. Your sister, your parents, your friends." My hands are wrapped around his corded forearms, holding on to him for support. "Luke cares. Jessica cares."

Say it, dammit.

Say the words, don't swallow them.

My heart pounds in my ears as my stomach knots. "I haven't known you long, but I…"

Noah drops his head forward a little and takes a shallow breath, but he keeps his eyes locked with mine. "What is it, Grace?"

"I care about you too."

My lip trembles as he raises his arm and I lose my hold—he brushes the pad of his thumb across my bottom lip, pulling it down a little.

"You shouldn't."

His words slice through me. They would totally wreck me if it weren't for the way he's looking at me right now—his eyes betray him. Emotion is painted on his face, thick and heavy.

"I told you I couldn't give you more."

He drops his hand, and I let go of his other arm as he steps back, offering a small bit of space between us, but tension fills that gap.

"Nothing has changed." I try to hide the disappointment in my voice. "We've spent a lot of time together this week. We learned a lot about each other."

He knows about Greece. My fears. The music. He knows more about me than Rachel. And he's been gradually sharing pieces of himself with me. Slowly, but they've come.

"And so, of course, I care for you. You've become a

friend. You offered your friendship, remember? Or do you regret that?"

"Grace…" His eyes linger on mine, thoughtful. Then his face hardens, and he's a sailor standing before me. A strict rule-follower. "Someone's bound to get hurt."

How did we get here? We rushed back to my place, anxious to have sex, and now we're talking about this?

I can almost hear my father's voice, or even Cade's, whispering in my ear that this is for the best, that it was going to have to end soon anyway. I don't want them to be right. I don't want my family making decisions for me about who I can care about.

"I'm willing to take that chance," I whisper-yell, surprised by my own words. "Even if everyone thinks we shouldn't, I'm okay with living for the now. Let's worry about tomorrow tomorrow."

"Who doesn't want us to be together? Who knows?" His lips part.

I turn away from him, not sure how to answer that. "People." I wave and start for my bedroom, irritated. My body is warm, rigid, and I'm ready to fight.

"Wait."

But I don't. I flick on the lights and cross my room in record time, needing cold water on my skin to cool off. It's not Noah I'm angry at; it's our situation—the fact that so many forces are keeping us from even trying to see if this thing between us could ever be something more than just sex.

"We need to talk. I don't want to leave things like this." He leans inside the doorframe of my bathroom, and I turn on the water and splash my face.

"Nothing to say." I grab a hand towel and dry myself. There's black liner beneath my eyes. How attractive—not that it matters anymore.

Some of the best moments of my life have been in this past week—but they'll become bitter memories. It's time to move on. I need to focus on work and figure out what the hell is going on with the business. I need to be a Parker-King again, even if the thought makes me nauseated.

"Go." I toss the towel at the laundry basket, not bothering to wipe my smeared eye makeup. I face him, cross my arms, and lean my hip against the marble countertop.

"This wasn't exactly how I meant for the night to end." His voice is low and has a flash more Southern than it normally does.

"Well, you shouldn't have screwed things up with your gift." I almost cringe at my words because I love the record player, more than he can possibly know.

He looks at the floor for a long minute, then he uses the tip of his shoe to kick off one black sneaker before maneuvering out of the other.

"What are you doing?"

He uses the side of his foot, covered in a black sock, to shift his shoes out of his way, off to the side of the door, then he comes in front of me.

My arms tense but go to my sides. "What?" I tug my lip between my teeth as his eyes darken.

"You're right."

"About what?" I snap.

"I fucked up. I got you the gift because I care too. I wanted to see you happy, to make you happy. *I* crossed the line." He shakes his head a little, and his hand sweeps up the back of my neck beneath my hair. The feel of his hand on me has me nearly forgetting what we're talking about. "It's been a long time since I've been in this situation, and I don't know what the hell I'm doing."

"We're doing that honesty thing again?" My brows rise.

"I never stopped being honest." He guides me a little closer to him and touches my chin with his other hand, as though he's demanding my attention—my eyes to be on his.

"But—"

"Someone will get hurt, that's the truth." He leans in so our lips are almost touching. "Do you still want this to happen—to let 'tomorrow be tomorrow'?"

His words are on my lips he's so close.

My eyes shut when his hand dips from my neck down my spine.

"Yes," I almost moan, my body arching up so my chest is flush against him. "More than anything."

And then he presses his mouth to mine, pulling me in tight where I belong.

16

NOAH

"IT'S TOMORROW." GRACE PROPS UP HER HEAD, ELBOW resting on the bed, and her smile meets her eyes. She has a killer smile. It gets me every time.

I copy her move to better face her. "It is."

"And you stayed."

"Is that okay?"

She stayed on my boat the other night, but that felt different. Last night was intense, though.

She nods. "I didn't have a nightmare."

"You didn't on the boat either."

"I guess I feel safe with you." She relaxes back down, her head on the pillow, her eyes on the ceiling. She combs her fingers through her hair, and I wait for her to say more, but she doesn't.

"Have you found anyone you can talk to about the nightmares, about what happened to you?" When this ends, she'll need to find a way to feel safe again.

"I'll see someone eventually."

I sit up in bed, leaning my back against the headboard, and clasp my hands over the sheet on my lap. "I know Bella wanted you to stay somewhere else before the big reveal, but I was thinking that maybe a hotel isn't the best idea." Given what happened to her in Greece… "My boat is a bit tight and you aren't a fan of the water. Otherwise, I'd offer."

She takes a breath. "I've been in a hotel since Athens. I'm not going to lie—I didn't sleep well. But I can't let what happened to me there give me yet another phobia, right? I've been obsessing about the water all my life, and somehow you managed to help me with that"—she snaps her fingers—"like that. So maybe I can put on my big girl panties and move forward."

"The hotel is a little different."

I don't know why she feels as if she has to ignore her feelings. This is why I really want her talking to a counselor or something. I've seen firsthand what PTSD can do to people. I don't want to lose her.

I almost drop my head forward and squeeze my eyes shut at the thought that just passed.

I will lose her. Jesus.

"I'll figure something out when the time comes. Just have Bella give me a day in advance before she kicks me out." She sighs and sits up, and her legs drop to the floor. She clearly doesn't want to talk about this right now. "Are you guys working on any other jobs or just my place? I never asked."

She faces me. She's only in a thong, a hot pink, frilly thong. I want to go to her, sink to my knees, and tug the strap of material down her legs with my teeth.

"Just yours since I'm the only labor she has. But now that we have an investment, we can hire a few people."

"That's great." She smiles. "So, um, what are you doing today?"

I want to say something stupid, like "you," but I refrain. I really would love to stay in her bed, to have her legs wrapped around me, to forget about our problems, but I also need to put a little space between us, to get my head on straight.

"I'm gonna try and see Lily."

I woke up in the middle of the night and checked the airport arrivals at JFK to make sure her plane got in as scheduled last night. I had memorized the flight information when Cindy flashed me the airline tickets on her phone last weekend. As long as they didn't miss their flight, they should be back in town. And I refuse to let Cindy keep me from her any longer.

"Oh. That's good. I hope it goes well."

"Yeah, you and me both." I get out of the bed, and her eyes dip south of my navel. Beneath her heated stare, I grow hard almost immediately.

"You're not dressed." Her eyes slowly drag up my chest and back to mine. They're a lighter blue today, maybe even grayer.

There's a little black beneath her eyes, and it only makes her sexier—the morning-after-sex look. I want to have morning sex now.

I glance around the bedroom for my boxers, but I don't even remember where they got tossed last night. I took her right on the bathroom counter, almost forgetting to sheath myself first. Remembering her taste, and the way she bucked and moved as I thrust in and out of her on the marble slab last night—fuck me, I need her now.

"You want to—" She comes around the bed to stand in front of me.

I palm her breast. She's the perfect size, fitting into my hand. This elicits a soft moan from her, and she shifts her hips forward a little as if she's desperate for my touch.

Her smooth center is tan. I wonder if she sunbathes in the nude because she doesn't look like she's got a spray tan. As my hand moves over her stomach and down, the doorbell rings.

"Expecting company?" I step back and scratch the side of my head, realizing I might need to calm my dick down. Not going to be easy. Her body—those lips…I need her.

"I don't even know what time it is," she says.

The bell rings again. She looks at the clock by her bed. It's a quarter past nine. I've missed my normal morning workout routine again, which is unlike me. Ever since Grace and I started doing whatever it is we're doing, I've been off. I don't think that's necessarily a bad thing, but it's thrown me a little.

"Want me to get it?" I cock my head and watch her firm ass in that little thong as she starts for her bathroom.

"Like that? You'll either scare off whoever it is, or they'll throw themselves at you. It depends on who's at the door." She laughs as she slides on a red silk robe.

"And what might happen with you wearing *that* when answering the door?" I move toward the bathroom to see if my clothes are in there.

"Just wait in here. I'll check the peephole to see who it is."

I find my clothes by the shower and get dressed. I'll need to go back to the boat and change before I show up at Cindy's door. I'm bound to come face to face with her fiancé today. I knew it would happen at some point, but I'm in no mood to talk to him. I had Luke run a thorough background check on her fiancé since that's part of what his company does, because I needed to make sure he wasn't some creepy pedophile. He came up clean. If he had been a psychopath, no one would have ever found his body.

Jesus, there's the killer in me again.

My body shakes a little. The very thought that some other

guy is stepping in for me right now has me almost ill. I've done my best not to think about it since I got out of the SEALs because I'll probably lose my fucking mind if I do.

When I come out into the bedroom, I hear a male's voice. Two maybe.

I go for the doorknob and open it without thinking first. Instinct kicks in, and the need to protect Grace seizes hold of me.

"Is this him?" There's a guy in jeans and a white untucked dress shirt behind the couch, and he points at me as I stand in the doorframe, not sure what to think.

I assess the scene, noting another man in the living room. He's standing beside Grace by the bay window.

She closes the record player top and faces me, then she tightens the sash on her robe and folds her arms. "This is Cade," she says while pointing at the guy by the couch, the one who looks as though he's ready to throw down with me. "And my other brother, Corbin." She tilts her head to the guy on her right.

"And this is the handyman? The one you're screwing?" Cade's brows pinch together. He comes around from behind the couch, starting for me.

"He's not *just* a handyman." The way she says the word handyman, it's as if she's embarrassed by me, by who I am. And I can't take my eyes off her to see how she'll react next, even though Cade is stalking my way. Her arms hang loose now at her sides. "Why are you here? Did Evan call you? Is that sick psycho listening through the walls to hear what I'm doing?"

As she takes a step in Cade's direction, Corbin stops her by touching her bicep.

"You need to go. You don't belong here." Cade's in front

of me now, his eyes drilling into me, trying to break me. Good fucking luck with that.

I don't respond to him as I look back at Grace. She looks conflicted, as if maybe she's going to tell me to leave. My shoulders tense, and my spine straightens.

"There's something we came to tell you. You weren't answering your phone, and we needed to talk to you." Corbin releases his hold on Grace, and she faces him. His voice isn't as edgy, and there's compassion in his eyes. He's a good guy. Thank God one of them is.

"What's going on?" she asks Corbin.

Corbin looks over at his brother, and Cade shakes his head.

"He should go, then we'll talk," Cade says.

"Is this about work?" she asks, her eyes darting to her older brother's.

"No," Cade answers.

"Then why does he need to leave?" she asks.

"It's about Greece." Corbin's voice is low, and I can tell his words have Grace's knees practically buckling as her face blanches.

I brush past Cade, wanting to be at her side to make sure she doesn't fall. I'm sure Corbin will help, but I can't be a bystander. It's not in my nature.

"He knows about Athens. Say whatever it is," she says in an almost shaky voice.

"You told him?" There's obvious surprise in Cade's voice, but I don't bother looking at him. I need to focus on Grace.

"Just tell me what's going on." Her palms press to her core, and I touch her arm, offering her support. She looks at me as she takes a few shallow breaths.

"They think they found the guy," Corbin says.

Grace starts to sink down, but I pull her against me, keeping her upright.

"They want you to identify him. They're sending someone here with images for you to look at. For me to look at as well."

Wow—I guess things really do work differently for the rich.

"So I won't have to face him?" Her hand goes to her chest, her fingertips burying into her collarbone as her pupils dilate.

"Not if you can ID him based on the pictures," Cade says from behind me.

"You should sit." I motion to the armchair near the couch, a silent request for Corbin to lift the dust blanket so she can relax.

He gets the message and is quick to act. I guide Grace to the chair, and she clutches the sides of it as if we're on a plane and suffering from major turbulence.

"This is a good thing. We can put this behind us," Cade says.

But Grace doesn't speak. I can see the fear, the stress— it's consuming her, and she's probably reliving the night at the hotel again. I want to comfort her, but I'm only the fucking handyman.

"You should go now," Cade says, and I lift my gaze to meet his. He tucks his hands in his pockets and arches his shoulders back. "We've got this."

"When do I need to ID him?" she asks, ignoring her brother.

"Tuesday," Corbin answers. "We'll be going together. They want to get the ID done as soon as possible so they can keep him locked up until the trial."

Grace starts taking quick breaths. She's in full panic mode. I touch her back and guide her forward a little.

"Put your hands on your knees. Try to slow your breathing." I look at Corbin. "Get her a bag or something to breathe into. She's having a panic attack."

Corbin remains staring at Grace, and I have to assume some sort of guilt is plaguing him. Even though he saved her, I wonder if he feels as though he should have ended this all back in Athens by not letting the asshole get away. I know that's how I'd feel.

"Now!" Cade barks.

Corbin shakes his head out of the daze and heads to the kitchen while I rub her back. I lean forward and press my mouth to her ear.

"You're going to be okay," I whisper, trying to keep her from going off the cliff.

"I'm fine," she says after a few minutes.

Corbin stands in front of her with a bag, but his eyes are on me. Curious, maybe? He's not staring me down like Cade, but he's also unsure of me; that much is obvious. His head is angled, and his eyes are narrowed on me as he remains standing before Grace.

I lift my hands from Grace's shoulders and step back from the chair. Cade comes to Corbin's side as Grace stands.

"You guys can go now," she says.

Cade's jaw clenches. "We should talk more about this."

"I need space." She moves around her brothers to the back of the chair where I'm standing. "Go see Lily. I'll be okay."

"You shouldn't be alone." I can't begin to imagine what she must be feeling right now, and the last thing she needs is to be alone with her fears.

"I'll stay." Corbin looks at me and nods.

"Please. We'll catch up later." She laces her fingers with mine, and the gesture, in front of her brothers, throws me a little. Is she really okay with them knowing what's going on between us?

"He's married."

I look at Cade. Did the son of a bitch look into me? How did he even know about us—did she tell him we were sleeping together? I highly doubt that.

Grace drops my hand and spins to face her brother. "Are you fucking kidding me?" She approaches him and jabs her finger at his chest. "Stay out of my life."

"How? You clearly don't know what the hell you're doing." Cade remains looking at me, ignoring her.

"Get out," she rasps and steps back. "And if you're in agreement with him, you too!" She looks at Corbin, but he holds his hands up in surrender.

"You know I've always got your back," Corbin says.

She releases a breath. "Cade, I mean it. Go. Now."

"If you hurt my sister, I'll kill you myself. You got that?" Cade's hands form into fists at his sides, and the vein in his throat throbs.

"Like you aren't trying to hurt me?" Grace looks Cade square in the eyes, and some unspoken message passes between them.

"We'll talk tomorrow," Cade grumbles and starts for the hall that leads to the front door. "Keep an eye on her, Corbin."

The tension drops once he's gone, and her shoulders relax. Corbin rests a hand on her shoulder and squeezes.

She shoots me an apologetic glance. "I'm sorry about him."

"It's fine." I should go, though. She should be with

Corbin right now, and I really need to see Lily. But… "I can stay if you want."

"No." Her response is immediate. "Please. See Lily."

"I'll be here. Don't worry," Corbin says then comes toward me and extends his hand.

I look at the potential peace offering and clasp palms with him.

"Nice to meet you," he says.

I only nod, because this entire situation is pretty damn awkward. "I'll call you later."

I grab my shoes from her room, which is even odder—going in her bedroom with her brother here. I shoot her one last look before I leave. A tightness stretches across my chest. Guilt. But I'm not sure if it's because I'm leaving or if it's because I'm worried that I'll do exactly what Cade's afraid of —hurt her. And that's the last thing I want.

But I guess we'll figure that out tomorrow—well, whenever our last tomorrow is.

* * *

OUR BOOTS HIT THE GROUND RIGHT AFTER WE'D PARACHUTED from a plane.

There were only five of us.

We entered the stronghold of a terrorist cell in Pakistan. Based on our thermal cameras, we had counted over twenty people inside the compound.

I was calm, though, in control as we had approached enemy territory.

And even after I took down six targets and got a bullet in my quad, I stayed resolute. Nothing rattled me. Mission first, emotions second. Hell, maybe even a distant tenth.

But as I approach Cindy's door right now, hoping not to

have it slammed in my face again, I'm on edge. Nervous. Scared even. I have no idea how to handle fear. It's foreign to me, and it's like a slow fire working through my veins, nearly incinerating my organs.

There's a tremble to my hand as I raise it.

I retract it for a moment, staring at my fist as if it doesn't belong to me.

I press both palms to the door and lower my head for a moment, trying to pull my shit together.

I go back to the ship—to the Navy—in my head. My heartbeat starts to slow to normal as I remember who I once was, who I still need to be.

I press the buzzer and wait.

Nothing.

I try again and add a few knocks.

Nothing.

Either she's not opening the door, or they're not home—but why wouldn't they be after being out of town for a week? Home sweet home, right?

I know they're not at church because Cindy divorced God long before she attempted to divorce me.

After a few minutes, I exit the high-rise as I contemplate my next moves, but I stop dead in my tracks at the sight across the street.

Lily's at the playground there. Her blond pigtails swish as she sails up on a swing then bends her legs and moves back, smiling.

I feel both relief and pain now. I almost don't want to move, to lose this moment of seeing her happy. I wonder how much she actually understands about what's happening between her mom and me.

I cross the street, ignoring the no walking sign, and go around to the gated entrance. Only a few kids are on the playground, but Cindy and her fiancé are on a bench off to the side, talking. I only know what the guy looks like based on the background search.

Lily's swinging by herself, and she's pretty good at it.

My breath hitches when Lily looks my way and her eyes grow wide. "Daddy!"

She jumps off the swing from way too high up, giving me a near heart attack, but she nails the landing. I start toward her as she runs to me, and I lift her into my arms and swing her around in a circle as she squeals with delight.

"I've missed you, baby girl," I say into her ear.

"Noah!" Cindy's voice is like nails on a chalkboard, and the hair on my arms stand.

"I've missed you so much. Mommy said you had to go back to sea and were gone."

What the hell! "No, I'm here. I'm never leaving you, I promise."

I squat to release her, but she keeps her arms wrapped around my neck, hugging me. She smells like sugar and honey.

I'm not much of a cook, but when I was home, I did my best to bake with her. She loves baking. Most of the time our cakes had a slow death in the oven, and our cookies were crispy as if in a fire—but she would always say, "You did your best, Daddy, and that's all that counts."

Am I still doing my best?

"How was your trip to Colorado?" I ask, hating that she went across the country without me.

"It was okay. I wish you could have come," Lily says.

"Me too—"

"You shouldn't be here," Cindy says from over my shoulder, cutting me off.

I stand back up, but Lily flings her body around my right

leg and hangs on as if she might lose me again. Jesus. How did I let Cindy keep me away from her like this?

"He's here, Mommy! You were wrong!" She lets go and rings her fingers together.

"Lily, go play. I need to talk to your dad." Cindy crosses her arms.

I work hard to keep a wrap on my anger since Lily's here. Cindy's fiancé comes up next to her and holds his arms out for Lily, and I instinctively reach for Lily's hand.

Hell no.

The guy looks like an ass. I might be biased, but still…

He squints his green eyes and assesses me beneath his dark-rimmed glasses before folding his arms as if he's trying to make his biceps—or lack of—pop and intimidate me.

It takes all my strength to say, "Go play, Lily. I'll be over in a minute." And I only do it because I don't want her listening to any vile filth Cindy might say.

Lily looks at me, and I can see her hesitance. She's afraid she might lose me again. How can I reassure her when her mother is doing her best to make that happen?

I let out a deep breath and try to ground myself, so I can remain composed. "It's okay. I'll push you way up high in that swing in just a minute."

"Promise?" She pouts a little.

I cross my fingers over my heart. "Promise." I wait for her to leave, and I do my best not to deck the bastard who's screwing Cindy and trying to steal my daughter.

To be honest, I'm over the affair, but this insanity about taking Lily from me—fuck that.

Once Lily is out of earshot, Cindy comes closer to me. Her fiancé, surprisingly, leaves us alone and goes off toward Lily.

"You shouldn't be here," she hisses.

I cock my head. "And you were supposed to call me as soon as you got back into town."

"I don't owe you updates," she says.

"And you can't keep me from Lily. I haven't seen a court warrant saying to stay away."

"I can get one!"

"How? What have I ever done that would justify keeping me away from her?" I ask in a low voice.

"I'm her mother. I get the final say."

"And who the hell am I?" I snap out.

She looks at the ground as her eyes close.

"There's no way you'll win this fight." I look over at Lily. She's playing with a girl who looks to be her age. They're laughing, and my heart swells.

"I don't want to do this here, not with Lily so close by," she says in almost a groan as her eyes flash open.

"Right now I'm going to spend some time with my daughter." I turn, prepared to head in Lily's direction, but Cindy's hand on my arm stops me.

"We were just leaving."

"Then you can leave. Lily will stay," I bite back.

She sighs. "Ten minutes, and I don't want to see you again until we have our lawyers present. I mean it."

I ignore her, knowing next Sunday I'll be back.

I leave the playground twenty minutes later, pissed about the short time, but I didn't want to fight in front of Lily. And then I spend the rest of the day drifting around the city like a man lost at sea.

As the sun drops from the sky and the moon makes its debut, I find myself lying on the couch on the deck of my boat, looking at a selfie I took of Lily and me earlier. She has her tongue playfully sticking out with bunny ears over my head.

A message pops up from Grace.

Did you get to see Lily today?

I focus on her question, surprised she's thinking about me after what happened to her today.

I sit upright and type a response.

Yes. At the park.

I send it and wait, my body growing strangely calm.

That's good. I hope you're doing okay. Sorry again about earlier.

Why is she apologizing? For her brother or for her panic attack? I really hope she sees someone for that.

Are YOU okay?

I delete the line and try again.

Can I come over? I don't want you to be alone.

I stand and delete the message again. Before I have a chance to write something else, Grace has sent me another text.

I'm not going into work tomorrow or Tuesday. Could you hold off on the remodel?

I squint at the message as if I didn't read it right. Shit, she must be worse than I thought. I should call her—or go to her.

I'm coming over.

I send it before I have a chance to hesitate.

No, I'm okay. Tell Bella if we fall behind schedule don't stress.

She seems a little cold. Distant. But it's hard to assess someone based on a few texts. But still, she must be struggling with what she learned today, and what if she has another anxiety attack? It's great news that the police found the asshole who almost—shit, I can't even finish that thought.

Don't worry about the remodel right now. I want to come over. Let me be there for you.

The message delivers, and I wait.

191

And wait.

And as I continue to wait, the minutes ticking by, I realize I've never sat around waiting for a woman to call or text me —EVER.

I've waited on ops. I've had to sit in the desert, in the bushes, in the freezing ass ocean and wait. I know how to wait for missions. *I did*—I keep forgetting I won't ever be on an op again.

But this type of waiting is god-awful.

No, scratch that. It's fucking horrible.

And this can only mean one thing—this thing between us…it's something more.

17

GRACE

"You're in your pajamas, for Christ's sake. You're not acting like the woman I raised," my mom says.

"At what point did you actually raise me? Nannies, boarding school…neither of you did anything. Maybe that's a good thing, though. Maybe I'd be more like you guys if you had," I snap.

Mom relaxes on my bed, but Dad remains in front of me where I'm sitting on the couch, his arms in his signature crossed pose to intimidate. I tuck a pillow against my chest and rest my head on the back of the couch, eyeing my father without a care in the world. But that's what four vodka tonics at three in the afternoon will do to you.

You become ballsy and stand up to your dictator father.

"What's wrong with you? Is this about the lineup tomorrow?" My dad shakes his head and waves dismissively. "Hell, it's not even a lineup. You and Corbin just have to look at a few photos. Make an ID." He sighs, but it comes across more like a hiss—like a hiss from a cobra. The king fucking cobra. "And it cost me an awful lot of money to convince them to come all the way here so you wouldn't have to go back. I don't see any appreciation."

Is he serious?

"Take a shower and get cleaned up. It's time to move on." He points toward the bathroom as if I don't know the way around my bedroom.

"Move on? Are you for real? The guy was going to kill me, and God knows what else." If he had rape—I can't finish that thought. There's not enough alcohol in me, yet, to allow myself to tackle that "what if" scenario. It's bad enough my nightmares give me a play-by-play of what could have happened if Corbin hadn't saved me.

"Well, he didn't. And right now, we have other problems to face." He crosses his arms and glances at Mom as if she's supposed to interject.

"Yes, dear, you have a guest coming later today." She plasters on a fake, tight-lipped smile.

"Who?" But I already know the answer. I can see it on my father's face. I never truly thought it would come to this— that I would have to tell my father "hell no" to his face.

"Patrick never left New York. He's still here, and he wants to see you again." Dad grips the bridge of his nose and closes his eyes. "I don't like asking you to do this. I don't want to force you into a relationship the way—"

"You two were?" I stand. "The way you pushed Cade into his engagement?"

"That's not fair. Or true," my mom rushes out while narrowing her eyes.

"I guess when you lie to yourself for so long, the lies become truths." I flick my wrist, move to the window, and hit the automatic switch by the blinds, opening them.

They slide up, but instead of beams from an afternoon sun blinding me, there's only a dense and overwhelming shot of grayness. Cloudy skies and a light rain that streaks down my window like the slow drop of oil on a canvas.

How perfect.

"I won't marry someone for the sake of a business merger. Maybe you could have bullied me into it a few months ago, but not now. Things have changed." My back is still to them because I don't know if I have the courage to say this to their faces. "This is 2017, F.Y.I. Maybe you didn't get the memo." I fake a laugh. Maybe it's the alcohol, or maybe I've totally lost my mind, but I can't grin and bear it anymore. "Perhaps you should fire your admin."

I bite my tongue and don't go as far as to mention the fact I know he's screwed her. So cliché. I mean, come on, if you're going to be a lying cheat, at least be original about it. Maybe fuck Greg, the doorman at our office building. Now that'd be interesting.

I cringe at my dark thoughts. This is my life, but I don't want it to be.

I get a taste of freedom every time I'm with Noah, and it's addicting.

I want to strip the chains of this last name, and I want to run. I want to dance naked while listening to the record player and not worry about what anyone would think.

I want…*Noah*.

"We heard about the carpenter. You've done this before." My mother is behind me. I can smell her sharp perfume, and it almost makes me feel a little dizzy. "You've dated men you know we would never approve of just to make sure we're paying attention." Her hand touches my back, and although I flinch, I don't face her. "And believe me, we're paying attention right now."

I can't look her in the eyes—a woman who's supposed to

protect me and do what's best for me. She only cares about what's in the best interest for the family name.

"Cade needs to mind his own business." I press my forehead against the glass, straining to hear the soft sounds of the rain.

"He didn't tell us—"

"Then who did?" I cut her off. There's no way Corbin said anything, and my parents don't know my neighbor that well. Cade only knows Evan because they belong to the same gym.

"Patrick saw you with him," Dad says.

Is the guy stalking me? My skin crawls with unease as I process what he said.

"You know you could never truly be happy with someone like him. He's not like us, dear." My mom presses her hand to my shoulder and squeezes as if I'll suddenly have an aha moment and be cured of my insanity.

"Someone like him?" My shoulders shudder, betraying the sudden emotions threading through me. "I hope you're referring to Patrick because then you're dead-on!"

I face my mom, and her hand drops.

"Don't be absurd. You know exactly who I was speaking about."

"And you know nothing about him," I say through clenched teeth.

"We don't need to." My dad comes next to Mom.

She shoots him a nervous look as if she's clueless as to how to handle my defiance.

"He's married, has a five-year-old daughter, and he makes less than fifty thousand a year." His brows slant. "Five. Zero. Did you hear me?"

He's not emphasizing the marriage part—it's the money part. Always.

"Leave." The intensity of my anger is piling up so high, I don't know if I'll be able to wrangle in my control much longer. "And tell Patrick I won't open the door if he shows up."

Dad makes a tsk noise. "Maybe once this Greek thing is behind you, you'll come to your senses again."

Greek thing? Yes, the annoying Greek thing where I was almost killed.

My parents finally start for my bedroom door.

"Wait." I step in front of them and hold out my hand. "I want your key."

"Key?" Dad's brows pinch together.

"I don't want anyone I don't trust having a key to my place." I raise my palm higher and closer to his face.

"You're being ridiculous." But he shoves his hand into his pocket and works the key off the chain.

"You too, Mom." I grip the key I'd given my father and assess my mother, trying to get a read on her.

"I don't even know what to say. I barely recognize you anymore," Mom says in a low voice as she digs into her purse.

"I think that's a good thing." And I mean it wholeheartedly. Once I have both keys, I wave toward the living room.

"Take some time off work this week and think, Grace. And when you have your head back on, make the right decision, because I don't want to have to make it for you." His voice has my skin pebbling and my chest tightening, because I know my father doesn't make empty threats.

* * *

I need less than thirty seconds to ID the man. His face has haunted me for weeks.

"That's him. I'm one hundred percent certain." I shut my eyes, not wanting to look at the photo any longer. He's already left an imprint in my brain, but having an image of him right in front of my eyes is suffocating.

The nightmares tonight will be more vivid than normal, more gut-wrenching and painful—if that's even possible. Last night my dreams shredded me, and I was all alone.

Thankfully Patrick never showed up, but neither did Noah. I'm sure it's because I never responded to his last message on Sunday night. I'm not sure why I'm afraid to reach out to him. Maybe it's because I feel that I need him.

He makes the monsters go away. I sound like a kid saying that, but it's true. The darkness slips away when he's around, and in its place is all this light. Bright and intoxicating light.

And I want it desperately. I want his light to wrap me up and take me away, out of this city.

But we're both married to this city in completely different ways.

Even if I turn my back on my family for a chance to be with someone like him, he said that he could never give me more.

He was always honest.

But I didn't expect this, to feel like *this*.

"Grace?"

I open my eyes to see Corbin approaching me.

"Are you done?" he asks.

"Yeah. You?" I gulp, chills spreading across my skin.

"Yeah." They didn't want us in the same room when we IDed the man so we couldn't influence one another.

"Did you recognize him?"

He nods. "You?"

"Yeah." I don't need to ask who he pointed out. Number one, two, three, four, or five. We both know it was Number Four.

Four. A number I'll hate maybe forever.

"Can we go now?" Corbin asks the officer next to the Greek official collecting the photos off the metal table, which looks like it doubles for autopsies.

"We'll be in touch about the trial. Here's my card if you need to reach me," the Greek officer, named Stefano, says as he hands Corbin the card.

I'm in a trance or something. "Trial?"

"Yes. It can take some time to have a trial, but you'll need to testify," Stefano answers.

"Like, how long?" Corbin asks.

"Two months." Stefano shrugs. "Two years. The courts are pretty backed up, but this guy was a very wanted man. We might try to process it faster to get him sentenced."

How can I ever face Number Four in person? How can I possibly be in the same room with him?

I can't go back to Greece.

"You okay?" Corbin wraps an arm around my shoulder and pulls me against him. "Thank you, sir." He nods at Stefano, but I can barely see straight.

I don't even remember walking out of the building.

I have no clue how I ended up in front of Corbin's apartment door.

Everything is one big blur.

Number Four—his face is all I can see.

The knife to my throat. The rough sound of his voice at my ear. His other hand sliding up my skirt as he held me in place and I was unable to move.

"Shit." He pats his pockets. "I either left my keys back there or at the office before I left for the meeting."

"I really should go anyway."

"I can get the super to let us in."

"No. I mean, yes—for you. But I think I have somewhere else I need to be right now," I say, in a bit of a daze still.

He presses a hand to the wall at my side and angles his head, studying me. "The handyman?"

"Don't call him that." I shake my head, now pulled out of my stupor.

"Embarrassed or—"

"No, I just mean…he has a name. And I expect that shit from Cade, not you."

Corbin drops his hand and steps back, his brows scrunching together. "Fuck. You really like this guy, don't you?"

"I, um…"

He exhales. "Don't let Dad or Cade stand in your way then."

I don't know what to say. I'm not even sure how I feel.

"I should go." I start to turn, but his hand on my forearm stops me.

"Are you sure you're okay?"

His words flit through my mind for a brief moment. "I will be," I say as the knot tightens in my stomach, locking all of my emotions in place where I'm fighting the current again —a battle I can't win.

Once outside, the sounds of the busy New York streets overwhelm me. The commotion, the lights, the people, the traffic. I need it to stop—all the noise. And since Corbin's driver brought us to his place, my driver, Frank, isn't here for a ride.

I hail a taxi and give the destination. And as I sit in the back of the cab, Corbin's words about Noah roll around in my head, playing on repeat like an annoying commercial.

"Ma'am."

I glance at the driver in the rearview mirror, realizing we've pulled up to the curb already. I grab a few bills from my wallet. "Thanks."

I get out of the car and look at the Hudson. I was having dinner nearby when that pilot landed his plane on this very river. The historic rescue without a single loss of life.

Miracles do happen.

That crash on the water is a testament to that.

So, anything is possible. Noah and I—it's possible, right?

I count the number of boats as I pass them on the docks. I don't have OCD, but they distract me from the water. It's cloudy out, and a strong breeze is making the water rise too high. The sound of it beating against the sides of the boats I pass has me on edge.

So, I count.

I focus on the yachts, the small fishing boats, the speed boats. I don't see anyone on them as I walk, and I assume it's because a storm is coming. How does Noah sleep on his boat in a storm? I can't imagine.

I stop counting when I find his boat. *Madeline.*

I wonder what Madeline was like. Was the couple truly, madly, and deeply in love? Does that kind of love even exist?

I hear Noah's voice before I see him. He's coming out of his cabin, his phone pressed to his ear. His eyes catch mine the second he's on deck.

"I have to go," he says into the phone and lowers it from his ear. "Hi. Are you okay?" He tosses his phone on the couch and steps onto the dock, closing the space between us. He braces my forearms, and I drag my gaze up to meet his intense eyes.

"I'm sorry you haven't heard from me...but it's done. I

identified the guy." My knees are weak, and if he weren't holding on to me, I'd fall.

"Come on." He helps me on board. Once we're below deck, he asks, "What happens now?"

I like that he knows the water is too much for me to deal with today. I sit on the edge of the bed and kick off my nude flats as he joins me. "I'll have to go to court to testify in the trial."

The same room as Number Four.

Face to face.

Speak before him.

Relive that night.

My hands cover my face as I try to fight back the emotions twining around my neck, cutting off my oxygen.

He touches my back. "When?"

"I don't know." I drop my arms and ball my hands on my lap.

"I won't let him hurt you," he says in a deep voice as our eyes meet.

"He'll be in handcuffs. I should be okay." I swallow.

"I don't care. I need to be with you." Slight lines appear on his forehead.

"You want to come to Greece?" I ask in disbelief.

He nods.

"That's not necessary. We're—"

"Friends. And I'm always there for a friend."

Friends. Can I ever be friends with him? Did I ever think it was possible to *only* be friends with Noah Dalton?

"We'll talk about it when the time comes." I try to shrug off the topic because I can't handle anything else heavy today.

"I want you to do something for me." He stands and holds his palm facing up.

I stare at his hand—the strength there. "What?" I rise, allowing our fingers to thread together.

"I want you to scream."

"Come again?" I rub my chest with my free hand as if I haven't heard him right.

"I want you to let it out. The anger, the pain. Let it all out."

"What?" I step back, trying to pull my hand from his, but he only tightens his grip—he won't let me go.

Don't ever let me go.

"Scream, Grace. It'll help." He nods. "Just scream."

Is he kidding? I can't—I just can't.

I shut my eyes, and now that he's holding both of my hands, I go back to Athens in my head. I wade through my nightmares. This time I don't get hurt by the man—this time I fight back.

I hit the son of a bitch.

His head jerks back.

I kick him.

Again.

And again.

And then I scream.

A blood-curdling scream. Louder. And louder until my voice is raw and there's barely anything left.

Noah's arms are locked around my body, holding me against his chest as I try to catch my breath. I'm not crying, though.

I feel…strong. Powerful.

I feel better.

After a few minutes, I pull out of his arms and look at him. "How'd you know that would help?"

He presses the pad of his thumb to my cheek and runs it down to my jawline. "When we'd lose someone—a team member—it helped to yell." His eyes flash shut, and there's a tightness to his face. "Sometimes I still scream. After each of my tattoos—I fucking let go. Otherwise, the pain will rip me apart. I can't let the assholes win." Noah opens his eyes, and they're a little red.

I can't imagine what this man has gone through.

"You're stronger than you realize," he says.

"With you I am," I whisper.

He shakes his head and points at my heart. "It's all you." He cups my face. "All you…"

I lean into his palm and close my eyes, giving in to the warmth of his touch, the safety of being near him.

"It's going to storm tonight."

"I know." I tilt my chin up and open my eyes. He's looking at me with parted lips. Lips I want on my mouth. I don't want this day to end with thoughts of Greece. I want it to end with Noah inside me.

"Do you want to stay?" His hand brushes over my bicep.

"Would that be okay?"

His chest moves up as he inhales a lungful of air, his eyes darkening—desire evident. He exhales and nods. I press up on my toes as he bows his head so our lips touch.

"More than okay," he says against my mouth.

18

NOAH

"You're no longer on the approved visitors' list. I'm sorry, Mr. Dalton."

It's Sunday. My day. She said to wait until we meet with the lawyers, but I'm sick of her rules.

I call Cindy.

No answer.

I text her and call again.

Nothing.

"Check one more time." I fold my arms, eyeing the security guard who looks as though he's still in high school. Slicked back blond hair, dark blue eyes, and a tall, lanky body. How is this guy going to stop an intruder from coming into the building? How safe is my daughter here?

The kid goes back to the computer behind the desk and taps at the keys. "Sorry."

I'm tempted to just walk around him, but the last thing I need is the cops coming and Cindy using that as ammunition against me. I shake my head and leave the lobby. I start to text Cindy again, but a message from her pops up on my phone.

I'll see you at the law office on Tuesday.

Sarah still doesn't think Cindy has a case, but she did recommend I sell the boat and try to get an apartment as soon as possible.

I may not need to sell right away, though, now that Bella and I have the investment from Luke and Jessica. Plus, we'll be able to take on more jobs since we've finally hired some people to work with us. I just need to find a place to live. I've been checking ads almost every hour, trying to find something affordable and move-in ready.

I tap out an angry response.

You can't keep me from my daughter. You're making a mistake.

But I delete the message and lean against the apartment building. She might interpret my text as a threat. I need to play it smart.

I stow my phone and resist the temptation to text back at all. It's what she wants.

Since I won't be seeing Lily today, I should spend it looking for apartments. Maybe Grace wouldn't mind tagging along? She didn't go to work the rest of last week, and since she didn't want to interfere with the remodel, she's staying at a hotel.

My job is done, and now it's up to Bella to style it up—or do whatever she does. The design part isn't my area of expertise. Bella's shooting for Wednesday as the big reveal day, which means Grace has another three nights in the hotel.

I've been staying with Grace, though. She said she was okay being in the hotel room alone, but I could tell it made her nervous. When I offered to stay with her, she agreed—as long as I promised copious amounts of orgasms.

I wasn't about to say no to that.

We've spent the last several nights together. She's been

keeping up with work from the hotel during the day while I wrapped up construction at her place.

It'll feel a little strange taking money from Grace when this is all done. I'll let Bella handle the finances.

My phone rings as I leave the apartment building, but it's not Cindy.

"What's up?" I answer.

"Are you ready for Tuesday?" Bella asks.

I finally told her about Cindy's insane attempts at full custody. I'll need her to testify on my behalf as a character witness. My parents might even need to fly up. I hate putting them in the middle of this, but once I tell them what Cindy's trying to do, I might have to hold my mom back from attacking Cindy.

"Yeah. I guess I am."

"Do you need anything from me?"

I shake my head as if she can see me. I'm in no mood to talk about Cindy. "No, not right now. Um, how are things going at Grace's?"

Bella spent the weekend decorating Grace's place to try to get things done quicker. "Good. I opened her storage closet outside the living room—seeing if she had anything I could use, you know, personal touches. And—"

"Shit, did you ask first?" Talk about a violation of privacy.

"No, but she has all of these instruments! I had no idea she loved music—and now I think I might want to change my design plan and make her place a little more artsy. You know, musical. What do you think?"

"I think you should have stayed out of her closet." I huff. "But now that you've already gone in there, I'd like to take a look."

"Why?"

"Just let me worry about it." I take a left and cross the street, heading to Grace's loft instead of the hotel.

I have an idea I can't get out of my head now, and it's got me lit on fire.

* * *

"Keep your eyes closed."

We're standing outside the hotel room, and I can tell Grace is peeking.

"You're bad at following instructions, but I came prepared just in case." I have two ties. One I'll use at the lawyer's office tomorrow, and this navy one I have rolled and hidden in my fist. "Put this on."

She opens one eye then the other. "A tie?" She chuckles. "Getting kinky on me, huh? When you kicked me out of the hotel room two hours ago, I didn't expect I'd come back to this."

I tip my chin up as I raise the tie between us, urging her to take it.

"Okay." She begins to wrap it around her head with my assistance.

"Good." I swipe the key in front of the electronic pad by the door, and it clicks and unlocks. "Can you see anything?" I ask while guiding her inside.

"No."

I've never done something like this before. But being with Grace is exciting and different—and I keep wanting more and more.

More of her.

The hotel is a suite. It has a living area, kitchen, and one large bedroom and bathroom. I take her into the bedroom and pause in the doorframe. I scan the room, making sure everything is how I want it. "You ready?"

"Are *you*?" She smiles, and I kind of want to keep her blindfolded as I explore every inch of her body.

Maybe later…

My fingers go to the knot, and I hesitate, suddenly on edge. Am I crossing the line?

But fuck, it's too late.

"Open your eyes," I say once the tie drops to the floor.

She slowly peels her eyes open as if she's afraid of what she might see.

A few candles are lit on each side of the bed and on the dresser. I didn't want to overdo it and set off the alarms. And although I'm not the rose-petals-on-the-bed kind of guy, I did place one long-stem red rose—without thorns—on her pillow.

But that's not where her eyes go.

She's looking at the chair by the window, a cello displayed next to it, the bow on the seat.

Her gaze darts to my face as her mouth opens—but no sound comes out.

"It's yours…obviously."

"I know." Her brows pinch together. "What's it doing here?"

She leaves my side and goes to it. Her fingers feather the polished wood, which I shined up, then she reaches for the bow.

"I want you to play for me. Put on a show for me only." I smile—she still isn't. And I'm worried I made a mistake. "Next time you can perform for a larger crowd."

She sets the bow back on the chair and angles her head, studying me. "Why would you do this? Why would you think I'd want to?"

"It was your dream to play, right? I'd have you sing for me, but you've warned me about your voice, so…" I tuck my hands in my jeans pockets.

"That's an old dream." She glances at the cello.

"I didn't know dreams expired." I want to go to her, but she seems guarded. I need her to come to me when she's ready.

"What if I don't remember how?" Her eyes are back on me, and there's a slight change in the way she stands now. She's less tense, more relaxed. She's warming up to the idea.

"It's just me. You only have to impress me." I untuck my hands and step in front of her. "And just so you know, you already impressed me a long time ago."

She rolls her tongue over her teeth and wets her lips. "This is crazy."

"Everything about us is crazy." There's a hell of a lot of meaning embedded in that sentence, but I can't dissect it right now. I just need this. This moment with her. I need this moment for us—in case we eventually run out of tomorrows.

It's how I lived as a SEAL. Today is what matters. Fight and make it through the "todays" because living that way means there will always be a tomorrow. But I don't know if Grace will always be in my life. I can't compare our relationship to being in the Navy.

Shit, I gotta stop thinking about all of this right now.

"Play for me," I say, cutting off my annoying thoughts. Fuck my brain. I just want her to play for me.

"Okay." She smiles and drops her purse on the floor then reaches for the bow.

"Okay," I murmur as triumph moves through me. I take a seat on the bed and watch as she examines the cello. "I want you to play naked."

She laughs. "You're joking."

"Do I look like I'm joking?"

She assesses me, her eyes roving over my body. Can she tell my dick is already saluting her?

"Naked," she repeats and scrunches her brow.

She moves slowly toward me, and her eyes never leave mine as she reaches for her hip and unzips the skirt she wore to work today—her first time back at the office in a week. She lets it fall. She's wearing black thigh-highs with black heels and a matching lace thong.

Her breath hitches as she touches the hem of that little strap of material between her thighs—aka underwear—and slowly slides it down and kicks it off.

Then she unbuttons her blouse, opens it, and tosses it to the floor.

Her strapless bra comes off next.

The woman is a goddess standing before me in only her thigh-highs and heels, and my hands turn to fists as I work at controlling my desire to pull her onto my lap.

"On or off?" she asks as her fingers glide down over her smooth V to the top of her black hose.

"On." I swallow, my heart racing, my body tensing, ready to go.

She eyes me playfully and cups her breasts before squeezing them. She's deliberately torturing me, and payback is going to be a bitch later.

I think about the tie.

She turns away, her tight golden ass on display.

Once seated, she stands the large instrument between her legs—and damned if I'm not jealous of the cello right now. She places the bow against the strings, her eyes closed, then begins to play. It takes her a minute to get into the groove, but when she does—it's beautiful.

And then she opens her eyes, capturing mine.

She's playing for me. To me.

Each time her bow swipes back and forth and her fingers almost dance against the strings, it gets to me.

Even though she's basically naked, all I find myself looking at is her eyes. The depth of those eyes—like crystals —sucks me in, taking hold of me, and eventually, I rise to my feet and go to her.

I stop a foot away, and she drops the bow, allowing it to fall to the floor. She takes in a deep breath, stands, and sets the cello back in its place. Before she's even turned around, I reach for her hips and pull her back against my chest. She looks at me over her shoulder, and I kiss her as my fingertips almost dig into her flesh. My need is unbearable.

The want for her is like nothing I've ever experienced.

She breaks the kiss and holds my outer thighs as she grinds her ass against me. Her head rests on my shoulder, offering her neck to me—and I inhale her soft jasmine scent before moving my mouth to her ear.

My hands slide over her hip bones and to her center before drifting up to her stomach, and I pull her even tighter against me. "That was amazing, Grace."

"Mm. 'Amazing Grace.' I know how to play that song," she murmurs.

"After," I say, my impatience, my need for her, too strong.

"I was hoping you wouldn't want to wait any longer." She shifts out of my grasp and faces me, her hands darting to my chest.

"I don't think I can wait another minute." I pull her lip between my teeth and suck on it.

Her hand goes to my jeans, and she works at the button, taking a step away from me to do so. "Then don't wait."

I watch her shove down my jeans and boxers. She frees my cock, holding it tight in her hand. She starts to sink to her knees, but I place my hands beneath her arms and guide her back to her feet.

"No. Tonight is about you."

"But you always make it about me." She pouts. "When will you let me spoil you?"

"Tomorrow," I say, but the word almost feels final, as though it will be our last time. I shove the thought from my mind. "Get comfortable on the bed." I look down at her heels. "Keep them on."

She moves for the rose and lies down, setting it in the center of her chest between her breasts. My gaze roves over every inch of her as I take off my shirt and finish undressing. She rubs the tip of her heel against her inner calf while resting a hand above her head. She looks so casual. So stunning.

And right now, she's all mine.

The bed sinks a little as I join her, and I brace myself on top of her, one hand on each side of her body.

Her chest rises as she takes a deep breath, holding my gaze. Her brows slant and her lips part. "This is something more, isn't it?"

I absorb her words. I allow them to sink deep inside me as I process what she's said.

Last week I would have said it can't be—because I didn't know if I could ever be with anyone again after what Cindy did to me. But saying that now would be a lie.

I brush a strand of hair off her face and nod. "Yes, it is."

The rose smashes between our bodies as I lower myself, feeling my cock pressed against her. I take her mouth, my tongue slipping between her lips as she shifts her hips up with need—the need for me to be inside her.

And I want it too. God, do I ever.

I keep kissing her, careful not to allow too much of my

weight to crush her…but I can't tear my mouth from hers. Her fingertips grip my shoulders then slide down to my biceps, where she squeezes the muscle. But the rotation of her pussy against my cock is making me lose my goddamn mind.

I pull up. "Grace?"

"Yeah?" She tilts her head up.

"I want to take my time with you, but if you keep moving like that, I'm not going to be able to wait."

"That's the idea. I don't want you to wait. I need you now. *Right now*." She slides her hands between our flesh and takes me into her hands, wrapping tight around my shaft.

She guides my tip to her center, and all I can do is look her in the eyes. I want to see the expression on her face when I fill her. She eases me in, and I slowly thrust until her pelvic bone meets mine. Her head goes back to the pillow, her eyes closing.

The feel of her…with nothing between us…I won't last long.

She hooks her legs around me as I shift up a little, and her silk thigh-highs rub against me, offering even more sensations. I run a hand over her breast and pinch her nipple, and she takes quick breaths. Her sex is clenching me—she's tightening, her body preparing…

"Fuck!" She grabs the sheets, her body jerking hard and fast.

Her loss of control has me close.

So close.

But I don't want to let go yet. I could stay buried inside her all night, all day…until the sun comes up and goes down and does it again.

And again.

My body trembles and the blood rushes through my veins,

to my tip, and I explode. I come so hard, spilling my seed inside her as my head drops forward.

When I open my eyes, I look at the crushed rose between us, and she raises it to her nose.

"I've never done that before." She inhales the scent, but I don't move.

I stay in place, knowing she'll become a sticky mess when I pull out. "Done what?"

"Sex without a condom."

Jesus. "Are you on the pill?" Shit, what was I thinking? I've never been careless. Ever.

"Yeah, I am, but I've always, you know, stayed safe." Her lips curve into a smile. "It was incredible."

"Sorry, I wasn't thinking."

"Neither was I—for a change."

I lift off her. "You want to clean up?"

"Mm hm." She slides out of bed and goes to the bathroom.

After a few moments, she comes back to me and gently wipes a warm wet rag between my thighs, around my tip. I pull my gaze from her and peer at the tie on the floor.

"And what dirty ideas are going on in that head of yours?" She stands, tosses the towel on the floor, and places her hands on her hips.

I want to grab her, pull her on top of me, and have her ride me hard and fast until she's screaming. A good scream this time, not like on the boat. Still a freeing one, though…

"Well?" She arches a dark brow.

I'd like to tie her hands to the headboard as I go down on her, but I'm worried the idea of being tied up will remind her of Greece, so I don't suggest it.

And then I get an idea.

"Pick up the tie," I say, my voice throaty and nearly hoarse as my body tenses.

She goes to the floor and bends down, and I have a beautiful shot of her ass. I grip my shaft and tug it a little, unable to stop myself.

"Mm. What do you propose we do with this?" She dangles it in the air and stands by the bed.

I keep pumping, preparing my body, while I take her wrist with the other hand. "We can pretend it's tomorrow."

She angles her head in curiosity, but then her eyes light up with recognition as her mouth forms an O. "I can finally have my way with you?" She bites her lip.

She really needs to hurry before I change my mind.

"Tie me up. Whatever you'd like."

"I want you to see the things I'm going to do to you." She shoots me a smile. "Hands it is."

I offer her my wrists as she climbs on top of me. She straddles my hips and binds my hands with the tie but keeps them resting on my chest.

She looks me straight in the eyes. "I want you to be able to pull my hair if you want to while I take you into my mouth."

I harden more than I thought possible as she lowers herself between my thighs. And when she darts her tongue up and down my dick, keeping her eyes on me—my neck lifted, straining so I can see her—I realize there's something different about her.

Something has changed.

I think she's finally free.

19

NOAH

"ARE WE SURE WE CAN'T RESOLVE THIS THROUGH MEDIATION? It seems a little crazy to drag this to court when we all know how it will end." Sarah doesn't waste time getting down to business.

I was supposed to be officially divorced today, and now I'm still married and—

"My client would love to if Mr. Dalton agrees to her new terms," Cindy's lawyer cuts off my thoughts.

"And what are your client's terms?" Sarah asks, her voice sharp.

"If the divorce is wrapped up in a timely manner, and Lily is allowed to take on the last name of Mr. Fletcher—your client can keep his Sundays," her lawyer explains, but I can't take my eyes off Cindy.

The rage inside me is hard to conceal as my hands clench into fists on the desk.

"No name change. And every weekend," I respond, even though I was supposed to let Sarah do the negotiating.

"My client is being very generous given the situation." Cindy's lawyer leans back in his seat.

What the hell is he talking about?

Cindy sighs. "Noah, you didn't open the envelope, did you?" Her green eyes find me, and her brows pinch together.

"The custody petition?" But the second I say the words, deep in my gut, I know I'm wrong.

"Not just that." Cindy closes her eyes. "Six and a half years ago, I got drunk three weeks before you came home from a tour of duty, and I slept with some guy."

Her betrayal isn't shocking. She's a cheat, I know this, but…

Her lawyer produces a piece of paper and slides it across the table to Sarah.

My whole world is spinning.

Bright lights flash before my eyes.

My stomach twists.

A pop-pop-pop in my head. Like gunfire.

My world fucking shatters.

I can see blood as if it's dripping down the window behind Cindy, instead of the rain.

"This is a paternity test, Noah," Sarah says, but her words are so faint, I can barely hear them.

I stand and find the door, rushing out of the room while pressing my palm to the wall to guide me.

And the next thing I know, I'm throwing up in a sink in the men's bathroom.

I grip the edges of the marble slab and finally look at my reflection. My body is shaky, my insides throbbing with a fierce intensity. Pain is everywhere. In my legs, my fingers, my head…

I cup the water beneath the faucet and splash it on my face.

Deep breaths. Deep fucking breaths.

I'm still in a daze when I finally make it back to the

conference room. I stand in the doorframe, unable to enter. I don't want to be in the same room as Cindy.

Everyone's still sitting, and Sarah's looking at me, her eyes narrowed with sympathy.

I swallow and blink a few times. I want to scream, to yell until I strip away the truth—I want to go back to the lie.

"I'm sorry, Noah. You should have opened the envelope. With the petition was the paternity paperwork," Cindy says. Her voice is calm. So fucking calm.

I press a hand inside the doorframe to keep myself upright. "How long have you known?"

"I had the test run after she was born," she answers so fast as if she's rehearsed these lines. But I doubt it because I don't think she would care enough to do so.

She's known the truth for years.

I remember questioning the doctor about Cindy's due date at the first ultrasound—the timing didn't make sense. He said they're not always accurate, and Cindy insisted the same.

"Now you see why you should walk away." Cindy stands and starts toward me, but I hold up my hand. I don't want her any closer to me. "She's not yours to fight for."

"The law suggests otherwise," Sarah says, but I can barely hear her. My pulse is racing. My heartbeat is like a ticking time bomb in my chest.

I take a moment before I say, "I'll see you in court."

"But—" Cindy starts.

"She's still my daughter." I glance at Sarah. "Nothing changes."

And I turn and leave before Cindy can say anything else.

I need to get the hell out of there before the walls close in on me and I lose my mind.

Lily *is* my daughter.

She's mine.

I don't care what anyone says. I won't abandon her.

As I move down Fifth Avenue, I think about Lily's smile.

I think about her laugh.

Her teddy bear with the missing eye that she used to love before her mother left it at our home when leaving me...

I'm her father.

Fuck blood.

I power off my phone and head to a bar.

I've only been drunk once in my life, but right now, I need something to dull the pain.

And five Jack and Cokes later, I end up in front of Jessica's door, ringing the bell.

She opens it as I press a palm to the wall. "Noah? God, are you okay?"

I exhale a deep, alcohol-infused breath. "No."

20

GRACE

"I'M SORRY I ASKED YOU TO MEET ME, BUT I'M WORRIED."
I'm standing in my own place as if I don't belong here, but
I'm also ruining Bella's "big reveal" that she was so excited
about. But that's the furthest thing on my mind right now.

"No, it's fine. I'm stressed too." Bella nods before dialing
Noah again on her cell, and I bite my thumbnail as I wait. She
shakes her head a few moments later. "Still going to
voicemail. And you checked his boat?"

"Yeah." I went aboard alone, which was frightening, but I
needed to know if he was okay.

"It's been nine hours since he met with the lawyers." Nine
long hours.

Bella's phone begins to ring, and we both flinch.

"Is it him?" I ask as she looks at her phone.

"Jessica." She answers it. "Hi." She looks at me, her lip
tucked between her teeth. "I should come over." She pauses
as, I assume, Jessica is talking again. "Okay, yeah—well,
keep me updated and thanks for letting me know. We were
worried."

It has to be about Noah.

"Yeah, Grace is here with me." Bella looks my way. "Yeah, okay, I'll talk to you later."

I sit on the couch in the living room and wait for an explanation, my pulse climbing.

The way Bella squeezes the back of her neck, her brows coming together, reminds me of her brother. "Noah's fine. He's at her place."

"Okay…" What does that mean? He said he'd come to me as soon as he left the lawyer's office, so why did he go to Jessica's?

My mind is racing, and I feel like a spool of yarn that's come unraveled and is rolling down a hill. I'm going to be a tangled mess when this is all over, aren't I? I knew this non-relationship with Noah was never going to be easy, but I couldn't stop myself—and there are so many strings attached now.

So. Many. Strings.

"Things didn't go well. Jessica says he needs some time. Some space." She swallows.

"Oh." But Noah kind of expected that, didn't he? Why—

"He's drunk," Bella cuts off my thoughts and her lips flat line for a brief moment. "He's going to spend the night on her couch. He'll call us when he's ready."

I don't know what to say.

"If it makes you feel better, he doesn't even want to see me." Her shoulders sag. "Jessica is asking Luke to fly in."

"Luke?" How bad could Noah be that he needs Luke here? What happened in that office today?

"Well, the thing is…Noah doesn't get drunk," she says in a low voice.

Her words have effectively paused my thoughts. The arm of the record player has lifted. The music of my mind has stopped.

Bella looks at the coffee table.

"What is it, Bella?"

"He doesn't talk about this, and it's not an issue anymore, but…" She blows out a breath. "Our father had a drinking problem. A long time ago. My mom stuck by my dad, though. But, uh, Noah doesn't let himself drink too much. I guess he's worried maybe he has the gene too."

His parents danced—they were happy.

Grass is always greener…guess not.

"Noah's a guarantee person, you know, so he doesn't get drunk. Not even when Cindy first laid the news on him. Well, he was on a ship off the coast of Iran when it happened, but still."

Coast of Iran?

"You think he's in trouble?" I stand, not sure what to do with my hands or feet. Hell, my body. I want to be there for him the way he's been there for me.

"He'll be fine, but if anyone can kick his ass to make sure of that, it's Luke. You know, SEAL to SEAL."

I've never been good at biding my time. Waiting can be brutal, but I've never met anyone like Noah, so I'll wait.

I'll wait for him because what other choice do I have? When you find someone like him, you don't let go.

* * *

IT SHOULDN'T AFFECT ME LIKE THIS. I MEAN, AT LEAST HE texted, but it's been forty-eight hours since he met with his ex and the lawyers.

I miss him. I want to know what he's thinking, how he's doing.

I read the message one more time as if the words might change.

I need some time. I'm sorry. I'll be in touch.

"Time," I mumble under my breath like an idiot before I look up to see Dad in my doorway. I've done well to avoid him since he barged into my home last week. But being at the office places a bull's-eye on my forehead.

He's in his jet-black suit with black pressed shirt and black tie—and no, he's not going to a funeral…well, maybe mine. When he wears this, his goal is to intimidate, to put the fear of God into someone. And it looks as though I'm the lucky winner today.

I stand and brace against my desk, knowing I'm in for a fight.

What I don't expect is for my mother to come walking in behind him, followed by Cade.

This has been planned. Everything they're about to say will have been choreographed in advance, like some theatrical production. My parents only know how to do big and splashy. They don't do subtle, not when it comes to family.

Cade sits in a chair and looks out the window at the city. He's not in some Grim Reaper suit, at least. Mom settles on the couch near him in her a white, fitted dress, but Dad comes before me.

"If we don't merge with Taylor Enterprises, I'm going to have to sell off a third of our assets." Dad's hand comes down on my desk, and I zone in on his thick platinum wedding band.

A symbol of love.

But not for my family.

"So sell. We can make up the difference." I drag my gaze up to meet his, knowing I'll find the eyes of a businessman, not my father, staring back at me.

His hand curls into a fist, and he pounds it on the desk.

My computer screen rattles, and I back away and cross my arms as if to protect myself, even though that's ridiculous. My dad's a jerk, but he would never hurt me. Well, not physically at least.

Emotionally—I'm pretty damaged.

All of us kids are…

But we're not kids anymore, right? I'll be thirty, Cade is pushing thirty-three, and Corbin is almost twenty-eight.

And yet, Dad always finds a way to bend us to his will.

Always.

"Do you not care about your mother or me? Your family? Things aren't so simple. We need this merger, and the Taylors won't sign unless you're included in the deal."

My shoulders shudder as his words whip my skin, nearly burning me. "Do you even hear yourself?"

My lips purse as I look over his shoulder at my mom. She's staring blankly out the window like Cade.

I can't ever become like her.

"I'm a person, Dad." I touch my chest and come around the desk toward him even though it feels like a dangerous move. "I'm your daughter." I have to remind him of this because I'm beginning to wonder if he's forgotten. "I'm not, and I will never be, part of a deal."

"Then get engaged to the guy until we sign the dotted lines and then don't follow through with it." My mom is standing now, facing us with her hands on her hips. "Isn't that the most obvious solution? You both get what you want. But maybe in time you'll change your mind about Patrick."

"No." That doesn't feel like a strong enough reply. More needs to be said. More is trying to seep through my bones, out of my body, and into the air. "I quit."

Cade's eyes are on Dad, curious for a reaction, which

means I truly spoke those words. I wasn't sure since Dad has yet to reply.

"I quit," I say louder this time. I'd like to shout the words for dramatic flair, but instead, I clutch at the material of my dress near my hips, gripping the fabric as if holding on to something will keep me grounded in my strength to stand up to this man.

"You can't quit." Dad lowers himself into the chair in front of my desk and angles his head to the side, studying me. He doesn't look the least bit worried.

He's got an ace up his sleeve.

"Corbin quits all the time." I swallow and release the hold on my dress. If I act like a kid, my father will keep treating me like one for sure.

"And he always comes back," Dad answers.

Blackmail? Fear? I don't know why, but he comes back to work within a week or so of walking out the doors of the building.

I won't come back, though. When I walk away, I'm done.

"What would you possibly do with your life?" Mom comes to my side, her eyes narrowed. "You were bred for this job."

Bred? Is Mom smoking some medical marijuana for all the migraines Dad must be giving her? What the hell is wrong with this woman?

She wasn't always this bad, was she?

"Think about what you're saying." Mom looks at Cade, but he's still quiet, aloof in all this. Does he remember when this happened to him last year?

"I've been thinking about quitting for years," I admit. And the honesty feels good.

Noah taught me that. He taught me how to speak my mind. My hand goes to my stomach when I think about him.

"Please tell me this isn't still about that carpenter." Dad pinches the bridge of his nose and shakes his head with disappointment.

"I almost died in Greece. That's what changed me. How can you not understand that?" And Noah helped me get back to who I once was—who I want to be.

"I don't believe you," Mom says. "This is about that man. I can see it all over your face." Her blue irises are darker than normal as they hold my gaze. "I told you she loved him."

She's directing her comment to either Dad or Cade. Probably both. They've clearly talked about all of this together.

Dad looks at her.

"Which means we only have one choice," she says as their eyes meet.

I look back and forth between them, my heartbeat elevating as I try to pick up on their unspoken communication.

"We won't let you throw away your life for a man like him. And if you really do care about him, then choose his happiness over being with him." Mom stands in front of me and reaches for my hands, but I retract them and step back.

"What are you trying to say?" I ask.

But Dad answers, "We can make his life hell if we have to."

I hold up a hand, wanting him to stop, but I know he won't. He's got the knife stuck in my chest, and he's going to do this slowly, painfully. He wants this to hurt.

"We'll have his company blacklisted. He'll never get another job in Manhattan," Dad says.

I take a shallow breath as my hands go back to my stomach as if it's going to fold in on itself and I'm going to be sick. "No." I shake my head. "You don't have that kind of power."

"Do you want to test us?" Dad lifts a brow. "And that daughter of his…you're guaranteeing he won't get custody if you keep seeing him."

Those words are the final blow.

"No!" I go straight to him and press my hands against his chest. "No, please."

"Cade's friends with the judge who'll be hearing Noah's case. What fucking luck." Dad grips my wrists and pushes my hands off his chest.

My lips part in surprise. I didn't know a date had been set —but I haven't heard from Noah, so…

I back away from Dad and face my brother, needing to focus on the big issue at hand—Noah's daughter.

"You wouldn't, would you?" I ask Cade, my voice pleading.

Cade tucks his hands in his slacks pockets, his jaw clenched, his head bowed—he won't look at me.

"You can't do that to him. He loves his daughter more than anything. Please." My voice breaks, tears pooling in my eyes at the thought of Noah losing Lily.

I'll do anything I can to prevent that from happening.

Anything.

"And if you think you can stay away from him until after the court hearing just to go back to him…that won't fly," Dad warns.

I don't know if there is even a "Noah and me" or if there ever will be, but how can I find out now?

My mom's fingers wrap over my shoulder, giving me chills. "It's time you start owning your name and who you are. It's your turn to make sacrifices for the family, for the company."

Like Cade…

"I won't marry Patrick." I jerk my body free of her touch. "Cade, please, don't let them do this to me." I start his way.

He finally looks at me, his eyes cold like his heart. "I have a meeting to get to."

My gaze follows his back as he exits my office, leaving me alone with two people I barely know or recognize anymore. His acceptance of what's happening to me is almost unbearable.

"Your engagement was announced in the *Times* this morning." Mom grabs her phone from her purse and taps at it.

I don't have to ask what she's doing. I already know. She's showing me proof of the betrayal—of my supposed sacrifice.

I should be in shock, but did I ever truly believe I could have more than a taste of freedom?

No. I've always known how this would go down. This shouldn't be a surprise.

But it doesn't change the fact that I'm close to throwing up on my mother's shoes, or maybe in her Louis bag. Pressure is increasing in my temples, and I'm sweating in my cleavage—hell, everywhere.

"We'll have a celebratory dinner. Maybe you'll come around to the idea eventually." Mom holds the phone in front of me—my engagement to Patrick is already trending on social media. "Don't forget, Patrick's family is a big deal in London."

How can she be so cavalier about this? They just threatened to hurt the man I…

"Only sixteen people have to die before Patrick's dad gets a shot to rule England," she adds.

"Good luck with that," I say under my breath, my body aching—the pain blinding. "Actually, I wouldn't put it past the Taylors to try to knock everyone off, including the Queen herself, to make it happen." But who's worse: them or my parents for blackmailing me into this?

"They're already dubbing this as a royal New York wedding." God, she almost looks happy. She's acting as though this marriage will happen.

"We'll be dining at our house with the Taylors a week from today. If you don't show, then Noah—" Dad begins.

I hold up my hand, begging him not to say anymore. I can't stomach the threats—not about Lily.

"Make Dalton believe you. I don't want him thinking he has a chance and coming back around," Dad says before he disappears from my office, leaving me alone with Mom.

I go to my chair and drop into it in a daze.

"You're making the right choice. In time, you'll be as happy as Cade," she says.

Happy as Cade?

Happy as Cade…

Oh God.

21

NOAH

"MORE COFFEE?" JESSICA EXTENDS ANOTHER MUG MY WAY.

"Nah. I think I'd better get going."

"And where are you going?" she asks as Luke comes into the kitchen.

He yawns and scratches the back of his head, squeezing his eyes a little as if waking up.

"You always sleep this late? What happened to you?" I catch Luke's eyes, happy to give the man a hard time since he's been poking and prodding me for the last few days.

Shit, it's already Friday.

"Don't tell me you're still doing five o'clock drills." He grabs the full cup of coffee from Jessica and lifts it to his mouth.

"Not this week, but yeah, normally." I stand and crack my neck. I haven't worked out in a while, and my body is protesting.

"So where are you going?" Jessica asks again as she sits up on top of the kitchen island and bites into a croissant.

"Grace's."

I disappeared with only a lame text, and Grace is

probably pissed. But it's taken some time for me to wrap my head around the blow Cindy delivered. I mean, somewhere deep down inside me, I always suspected Lily might not be my blood, but she'll always be mine—that will never change.

It still fucking hurts, though.

The truth hurts.

"You know, Luke kind of warned Grace to stay away from you." Jessica takes another bite before she dusts crumbs off her lap and onto the floor.

I turn to look at Luke, who shrugs before sliding into a chair at the table. "I was worried about you, man. I didn't want another woman screwing with your head."

"She's not like that, but thanks for the concern. Remind me to interfere in your love life next time I'm down in Nashville," I say.

"Love life?" Jessica grins.

We haven't done much joking around since Luke came. I've been doing my best to simply hang on to my sanity, but I'm finally feeling like myself again, and all I want to do is see Grace.

I have to assume that means something.

"Hey, before I fly out tonight, I wanted to let you know I heard back from my contact about the thing we were discussing last night." Luke looks at his sister before his eyes dart back to mine.

"The *thing*?" Jessica laughs. "Please tell me you're not talking about a penis."

"Jesus Christ, Jessica, I don't want to hear that word coming from you." Luke leans back in the chair and folds his arms.

"Well?" I cock my head, waiting, my heart rate kicks up a few notches.

"It can be done." He lets out a deep breath. "You sure about this? It's a little different."

"I have zero doubts, but if I need to handle it myself, then I—"

"No, no, I've got it covered. I just wanted to double-check with you," Luke says as Jessica looks back and forth between us.

She shoves off the counter. "You care to enlighten me?"

Luke shakes his head. "No."

"Jerk," she mumbles as her phone pings incessantly.

"Damn, who's blowing up your cell?" Luke gets up.

Jessica's brows furrow and she swipes at her screen, tugging her lip between her teeth while tapping on her smartphone.

"What is it?" Luke asks.

"It can't be true," she says a moment later before offering me the phone. "People are texting me asking if I knew about it…"

"About what?" I look at the screen—at the headline: ***Manhattan Millionaire Heiress Grace Parker-King and Lord Patrick Taylor of London to be wed.***

As I step back, trying to figure out what the hell I just read, Luke takes the phone. "It has to be a mistake," I mumble.

"Probably. I didn't even see any pictures of them together. All split-screen shots," Jessica notes.

"I've gotta go to talk to her," I say.

"You want me to come with you?" Luke asks.

"No, I'm good."

I clean up, hurry out of Jessica's loft, and hail a taxi.

Grace isn't at the hotel anymore because I finally talked to my sister yesterday about everything—and in between her yelling about Cindy, she mentioned Grace was back at her own place. I screwed up the reveal Bella was so excited about, but at least she gave me a pass, given what happened this week.

I make my way to Grace's loft, but after three rings and no answer, she either doesn't want to talk to me, or she's at work.

Can I go to her office, though? Would that be officially crossing the line?

Shit, I'm pretty sure we crossed the line the moment we created it.

I think about her brother Cade—a run-in with him wouldn't go so well, but I don't want to wait until tonight to talk to her. I need to see her, to hear from her that the engagement is only a rumor.

Of course, I don't hold any claim on her, but there's no way in hell she'd up and marry that asshole. No goddamn way.

After another cab ride, which takes forever in the traffic, I find myself standing in front of the tall glass skyscraper that holds her company—I checked my phone while in the taxi. Her office is on the thirtieth floor.

I don't even know if I'll be allowed up.

I eye the security guards in the lobby and start past them toward the elevators, but they're busy talking with people and don't say anything. Maybe I'm in the clear.

I wait impatiently on the trek up to her floor, and when the doors open, I'm greeted by more security. I figured it wouldn't be that easy.

"Can I help you?" the man asks while looking up from his computer screen.

"I'm here to see Grace."

"Miss King?"

Maybe she prefers only to use her last-last name. I know

how much she hates the hyphen. She's joked around a few times about being anxious to marry if only to get rid of her name.

And some part of me has wanted to say, "Dalton would sound nice."

"Yeah, I am."

"Is she expecting you?" He drags his gaze from my sneakers up to my graphic tee. It's Luke's shirt since I haven't been back to my boat.

"Yes, she is," I lie, hoping she'll be available and have my back.

He lifts the phone, but I can tell he's not buying it. I guess Grace doesn't get many visitors dressed like me.

"Dalton?"

I look over the shoulder of the guard and see Corbin—the *good* brother.

"What are you doing here?" His eyes narrow in surprise as he heads my way. He's in similar clothes to me, which catches me off guard. I guess Grace wasn't joking about him being a hell of a lot different than Cade.

"I need to talk to Grace."

Corbin nods at the guard. "I'll take him."

"Yes, sir." The guard smiles.

"You know better than to address me like that, Jimmy." Corbin grins. "Oh, and I got you tickets to the Mets game next weekend. Remind me to get them to you."

"Aww, thanks, man, my son will be so excited."

Corbin fist-bumps the guard before redirecting his attention my way as we walk down a hall. "Does she know you're coming?"

"No."

"I'd make it quick then. If my family sees you around

here, it won't be good. Sorry, man." He clears his throat. "Next door on the left, and good luck."

Do I need luck?

I stop in front of her closed door once Corbin is out of sight, then I knock.

"Come in," she calls.

I slowly open the door and find her standing in front of a window overlooking the city, her back to me. She's in a black dress and red heels. I remember the first night I met her— Miss Fourth of July.

I look at the massive desk then take in the size of the room—it's a hell of a lot more spacious than my boat. "Hi."

Her shoulders flinch, and she swivels on her heel to face me, her lips parting. "What are you doing here?" She looks behind me. "Um, could you close the door?"

"I shouldn't have come. Sorry. But we need to talk." I follow her request and shut the door, but she remains by the window, not moving an inch.

"How'd it go on Tuesday? I've been worried about you."

I want to talk about that, I do, but I need to get this engagement issue straightened up first. "I know, and I'm sorry. I've had a shit week."

She looks at the floor.

"But what about you?" I take a few steps closer, but I don't quite close the gap. "Tell me you're not actually engaged to that guy."

Just saying it sounds ridiculous. I'm waiting for her to laugh and wave dismissively—but she doesn't.

Her gaze skates up to my face, and she swallows. "I don't have a choice."

"What?" I'm in front of her almost immediately, reaching for her forearms, but she steps back, bumping into the window.

What the hell is going on?

I drop my arms like dead weights. "It's true? I was with you Tuesday morning before the lawyers. What happened between then and now that has you marrying that guy?" Mr. Armani from the first night we met…

"I can't explain." She closes her eyes. "This thing between us is over, Noah." She can't even look at me when she says it.

"I still don't understand."

"This engagement isn't what I want, and you know it." She finally peers at me.

I shake my head, confused. "Then why are you doing it?"

"It's complicated." She starts to turn away, but I stop her.

"Is it about your family? They're forcing you into this?" I keep my hand wrapped around her bicep.

"They're not giving me an option. Please, don't make this harder for me than it already is."

"I don't accept that." Jesus. I release my grip and step back, raking my hands through my hair, trying to make sense of this. "You can't marry that guy. You can make your own choices in life—remember?"

We've talked about this before. I thought she finally accepted she can control her life. What changed since I last saw her? I shouldn't have ever disappeared. This is my fault.

"You need to accept it," she says in a broken voice, a slight sheen over her light blue eyes. "Please."

"What about us?" I need to reason with her, to get her to remember who she is.

"What us? There is no us. It was always sex," she says with a strained voice.

"So we're lying to each other now?" I turn away and catch sight of Cade in the hall outside the door—he's observing us through the narrow window at the side.

"We were always lying to each other."

Her words are like a hot lash to my skin.

"I don't buy it, Grace." I face her again, but her eyes are directed across the room to where Cade's standing. "I'll fight for you. I'll stand up to your family with you. Just give me the word."

I didn't know I was capable of handling something this intense right now, after what's happened this week, but I can't imagine losing her—not like this. I need more time to see if anything can ever happen between us.

"I can't...I'm sorry. The decision's been made. I'm marrying Patrick." There's an obvious tremble to her voice as if she might cry, and yet she's speaking about her life as if it's a business deal.

"No."

I don't give a damn her brother is out there. I cup her face with both hands. She bites her lip as she traps me with her gaze.

"Tell me you don't want me." I edge my face closer to hers. "Tell me you don't want to fight for *this*." Both palms rest on her cheeks as my mouth finds hers.

She kisses me back, her fingertips burying into my shoulder blades as I deepen the kiss.

When I finally step back, she's slightly breathless, and her lips twist at the edges. She bows her head and places her hand over her mouth.

But when she looks back up at me, I see the pain in her eyes—and I see the answer to my question on her face.

"I'm sorry, Noah. But we were fooling each other to think this could ever be more." She sniffles. "You and I both know I could never be with someone like you," she says so low I barely hear her.

I back up, swiping a hand down my face and over the light beard I now have.

She turns and goes back to the window then raises her palm to the glass as her forehead rests against it.

I don't know what else to say. Maybe I always knew this day was coming. This day was supposed to come. That was the deal. But somewhere in that time, I started to believe it was possible for us to be together.

I was wrong.

"Goodbye, Grace." My chest is tight, and the blood rushes to my ears as I exhale a breath and go to the door.

"I'm sorry," she cries, but I don't respond.

I can't respond. I can't be with another woman who won't fight for us. I can't be the only one in it.

First Cindy and now Grace.

I'm fucking done.

22

NOAH

I STUFF MY CLOTHES INTO A BOX WITH A LITTLE MORE FORCE than necessary, cramming everything as far down as it can go to save room. Plus, I need to take my anger out on something after seeing Grace yesterday. I've bounced back and forth between anger and—no…just anger. I don't know how else to feel. Angry at her for surrendering to her family and pissed at myself for ever allowing anything to start with her.

Bella sinks onto my bed next to the box.

"What's wrong?" I stand upright and focus my attention on her.

"Just sad about Grace." She tucks her lip between her teeth and fidgets with her hands on her lap.

"She made her decision." I grab another stack of T-shirts and set them in the box, then I use both palms to press them down as if that'll actually make them fit.

"I'm sorry. I guess you two just weren't—"

"You were right." I grab the shirts from the box and toss them on the bed in frustration. I move the box and sit next to her.

She finally looks at me. "I didn't want to be right."

"Well, I wasn't in the best place to be getting involved with anyone—especially someone like her."

"You'll meet someone someday. Give it time." She stands, grabs another flat box, and starts folding it.

I grab the tape roll and toss it to her. "I don't want to meet anyone." It hurts too goddamn much. "Let's just pack and not talk about this anymore. Okay?"

She sets the box she's taped together on the bed and reaches for the T-shirts I tossed. "Sure."

"And, Bella?"

"Yeah?"

"Do me a favor. Never mention her name again."

"Cindy?"

My jaw tightens. "Grace."

* * *

I HAVE NO IDEA WHY BELLA AND JESSICA BROUGHT ME TO this place. There's not a chance in hell I can afford it. I leave the master bedroom and head back into the living area, where the realtor is talking to them.

"And we're here because…?" I lean my hip against the kitchen island.

"You need to live close to Cindy's. It will increase your chances of getting joint custody," Bella says, and the realtor just raises her blond brows and smiles.

The court date is in two weeks, which means I need to get my shit together. "I can't afford this place. I don't even want to know how much it costs." I push away from the counter and start for the door.

"We have the investment. We can put some of that money toward the rent here," Bella says from behind me, and I turn to face her.

"No. We need that for the business."

Jessica steps in front of me. "Let me help you."

"No."

"Don't be a stubborn ass. Do you want Lily to be able to stay with you or not?" She crosses her arms, trying to stare me down. "Cindy might win if you rent some one-bedroom place across the river."

"Better than the boat," I grumble, hating that I'm getting rid of the thing.

I was planning on keeping it since I'm taking an actual paycheck from the business now, thanks to Jessica and Luke's investment, but it's nowhere near enough to cover a place like this. And...the boat reminds me of Grace now.

I don't need any reminders of her, of the way she made me feel during those few weeks we were supposed to be only screwing. Yeah, sure...as if that's all it was.

"I want to help," Jessica says.

Bella comes up next to her, and the realtor disappears, giving us some space to talk.

"And I said no."

"Then work for me." Jessica's shoulders lift as she exhales a frustrated breath.

"What?" Bella looks at her.

"We could use another guy for a job. It shouldn't take too long. Five days. Maybe seven. You'd be done in time for the court hearing," Jessica says. "It pays fifty thousand."

Fifty thousand?

My fingers rush through my hair as I process the amount. How can I turn that down?

But I promised myself I wouldn't do anything dangerous anymore, risking leaving Lily without a father.

But Lily might lose me anyway if I don't do this.

"I'll give you the money up front so you can put a deposit

on this place." Jessica places her hand on my forearm. "It's an easy job."

"How easy can it be if it pays fifty Gs?" I need to say yes, though. She's right about this apartment. It might help me secure at least the weekends with Lily. It's less than five minutes from Cindy's, and it has two large bedrooms, a great kitchen, and even a pool on top of the building, which Lily would love.

"Then take the fifty and don't do the job—that works for me too," Jessica says, avoiding eye contact with Bella.

But she already knows I won't take a handout.

I raise a brow. "Do I get a gun?"

"Maybe even two," she says as her hand leaves my arm.

I shut my eyes. It's been eight months since I've been in the military. Eight months since I've shot a gun or suited up. If I go back into this world—will I ever be able to leave it?

My eyes flash open as my body tenses, and my heart starts hammering. "I'm in."

* * *

"I THOUGHT YOU ONLY DID BODYGUARD GIGS AND STUFF." I look at Luke as a broad grin spreads across his face.

"This is the 'and stuff.'" He points at an image on a computer screen. We're in a hotel in Boston's South Ward. "Timothy. Age five. He was taken three days ago."

"Ransom?" I ask, eyeing the kid who's the same age as Lily. My stomach tightens at the thought of any asshole ever kidnapping my daughter.

"Yeah. Parents were told if they contacted the Feds, they'd kill their son."

"How'd they find you?"

"The father is friends with a buddy of mine."

"The two of us against an unknown number of kidnappers, huh?" I fold my arms. I've been in much worse situations, but they were a lot different. They were government-issued ops.

"I've got them tracked to within a square mile of this area," he says while pulling up a map and zooming in on the screen. "Once we narrow it down, we'll go in."

"Rules of engagement? Because last time I checked, shooting people was still illegal in the US."

"Not if it's self-defense. And I'll give my friend at the Boston FBI office a call right after we've secured the kid."

"Not before?"

"I don't want any Feds fucking things up for us. I want this to be a quick in and out."

Yeah, that'd be ideal.

He cocks his head, studying me. "You sure you're good?"

Do I look hesitant?

Shit, I have a lot on my mind, which isn't good. When I was a SEAL, I had learned to become two different people because the person I needed to be on the field couldn't worry about dying or leaving a widow or a fatherless child…

"You can back out. I can handle this."

I glance at the bed where he's got pistols and rifles laid out. There's a slight twitch in my hand as I go to them and reach for a Sig P220. I run my fingers over the gleaming metal and look at Luke.

"I've got your back," I say, and he nods. "Is this going to be a kill or capture mission?"

"Guess we'll find out when we get there."

23

GRACE

I SLIP ON MY BLACK SLACKS. I HAVE ZERO DESIRE TO DRESS up for dinner with Patrick and his family at my parents' tonight. No dress or skirt—nothing to give him any glimmer of hope that he'll ever touch me. It's almost eighty outside, but I'm tempted to put on a turtleneck just to cover as much skin as possible.

I zip the pants and look at my phone on the bathroom counter in front of me. It's a message from Bella.

Unfortunately, we'll be passing on the Hamptons job. Thank you, though, for the consideration.

My hand darts to my stomach as I go into my bedroom and read the message again. I settle down on my bed. I've been expecting this after what happened between Noah and me, but it still hurts. Part of me was hoping I'd get to see him again.

If he remodeled my house, maybe there'd still be hope for us.

But how?

I have to pull myself out of this mess without Noah getting hurt in the process.

Well…*more* hurt. I already stuck a knife in him with what I said. I don't know if I'll ever be able to forgive myself for recycling the words my parents said to me about him —*to him*.

But Noah's not the type of man to give up so easily. I witnessed that during his fight for Lily, and even when he stood in front of me, offering to fight my family with me.

I had to say what I did to make sure he would give up on me, give up on the idea of us, even if *I* never want to give up on the idea. It was a crazy idea to start with—there ever being an *us*.

But somehow it became crazier for there not to be.

I stopped caring about my name, what my friends or family would think—I just knew I had to be with him.

And the second I gave in to that, he was taken from me.

The goddamn world was against us from the start. We never had a chance.

I've never cried over a man before. I've never cared enough about one. But my insides have been a shaky mess, my stomach doing a gymnastic routine as my eyes have been blurred by tears every day since Noah left my office.

I want to type a message back to Bella to apologize or say something to make this right. But what can I possibly say? The truth?

"The truth is kind of our thing, right?" Noah's words come back to me as I stand and toss my phone on the bed, my stomach squeezing as though I might be sick.

I've barely slept in the week since I ended things with him. Between the pain and the nightmares about Number Four…I'm beginning to feel as though I'm losing my mind.

I try to figure out how I'm going to keep my shit together as my driver takes me to my parents' place.

"You okay?" Frank asks, his eyes on me in the rearview mirror.

Frank has been with our family since before my father took control of the company thirty-three years ago. He started as my grandparents' driver, then Dad's driver before he switched to me. I don't know how he's tolerated being with our family for so long.

"I'm being forced to marry someone I hate," I admit without hesitation. Frank has known me forever, and he would never betray me. It feels good, to be honest.

"The Grace I know would never be forced to do anything."

I wonder if I ever let Frank know the real me. Which person have I been around him? The Ice Queen Bitch or the woman beneath the mask—the woman Noah revealed again? Noah chipped away the ice. It became nothing more than a puddle at my feet. All that was left was me. The *real* me.

"You know my father. Once his mind is made up…"

"Yeah, and I also know he was in love with someone else before he was forced to marry your mother." He parks the car at the curb, but he doesn't get out.

"What are you talking about?" My breath hitches as I lean forward and press a palm to the edge of his seat.

He shifts and faces me, his eyes finding mine. So much warmth there. "Her name was Jane. She was taking night classes at an art school while waitressing during the day." His brows pull together, and my heartbeat quickens as I wait for him to finish. "Her dad swept the floors at the high school. Her mom was a teacher."

I swallow, thinking about my hard-ass grandfather. "And grandpa didn't approve?"

He shakes his head. "It was your grandmother. She refused to allow him to see her anymore once she found out."

"No. That can't be…" My house in the Hamptons was hers. She was different than everyone else. "You must be mistaken."

I reach for the door handle, my fingers trembling because I can't possibly imagine my grandmother denying true love. I only remember her telling me about her hopes and dreams for me, ones that involved being the opposite of my dad.

"Your father was pushed into the marriage with your mom a few months later. And your dad never forgave her for that." He sighs.

"She wasn't like that, though." I drop my hand to my lap.

"When she saw what your father became after his marriage—cold, hard, ruthless…like her own husband—I think she changed." He smiles. "She became carefree. A little crazy at times, but in a good way."

Holy shit. "And now he's doing the same thing to me."

Frank gets out of the car, comes around to open my door, and holds his hand out for me. "The question is—are you going to let him?"

I take his hand and get out, looking at him as I do. "It's never that simple."

"Nothing worth fighting for ever is."

"SHALL WE TOAST?" MOM RAISES HER CHAMPAGNE FLUTE, but I can't bring myself to celebrate this sham of a marriage.

Everyone looks at me, though. Waiting.

Patrick's sitting opposite me, his head angled, his cold eyes narrowed. "To our engagement." He extends his glass my way.

My stomach twists. "I, uh, need some air. Excuse me." I push back from the table.

"Grace," my father rasps.

I look at Corbin, not Cade, for some sort of interference. If I don't get out of this dining room, I'm going to suffocate —officially drown like I almost did twenty years ago.

"Cade pissed off the mayor last night by taking all of his money in a card game," Corbin says and winks at me.

"What?" my mom shrieks.

I hear Dad call my name, but I've already rushed into the kitchen and am headed straight for the closest terrace. Their home occupies the entire floor of the building, and their massive outdoor living space wraps around the outside like one big Saturn ring.

An outdoor garden thirty stories above the ground. I used to love it when I was a kid. I'd play my cello outside when I was home during the summers in order to escape the noise inside—the noise of complete silence. I never knew silence could be so loud…but it's possible.

I go over to the edge of the deck and grip the railing, looking onto the city and feeling a little like Rose in *Titanic,* when she makes her quick exit from dinner.

But that was a movie, and this is real life.

And Jack isn't about to rescue me. I'd give anything for Noah to, though.

"You shouldn't have taken off like that."

Patrick's voice slides over my skin, burning me, and when his hand touches my back and starts to slip south, I spin around and reach up to smack him. He catches my wrist quickly and pins me to the railing. My arm is caught between his chest and mine, so I try to use my other to shove at him, but he grabs that one too.

"Let go of me," I hiss as he presses his body even harder against me.

"Or what? You're going to be my wife in three weeks.

And then when we're in London, I'll make you scream my name, beg me for more."

"Let go," I demand again, ignoring his disgusting words as I struggle.

"Take your fucking hands off my sister."

Patrick's forehead creases in surprise, then Cade's hand is on his shoulder, ripping him away from me.

Cade's jaw is locked tight, his chest slowly expanding as he takes a deep breath. He grabs the lapels of Patrick's blazer and yanks him forward. "Get the hell out of here!"

"She's mine. What's wrong with you?" Patrick shakes his head and tries to back away. "And you can't do a goddamn thing about it."

I stare at them as I try to digest what's going on. My body tenses and I'm back in that hotel room in Greece…only this time it's Cade there to protect me.

"I'm not going to ask you again," Cade warns, even though I barely hear him.

My shoulders tremble, and my hand goes to my chest as Cade punches Patrick in the face.

"Bloody hell!" Patrick's hands go to his nose, and he looks at me then back at Cade before heading into the house.

"You okay?" Cade comes my way, but I flinch.

"Why'd you help me?"

He doesn't say anything. His lips draw tight, then he reaches for my arm and gently grabs my elbow. "Come on, you took off right before I was about to make an important announcement."

I blink a few times, surprise warming my skin as I allow him to lead me back inside—terrified of how this will all go down.

"What did you do?" Richard Taylor yells the second he sees Cade.

Patrick's not in the room, nor is his mom, so the bastard is probably getting cleaned up in the bathroom.

"Nothing he didn't deserve." Cade scratches the back of his head and looks at Corbin and nods.

What am I missing?

"You better start talking, or the engagement and merger are off!" Richard comes around in front of Cade.

Cade shakes his head. "You won't call it off. You need us. You're so goddamn desperate that you thought marrying your son off before the merger would be the only way to ensure we didn't back out of the deal when we found out about all of the shit you're in."

"What the hell are you talking about, Son?" Dad grips the back of his chair, his knuckles whitening.

"You did your due diligence on these guys—but you didn't look deep enough." Cade tips his head Corbin's way and Corbin pulls out his phone, taps the screen, and tosses it to Dad.

Everything is happening so fast, and I'm afraid I'll miss something from the loud sound of my heartbeat pulsing in my neck.

"I have a friend at MI5 in London, and I had him dig a little deeper into your company. Apparently"—Cade looks at my Dad—"he lied to us about his financials. He's facing major tax evasion, among other things, and he's been using his name and title to bail him out for the last few years. But at some point, he'll need a deal or the company will collapse." Cade points at the phone in my Dad's hand. "It's all there."

Dad reaches into his pocket for his glasses, slips them on, and swipes at the screen.

Patrick comes back in the room with a bandage covering his nose. "That's not true."

"It looks that way," Dad says under his breath.

"And you," Cade says while winding around the table toward Patrick, "better stay away from my sister. If you ever touch her again, your nose will be the least of your worries."

Patrick, the sissy with the shrunken testicles that he is, swallows and steps away from Cade, clearly scared shitless. My heart has grown wings, my mind's a little dizzy, and for the first time in a week, hope bubbles up inside me.

"This has all been one big misunderstanding." Richard raises his palms, but he doesn't look all that aristocratic right now—just looks like an asshole in a suit.

"Who approached who? Who suggested the proposal? Who pushed for all of this to happen quicker than normal?" Corbin comes up next to Dad. "They've been using us."

Dad closes his eyes for a moment. "Get out of my house. Now."

Richard looks at his wife then at Patrick, and they start for the exit.

Dad opens his eyes once the Taylors are gone. "This doesn't change anything, Grace."

Panic wraps around my throat, tightening. I can't breathe. I was so close to a way out.

No…

"Why? I don't understand." I look at my mom as if she might help, but that's absurd.

All she does is shrug and go out the door leading to the kitchen.

"Dad." Corbin comes up next to me. "This needs to stop. Don't do this to her."

"You're no one to talk, Son. Your life is a fucking mess."

"Is this because of Jane?" I take a hesitant step in Dad's direction. "Do you want Cade and me to suffer because you lost the woman you cared about? Because you had to marry Mom?"

Both Cade's and Corbin's eyes are on me now. I don't have to look at them to know—I can feel it. Dad slowly drags his gaze to meet mine, and there's anger there. So. Much. Anger. But with whom?

"Who told you that?" His eyes are thin slits, his nose flaring. There's a bead of sweat at his hairline.

"It doesn't matter. What matters is that you're going to destroy your kids, your own flesh and blood, if you make us suffer the same fate as you." I need to say this—I need to stand up to my dad and fight.

Fight for myself.

Fight for my happiness…

For there to ever be a Noah and me, I have to do this.

"I can't do this right now," he grumbles and heads toward the kitchen. "Go home."

When the door closes, I lower my head and stare at the floor, my mind reeling from everything that happened tonight.

"Well, that was intense." Corbin squeezes my shoulder. "You okay?"

"Yes." I shake my head and look up. "No."

"This was never supposed to happen." Cade runs a hand through his hair as his eyes flicker to mine.

"What are you talking about?" I look at Corbin, but he only shrugs.

"Dad said he'd leave you two alone if—"

"If what?" I whisper, focused on Cade.

"If I agreed to marry Veronica, he promised not to do the same thing to you and Corbin. It was part of the deal."

"What the hell are you saying?" Corbin grabs ahold of Cade's arm, his brows pulling together.

"I was trying to protect you both. That's why I knew we needed that deal with Alexander & Sons so damn bad. The second I learned Dad was talking to the Taylors, I realized he'd betray his promise if we had to merge with them."

"You mean all this time…" It doesn't add up. Has Cade always been in my corner and I just didn't know it? "But you didn't want me with Noah, you—"

"I was trying to protect you from falling for someone before it was too late."

"You really proposed to Veronica to try to save Grace and me?" Corbin asks as his arms fall to his sides.

"In part. Dad had a few other things to throw at me."

"He always does," I say. "So when Dad was in my office last week threatening Noah—you were never in support of that?"

"No, I've been trying to find a way out for you."

I've hated Cade, comparing him to my father—but he's nothing like him. He's been wearing a mask too, and I've been too blind to see the real him. He might be a bit of an ass, but there's more beneath the surface. I don't know if I even truly know my own brother, which is sad.

"I need to go," I say as I blink a few times, realizing there's somewhere else I need to be.

Cade takes my arm. "You can't go to him. Not yet."

How'd he know? "Why not? If you're not going to help Dad—"

"You and I both know that if Dad wants something done, he can do it without me." Cade angles his head, studying me, trying to get a read on me. "Do you really care about this guy?"

"I do."

"And you want out of the company?" he asks.

I nod.

"Then give me one week."

At what point did Cade become my savior?

"A week for what?" I say, my voice shaking a little.

"A week to get you your freedom."

24

GRACE

I don't listen to Cade, though. I can't wait any longer. Now that I know Cade is in my corner, I have to see Noah.

As long as no one finds out, he'll be safe.

Frank drops me off at the docks and tips his hat my way.

"You don't need to wait," I say then hurry out of the car before he has a chance to open the door for me.

I take off my shoes and hold them as I go into a full-on sprint down the dock. Noah's phone keeps going straight to voicemail, so he doesn't even know I've been trying to get ahold of him.

Not that I think he'd answer anyway.

The wind kicks my hair back, probably tangling it as I rush past people. My purse slaps hard against my side with each step.

And then I realize I've run too damn far. Or maybe I didn't.

Something isn't right.

I thread my fingers through my hair and spin around.

There's an empty space between two boats where Noah's used to be.

He's gone.

Did he already sell his boat? It doesn't work, so he can't be out on it now.

My mind scrambles to think of where to go, how to find him.

I press my palms to my face and groan against them. I want to scream—to let it all go. I want back on Noah's boat, in his arms—to yell at the top of my lungs as the waves I used to fear crash over me, washing away the bullshit of what's happened, the pain and lies.

My hands drop down as I look at the water and approach the edge of the dock where his boat used to be tied up.

"Where are you?" I must sound crazy, asking the water as if I'll get an answer.

But a moment later, Jessica comes to mind. She'd know where he is, wouldn't she?

She's been avoiding my calls and texts all week, so she might slam the door in my face—if she even opens it—but I have to try.

The sense of urgency, the need to strip away the lie of this last week and be with him again, is overwhelming, so I take off, my legs carrying me fast—and I ignore the pain in my feet from running without shoes.

I slip the heels on once inside a cab, and my fingertips dig into my quads on the ride over.

Within twenty minutes I'm standing on the other side of her door, my hands tapping the sides of my legs as I wait for her to open it.

Please be home.

I ring again.

My heart snaps up and into my throat when I hear the sliding of the chain. Thank God.

She slowly opens the door but not too wide. "What are you doing here?"

I knew she'd be pissed, but we're also friends, so the fact that she hasn't even given me a chance to explain is a bit of a slap in the face to our friendship. But...maybe I don't blame her.

"I need to see him."

"No. You don't get to see him after what you did." She starts to close the door, but in a panic, I thrust my arm in the opening, blocking her.

"Have you lost your mind?" She opens it up again.

"Yes," I admit. "I really, really need to see Noah. Please, Jessica."

She folds her arms across her chest, but she won't budge out of the way, which makes me wonder if he's here. I look over her shoulder but can't see much of anything.

"How could you do that to him after what he went through? The man is never going to trust another woman again." She takes in a lungful of air, her shoulders rising, her eyes steadying on me as if she's in disbelief I could be so— Parker-King like.

"That's why I'm here, Jessica. I need to explain to him what happened. He needs to know the truth," I plead. "I'm not engaged anymore."

She rolls her eyes. "Wow. You mean you pulled your head out of your ass and realized you can make your own choices?"

I was wrong about Jessica being pissed. She straight-up hates me.

"The man finds out his daughter isn't his, then you go

break his heart to be with some douchebag you hate. I can't even look at you."

"What are you talking about?" I replay her words in my head again because I'm sure I misheard her. I step back, my eyes widening, my body tensing. "Lily isn't his?"

"I thought he told you." She opens the door wider and steps into the hall.

"I never gave him the chance." I take quick, shallow breaths, trying not to have another panic attack.

Oh, God. I want to fall to my knees and fucking sob.

The man was hurting—hurting so damn bad—yet he still wanted me that day in my office, right after he got one of the biggest blows of his life, and I...*shit.*

"Where is he? Please." I swipe at tears. "I need to see him, to make this right. I was trying to protect him," I whisper as my body goes weak, my knees giving out.

"Jesus, you're going to collapse." She grabs my arm and guides me into her house, urging me to sit at the kitchen table.

I look around, hoping Noah will appear, but the place feels empty. Anywhere that Noah isn't—always feels that way. She hands me a glass of water a minute later, and after taking a sip, I look at her.

"Tell me what you're talking about—what do you mean by 'protecting' him?"

"My parents threatened me," I say, but I don't want to get into too much detail. It's too hard for me to stomach the words —or the idea that my mother and father could ever be so truly vicious. "To keep Noah safe, I had to agree to marry Patrick."

"This is Noah we're talking about. He can take care of himself. That doesn't add up." She comes around to the other side of the table and sits down.

"They know the judge who will be hearing Noah's custody case."

There. I said it. The evil is out there. The darkness of my family name that swallows and consumes everything—spreading everywhere…I can't even look her in the eyes to see her response, and I don't need to elaborate. She'll understand what I'm saying.

The chair legs screech on the floor, and I finally look at her. She's cupping the back of her neck with both hands, her hair swept up into a messy bun atop her head, and she's staring at the adjoining living room.

"And now?" she asks after a few minutes of silence.

I was expecting more of a reaction, but she probably doesn't even know how to stomach a response.

"Cade is helping me get out of this mess."

"Cade?" She faces me as her arms drop. "You trust him? Really? Corbin, yes, but—"

"I do." I nod. "So tell me where he is so I can explain."

"Yeah, and then Noah will go and kill your dad." She sighs. "That's what I'd do if I were him." Her lips go tight for a moment, and I can tell she's contemplating what to do.

"If you don't help me, then I'll look up where Bella lives and go harass her until she tells me, because I won't give up."

Not now. Not ever.

"He's in Boston," she finally sputters.

A parade of questions litters my mind as I stand. "What? Why? What's in Boston?"

"A job."

"A remodel?" I mentally calculate how fast I can get to Boston in my car even though I'm a terrible driver.

"He's on a job with Luke."

My heart drops, and I'm seeing fucking stars. "No…"

"It should be pretty routine. He'll be back in a couple of days, I'd guess. You'll need to wait until then to talk to him. And let me get the guns back first, so he doesn't actually shoot your father."

I don't think she's joking either. When it comes to Lily— Noah will do anything for her.

And oh, God, she's not his daughter…how is he handling this?

"Why is he doing it?"

"For the money, so he can have a better shot at joint custody."

"So he still wants—"

She arches a brow. "Do you really need to ask that question?"

"No, you're right." Noah—the good guy. Always. And I'm the darkness… "What kind of case?"

My chest constricts, worry eating at me. How would I ever have survived waiting on the other side of the world if he'd been a SEAL when we met? The spouses, unlike his ex, must be so damn strong to marry Teamguys. Could I ever be that strong?

"It's a kidnapping case, so it's pretty routine."

"Routine?" I'm going to be sick.

"It's gonna be fine." She waves dismissively, and it's obvious her anger with me has weakened. It's not totally gone, but I don't think she wants to ram her fist into my face anymore.

And I know she can. She's learned a lot of moves from Luke.

"You promise?" I hold my breath.

"Of course."

I sit back down because the weight of my emotions is too heavy for me to remain standing. "How do you do this? How

261

do you handle the stress of waiting for your brother while he's out there risking his neck?"

She grabs a bottle of wine off her counter and holds it up. "I drink." She smiles. "You'll get used to it."

"What do you mean?"

"If you and Noah get back together, then you'll need to get used to it."

"Is this permanent? Is he going to keep working with Luke?" I'm in full-on panic mode, and I desperately need that wine.

Jessica shrugs. "It's in his blood. Like Luke, his need to help people." She pours me a glass and slides it across the table. "I'm betting once he starts, he won't be able to stop."

25

GRACE

I CAN TELL IT'S HIM. TALL, BROAD SHOULDERS, DARK HAIR, gorgeous arms. Military-looking black cargo pants, a hunter-green tee, and black combat boots.

He turns around, and when his eyes find mine, they narrow in obvious surprise, his mouth parting.

He looks lethal.

I shake my hands a little at my sides as if they've gone numb.

Jessica moves past me, and I stop walking, leaving a good thirty feet between Noah and me. He doesn't say anything or even move—he just keeps his eyes locked on mine.

"Where is he?" Jessica asks.

Noah tips his head to the left, motioning to the hospital room at his side. She nods and pats his shoulder before slipping out of sight into the room. Noah takes one last look at me then goes in, not saying anything. And that moment hurts more than if he had yelled.

But I suck it up. Although my nerves are out of control, I force myself to follow.

"What happened?" Jessica's standing next to Luke's bed, eyeing the monitors, when I walk in.

"Your idiot brother jumped in front of a bullet for me," Noah says from the other side of the bed.

"Weren't you wearing vests?" Jessica looks at the bandage spiraling around Luke's bicep. A vest wouldn't help his arm, though.

"Yes," Noah answers in a clipped voice, clearly agitated.

"I didn't want to take any chances that you'd get hurt, man. It wouldn't look good in court. You know Cindy. She'd even turn rescuing a five-year-old into something to use against you." Luke shakes his head and curses under his breath as his hand goes to the wound.

"You shouldn't have done it, is all. I would have been fine," Noah grumbles as his eyes sweep back across the room and over to Jessica.

"So you saved Timothy?" she asks.

"Yeah, he's good." Noah nods.

"And the kidnappers are all still alive—well, unless one or two don't make it through surgery," Luke adds.

"Why'd you bring her here?" Noah asks, taking a complete detour from the current conversation.

"I needed a ride. I called her when I found out Luke got shot."

"You have a car," Noah challenges Jessica, and I can tell he's trying to get a read on her. He must assume she has ulterior motives for bringing me.

After waiting three days since I learned the truth from Jessica, I was more than eager to drive to Boston with her—I just hadn't expected I'd be heading to a hospital. But now that I'm standing in the same room as Noah, I'm at a loss for what to say or how to act.

Jessica crosses her arms. "My car is getting work done."

"Yeah, sure," Noah says.

The room fills with silence for a few minutes before Luke raises a fist to his mouth and coughs—a fake and obnoxious one.

Way to be obvious...

My eyes dart to Noah's arm, and I resist the urge to go to him when I notice red marks on his bicep. "Are you bleeding?"

"It's not my blood," he says without even glancing my way.

And the tension in the room springs back into place. It's molasses-thick.

Jessica peers at me with a lopsided smile. "You should probably spend the night here before heading back home. I'll stay with Luke."

"Get some rest. You can check in on me in the morning if you're that worried." Luke flashes me a grin.

I was expecting a little more anger from him, especially after how he warned me to stay away from Noah to begin with, but he must assume that if Jessica brought me here everything is okay.

Now I just need to figure out how to make it okay.

"Well, I'm glad you're not too badly hurt. I'll, uh, see you in the morning." I steal one last look at Noah, but his jaw's tight, the muscles clenched, and his eyes are focused on the floor.

"Thanks. Good night," Luke says as I head for the door.

This isn't how I planned for the night to happen. Shit. I close my eyes for a moment as I walk out of the room. Part of me is expecting Noah to follow, to yell at me even. I'd take any kind of contact from him.

But he doesn't budge.

Once down the hall, I jab the call button and wait for the

elevator. I slip inside as soon as the doors part and press the number for my floor. I lean back against the wall and bite my lip, trying to keep the tears at bay as the doors close.

But I startle as the doors touch together only to pop back open.

Goose bumps spread across my arms at the sight of Noah on the other side.

He keeps his eyes on me as he comes in. "You shouldn't go to the parking garage alone at night."

He turns his back and stands off to the side as if he doesn't want to be close. A moment later, we're on the next floor, and two more people join us, which has him stepping to the back, his arm brushing against mine. That slight bit of contact makes me shut my eyes as my body absorbs the shock of his simple touch.

I look at him from the corners of my eyes and find his eyes are closed and his chin tipped up a little. He's tense, his breathing slow.

I flinch when the doors open, and I wait for the others to exit before I do.

Noah stays a few feet behind me as we walk into the parking garage. And the silence hanging between us is killing me, so I stop and spin around to face him. I think he was expecting this, because his hands are hidden in his pockets, and he's just standing there, eyeing me as if I'm dangerous, an enemy.

"Noah."

"Don't," he warns.

This can't go down here, not in a garage of all places. It's late at night, and surely not many people will be coming out here, but still...

"I was going to ask if you'd ride with me to a hotel. I'm

not sure I'm up for driving," I lie, knowing he'll see right through my flimsy, paper-thin words.

"Then call a cab."

I take a cautious step his way, my eyes scanning the area to make sure we're still alone. "I'm sorry." But the words feel like they can never possibly be enough.

"For what, Grace?" And it's not a real question—sarcasm wraps a tight ribbon around his words. His hands come out of his pockets, and he rubs his jaw and his dark beard.

"There's so much I need to say. Please, can we talk at the hotel? Or even in my car?"

He closes the space between us, and it's as if the garage has shrunk to the size of a tiny six by six jail cell, and there's only us. His strong presence controls the room, it controls everything—especially me at the moment.

He stands before me, observing me, his chest moving with slow, deep breaths. His eyes remain on mine for a moment before he shifts back a step. "We can't go to a hotel."

And now I notice the lust in his eyes. I can hear it in the slight strain in his voice.

Even after everything, he still wants me. And it gives me hope.

"I stood up to my father. I'm not marrying Patrick." The truth, even in here, is better than not at all, I decide. I need him to know that if he takes me into his arms like I want him to, he won't become the "other man." He was cheated on, so I know Noah would never allow himself to be *that* man.

"It doesn't change anything. It's too late." He turns, but I reach for him, desperate not to lose him, to lose this moment.

"I'm begging you to hear me out."

He bows his head. He's thinking about it.

The feel of his warm skin beneath mine wakes up my

body, and it's as if a thousand little wings beat inside my stomach and flutter south.

"There's nothing to say." He lifts his head. "You're *you*." He shifts to face me as my hand drops, going cold at my side. "And I'm *me*."

His words cut me. The pain I've caused him is chilling, but I refuse to surrender. Not this time.

"We have to talk. I won't leave here without you talking to me."

"And I *can't* go to a goddamn hotel with you," he bites out, and the flair of emotion and grit in his voice has me stepping back.

"Why not?"

"Jesus Christ—just leave," he says in a lower voice. He puts a hand to his forehead and grips his temples with his thumb and middle finger.

"No." I step in front of him, reaching for his wrist in an attempt to unmask his eyes. I need him to look at me, to see me. To trust me, even if I don't deserve it.

He says my name like a hiss as he shifts his hand in one fast movement, so it's now him holding on to me. Lightning-fast reflexes.

"Why can't you come with me?"

"Because I'm mad as hell at you." He releases his grip, and I don't want him to. I don't want to lose his touch.

"You hate me so much that you can't be alone with me?"

"Yes." He shakes his head. "No…"

"Well, what is it?"

His eyes flash to mine. "Because I want to fuck you. And I shouldn't want to."

The rawness of his words and the gravelly sound of his voice makes the hairs on my arms stand.

He means *just* sex, though.

"So do it," I whisper.

The heat radiating from his body blasts me. He takes me by the elbows, gently holding on to me, and I watch the movement in his throat—the emotion being swallowed. He leans forward and my lips part, my nipples tighten, and my eyes close as I wait.

But instead his breath is at my ear. "You know I'm not that kind of man."

Then his hands are off me again, and when I open my eyes, he's walking back to the hospital.

"They threatened me with Lily," I say in a rush.

I'm screwing everything up. This isn't how I wanted to tell him, but I'm so afraid if he walks away from me now, I'll never get another chance.

His palm rests against the door, and he keeps his back to me for a moment.

"If I didn't stop seeing you and agree to marry Patrick…" God, I can't say the words, they're so vile. Will he ever be able to look at me knowing my own blood is so ruthless? I stop a foot shy of him, a little terrified of his lack of a response. "My parents promised to make sure you lose your custody case."

No movement at all. He remains still.

"I quit. I tried to get free of the company, but then my parents hit me where they knew they could hurt me." I close my eyes. "You." I draw in a shaky breath. "Lily."

When I finally peel my eyes open a minute later, I find Noah looking back at me.

"What choice did I have?" I ask, my voice trembling.

He angles his head, his eyes narrowing. "You should have told me. We could have figured this out together. You took the choice from me. You made it on your own."

His words have my eyes widening in surprise. "But—"

"You know I would never let anyone hurt Lily—or take her from me. I'd walk through hell and back for her." He turns, his biceps tightening. "I would have walked through fire for you too."

My hand darts to my stomach at his words. Did I mess everything up by not trusting him to help? God, no. I thought I was doing the right thing, but...

"Did your father threaten you too?" he asks a moment later and slowly faces me.

I notice his hand curve into a fist at his side.

Is Jessica right? Is Noah capable of killing my dad? He's one of the sweetest men I've ever met, but there's still a dangerous edge to him. Maybe it's from being a SEAL, but I don't doubt for a minute he won't kill for someone he loves.

I close the gap between us, wetting my lips as I look into his eyes. This side of him—this bit of dark—it doesn't scare me. Nothing about this man scares me, except for the idea of there never being a tomorrow with him in it.

"No, he didn't threaten me," I say. "I should have told you. You're right. I thought I was keeping you safe, but we've always been honest with each other, and I—"

His mouth captures mine so fast that I almost stumble back, but he catches me, his hands swooping around to my back, pulling me in closer to him...to where I belong.

* * *

"I NEED YOU," I CRY INTO HIS EAR AS HE PINS ME TO THE wall inside the hotel room. He's holding on to my hips as he kisses my neck, and my eyelids fall, heavy as desire swells inside me.

He inches away so he can lift my blue blouse over my head and toss it to the floor. "I've missed you so much."

He holds my face with both hands and kisses me again, his tongue coaxing my lips apart, finding mine. I want to buck and grind against him, so desperate for him to be inside me. His tongue only makes me want it that much more. I press my palms against his chest and gently shove. His lips break from mine as his eyes meet my now-open ones.

"I. Need. You. Now." I try to catch my breath. "I'm not going to repeat myself again."

His lips curve up a little, and the sight of a smile on his face does me in.

He reaches behind my back and works at my bra. "I can assemble a rifle faster than I can get this thing off."

I chuckle as I assist, but this moment isn't lost on me—the way his eyes remain on mine, his brows drawn inward the slightest bit as if there's still some question in his mind about what we're doing...

But when my bra falls to the floor, and he palms my breasts with both hands, I forget everything.

And I mean everything.

His name.

My name.

My birthdate.

"Oh, God," is about all I can manage when I observe the SEAL stripping out of his cargo pants and boots—following orders.

I stand before him, naked myself now. He takes my wrist and kisses the inside of it, his lips gentle there, and my thighs tighten as his mouth trails to my thumb. He tugs it between his teeth and applies a little pressure.

"I'm going to fuck you now," he says in a low voice, his eyes darkening.

And I'm so turned on.

He lifts me, and I cradle his neck as he carries me to the

bed and sets me down. He parts my legs, urging them to open wide. His eyes sweep over every inch of my body as he holds his shaft. He finally braces himself above me, his biceps flexed as they hold the weight of his body.

I try not to look at his tattoo, to think about the people he's lost—and that he could have been hurt or worse tonight.

"You okay?"

"Yes," I cry as he reaches between my thighs and strokes my flesh. I immediately respond to his touch and lose myself in the moment again.

I almost expect him to slam inside me harder than he ever has—to make it hurt. To make me scream. And I want him to. I screwed up, even if I thought I was doing the right thing. I deserve some pain.

But this is Noah we're talking about.

He slowly eases all the way into me.

But when our eyes connect, he pulls back out for a moment before he thrusts so deep and fast that his pelvic bone hits mine. Then he does it again with even more intensity.

My eyes...I can't see. The sensations of his movements have me seeing bursts of color in my mind since I can't focus my sight.

Hard.

Fast.

Carnal and pure.

Everything is stripped free, and we're two people who need only one thing—each other.

I writhe against him and bite my lip when his hand shifts from my hip to my ass.

"Yes. Yes. Don't stop. Oh, God." I tense. "Don't. Fucking. Stop." My toes curl, my body shakes...and I come.

A few moments later, a deep rumble escapes from his chest, and his body jerks as warm liquid fills me.

I don't want to move even if I'm filled with his come. I'm mush—boneless.

Totally sated.

The last time we had sex, it was wild and even a little kinky, which I hadn't expected of the good sailor—and it was incredible.

But this…*wow.*

"Grace."

"Hmm?"

He lowers himself next to me. "I need to know something before we do this again."

"Do *what*?" I point at my naked body like an idiot because my limbs are like jelly, my body limp—I need a few minutes before we go again, and I'm a woman. How can he be ready again so fast?

"Before we become an us."

Become an us. I repeat his words in my head, loving the sound of that last one—us. *Us.* I want to bottle that word up like an oil and rub it all over myself.

He clears his throat. "I need to know you're going to fight for us." His brows pinch together as if he doesn't like his own choice of words. "I understand what you tried to do for me, for Lily, but I have to know that if things get hard again or something else happens, you won't bail. I'm a father. I can't fall in love with someone if she won't be around tomorrow."

His mom stayed when things were rough.

Cindy bailed.

I bailed…

"This was supposed to be just sex," I say. "But that was the only real lie I told you. Well, up until that day in my office."

His eyes remain intense and focused on mine. "These last two weeks were the worst of my life, and regardless of what I said to you that day, I was always going to try to find my way back to you. And that's the truth," I say.

My heart skips into my throat, and I sit up. I'm only just now stringing all of his words together as if I didn't have all the musical notes in the right order. "Wait, did you say the word love a moment ago?"

He smiles and takes my hand, lacing our fingers, and he gently squeezes. "It's been a whirlwind since I met you. The timing of this...it's clearly not great." He looks at our hands for a moment.

"There better be a but coming."

He laughs and raises our clasped hands to his lips and kisses my hand. "*But*"—he smiles—"now that I have you back, I'm for damn sure never going to let you go."

26

NOAH

"WHAT'S HE DOING HERE?"

Grace's father looks up from his desk, and it's the first time I've laid eyes on the man. I'm doing my best to trap my anger about his threats deep inside me, but it's going to be hard.

Grace is at my side, and both her brothers are sitting across from her dad's desk. Cade tips his chin her way, giving her the signal to come all the way in.

Her father stands and braces against the desk. "Have you lost your mind bringing him here?"

Maybe she has, because testing my limits in regards to my anger toward him might not be the best idea. I don't have a gun, but I don't need one to do what I'd like to him. My jaw locks tight, and I remain closer to the door as Grace walks up behind her brothers.

She wanted me with her. She wanted her dad to truly understand that he wouldn't be able to come between us. We may have been all wrong for each other when we first met, but it doesn't matter anymore. All that matters is that we're right for each other now.

Cade rises, and so does Corbin. I'm still furious with Cade, but knowing he punched Patrick in the face and had Grace's best interest at heart all along makes me feel a little better.

"What's going on?" Her dad narrows his eyes at Grace before shifting his attention to her older brother, attempting to demand answers by staring them down.

"It's over," Grace says softly. "You won't be threatening us anymore."

"What?" Her dad laughs a little and eases his stance. He moves to the side of his leather chair and casually rests a hand on top.

Cade slides a folder across the desk to his father. "The board members are meeting in ten minutes, and they'll be voting in favor of you stepping down as CEO."

Her dad eyes the folder before his gaze darts back up to Cade, his eyes darkening. "They wouldn't."

"You think we're the only ones who can't stand you?" Corbin walks away from the desk to the window.

"Corbin, Grace, and I—along with nine of the other members—will vote to terminate your position. I'll be taking over." Cade tucks his hands in his pockets, his jaw tight, and there's not an ounce of fear on his face.

And not on Grace's either…it's about time. Her father has been pushing her around too long. She deserves to be free of him.

But he's still her dad, so this must be hard. And *because* he's her dad, and *because* I don't want to go to jail, I won't touch him, even if I do want to wrap my hands around his neck.

His face is blank as he says, "You can't do this to me. You wouldn't dare."

"I figured out how to save the company without merging

or cutting back on our assets. And the first step means eliminating you." Cade shoots me a glance over his shoulder. I don't know if it's his version of a peace offering, but he nods before looking back at his father.

"Look in the folder," Grace says while motioning to it. "You've been blackmailing all of us so long, it's time you know what it feels like."

"All the shady shit you've done in the last ten years, well, I've been paying attention, keeping track. And you don't really want to go against me, do you? I'm marrying the governor's daughter, after all."

Her father pushes his glasses farther up on his nose and snatches the folder. He flips through the papers before tossing the folder back on the desk, grumbling. "How could you do this to me? I'm your father."

The second the man starts for Grace, I move across the room, prepared to defend her.

He's face to face with me now. "You going to hit me, boy?"

My hands go tight at my sides. "Call me boy one more time." I swallow. "Please." I look down at him, my rage barely concealed…but when Grace's hand touches my back, my pulse slows a little.

Grace. Lily. Two reasons why I need to keep my shit together.

This never happened to me when I was in the military. I didn't lose my control. I guess love does something to a man. When someone threatens the people you care about…

Her dad hisses and makes a clicking sound with his tongue. "This isn't over."

"Oh, it is." Cade comes up next to him and rests a hand on his shoulder as if daring him to say more.

"Maybe if your mom didn't force you away from the woman you loved, you wouldn't be such an asshole, Dad."

I'm not sure what Grace is talking about, but she reaches for my hand and threads her fingers with mine. It's a little hard to believe we're standing in front of the man who tried to rip us apart. His eyes go to our hands, and he exhales a shaky breath.

"Retire. Go enjoy a sunset. On an island—far away," Corbin says while turning away from the window.

Silence stretches across the room for a minute before her father's brows pinch together, disappointment evident in his eyes. After a minute, he turns his back on his kids and leaves.

Grace's free hand darts to her stomach as her eyes close.

"It's over. Are you sure you still want out now that Dad will be gone?" Cade asks.

"More than anything," she says while nodding, her eyes opening.

Cade drags his hand down his jaw and throat before he extends it to me. "We good?"

I eye his hand for a moment and look at Grace. She's observing us, probably curious how I'm going to respond.

I gently pull my hand free of hers and take his. "Yeah, we're good."

I STAND IN FRONT OF THE MIRROR, MY SLACKS ON, BUT MY dress shirt is still open. My gaze shifts to the scars on my chest, my side, and beneath my ribs. Some are prominent, whereas others are lighter, fading from time.

I drop my hands to the counter, bracing against it as I find my eyes in the mirror, thinking about Luke's phone call yesterday. A few jobs a year—just a few...I'd make more money on three ops with him than in a year working with Bella.

But can I really go back into the line of fire?

"You ready?" Grace comes up behind me, places her hands around my waist, and rests her chin on my shoulder, finding my eyes in the reflection.

"I think so."

"Everything is going to work out, I promise." She smiles at me. "Let me help you with the buttons." Her arms drop, and I face her. Her lip catches between her teeth and her eyes focus on my chest as she works at the buttons. "Where's the tie?" She raises a brow.

The tie. Jesus, I can't wait to use that again in bed with her. Maybe tonight. Well, if everything goes well in court, that is. Otherwise, I might get fucking drunk again—feel the slow burn of liquor lighting a fire in my chest.

I don't think the idea of drinking too much even makes me nervous anymore, not with Grace in my life.

"I know what you're thinking." She presses a quick kiss to my lips, her hands on my chest, and I nip her bottom lip as my hand curves up to her firm ass.

"Oh yeah? What?" I arch a brow, my cock hardening against her.

"You want to tie me up this time, don't you?" She smiles, her face so close to mine that it's hard not to pull her back in and kiss her, to feel my tongue in her mouth.

"Grace." I touch her cheek with the back of my free hand. "I want to do much more than that."

27

GRACE

Noah's arms are wrapped tightly around Lily out front of the courthouse, and I can tell this big, strong man is close to crying.

I'm standing off to the side because he hasn't introduced me to Lily yet. Today isn't exactly the best day to do it, but the fact that he wanted me here with him means a lot.

Noah stands up after hugging her, his back to me now, but he keeps hold of her little hand as he looks at her. "Are you excited about seeing my new apartment this weekend?"

"Yeah, but I'll miss that boat of yours. I love the water, just like you, Daddy."

I press a hand to my chest, my heart melting.

"We'll get another one someday." He glances over his shoulder, finding my eyes, and it's at that moment that I know I love this man.

It doesn't matter how long we've known each other. I've been waiting for someone like him my entire life.

I look at Noah's ex, who is standing off to the side, and her eyes are on me—shooting damn daggers my way. When she saw me in court with Noah, she had the nerve to approach me and accuse me of cheating.

Cheating on Patrick Taylor. Apparently, she follows social media, but she missed the part about the announcement being an error.

"Hi." Noah is in front of me now, and I look at Cindy as she walks with her fiancé and Lily toward a town car.

"You okay?"

His face is stoic, his body a little tense. "Every other weekend isn't a lot, but it's better than nothing. And at least I get a couple of weeks in the summertime."

"And you'll make the most of that time, I'm sure." We start down the street.

"I'm a single man now," he says after a minute.

"Single?" I stop walking and face him.

He chuckles. "You know what I mean." He takes my hands and pulls me off to the side near a storefront, out of the way of foot traffic. "What are your plans this Saturday?"

"Nothing, but you'll have Lily. Which reminds me, we have a lot of unpacking to do at your apartment before then." I make a mental note to call his sister to ensure she's on the job of decorating his place.

"I want you to meet her."

I knew this would happen eventually, but that doesn't change the fact that my palms are now sweaty.

"You sure?"

The pad of his thumb traces my bottom lip. "More than ever."

A house. A white picket fence. Kids. A family together at dinnertime. These are things I always wanted but never thought I could have. Okay, so the fence isn't all that important, but maybe a dog would be nice.

"What are you thinking about?" He smiles. He can always

tell when my mind starts to get a little derailed. But he does that to me. He makes my thoughts race. Excitement always fills me when he's around.

"Thinking about the future," I say.

"Oh yeah? And am I in it?"

"Do you even have to ask?" My eyes narrow in a playful way, and he pulls me against him and kisses me.

In front of everyone.

And it doesn't matter if all of New York sees us.

"HAVE YOU MADE A DECISION?"

Noah looks up from his newspaper as I come into his living room. I love that he's so old school he reads the actual paper. Not the news on a tablet.

"And are you seriously asking me that question while wearing *that*?" he asks in a silky voice.

I smile and play with the knot of my black satin robe before untying it.

"You're not playing fair." He rises from the couch and stands in front of it but doesn't come to me.

Not yet at least.

So, I allow the robe to slip from my shoulders and fall to the floor.

I'm naked now, and the blinds are open.

He looks over at the window, and his jaw tightens. He shakes his head and goes to it, and I watch as the blinds scroll down before he faces me.

"So? You've been thinking about the decision for three weeks now. You said yesterday you'd have an answer for Luke by tomorrow." I step over the robe. "Well, it's tomorrow."

"I can see that." His naked chest rises and falls as he takes a breath, and I look down at his black pajama bottoms. His desire, his want, is evident. His eyes are on my nude stilettos before his gaze drifts up my legs. "And you expect me to answer the question while you're wearing only your high heels?"

I cross my arms, purposefully covering my breasts while also pushing them up and together, drawing his eyes.

He comes in front of me. "I won't work with Luke."

Relief swells in my chest.

But also guilt.

He holds my hips as he looks me in the eyes.

My fingertips dance up his chest, and my palm settles over his tattoo. "I don't want to lose you," I say and swallow, "but I'll support you either way."

"You and Lily are all that matter to me. I don't need to live that life anymore." He nuzzles my nose with his before kissing the tip.

"You help people. That's who you are. So, if you want to work with Luke every once in a while, you should—"

He cuts me off with his mouth, his tongue finding mine, stealing my breath.

"What was that for?" I ask, a little breathless.

"For letting me be me. For understanding who I am." His hands are on my shoulders now, warming my skin. "It doesn't mean I'll do it…but thank you."

His hands slide up my neck and to my cheeks where he holds my face, his eyes on mine.

My damn phone rings, startling me, but he doesn't flinch.

"Don't answer it," he says with his mouth so close to mine.

I press my lips to his, kissing him again—but the phone won't stop ringing.

After our lips part, he says, "I'll turn it off." He grabs it off the table, but his brows pull together. "It's Corbin."

"Shit."

He knows by now that if Corbin is calling me, especially this early, it can't be good. *Please don't be in trouble—again.*

Noah hands me the phone, and I answer. "Hello?"

"Hey, I have something to tell you. You might want to sit down for this," Corbin says in a rush.

My skin pebbles and I sink onto the couch behind me, my eyes on Noah. He must see the worry on my face, because he reaches for my robe off the ground and comes in front of me, handing it to me as he waits to learn what's going on.

"Tell me." I clutch the material tight to my chest.

"He's dead."

"Dead?" Panic hits me, and I suck in a breath, dropping the robe.

"Number Four."

Number Four…? Oh, God. "I don't understand."

"The lawyer called to let us know they won't need us anymore since there won't be a trial."

"What happened to him?" I ask.

Noah's squeezing my hand, offering support.

"Suicide, maybe. They're not sure. They don't really know how he was strangled. They didn't find anything in the jail cell with him." There's a crackle from a deep breath through the phone. "It's over."

"It's over," I repeat in shock, trying to absorb the words, to make sense of them. My mind flashes back to Greece, to the man's hands on me—the knife… "I have to go." I end the call and drop the phone, pressing my palms to my face.

Noah is sitting next to me now, and he pulls me into his arms. "He can't ever hurt you again."

His words have my hands falling to my lap as I shift out

of his arms so I can look into his eyes. "How—how'd you know?"

Is he so smart that he inferred what Corbin said to me? Or could he hear Corbin through the phone?

And then I take a deep breath as it comes to me—the realization hits me like a freight train.

He'd walk through fire for me.

Kill for me.

"Noah, you didn't—did you?" I stand and hold my arms tight to my chest, freezing.

He rubs a hand down his jaw. "Didn't what?"

"Did you kill that guy in Athens?" But that's not possible. He hasn't left New York. I've been with him almost every day.

He stands, his brows stitching together. "Of course not."

"Did you have anything to do with it?"

He doesn't say anything, and he doesn't need to. We don't lie to each other—always honesty. It's our "thing."

He's torn. Maybe he's afraid of what I might think.

"I love you," I say. This wasn't how I planned to say those words for the first time, but they're the only words he needs to hear right now.

"I love you too." He places a hand on my face, cupping my cheek, and angles his head a little as he traps me with those sapphire eyes.

Hearing it back from him…my heart—there are wings there. Jesus. My eyes are blurred by tears, by the admission, by the fact that this thing is really over with Number Four.

I can move on.

A huge weight has been lifted from my chest, and whether Noah truly had anything to do with it or not doesn't matter to me—all that matters is that he loves me.

285

"I'm naked, Noah." And finally free. "Are you going to do something about it?"

He chuckles and lifts me into his arms in one fast movement, which has me squealing.

"Hell, yes."

NOAH

"Bella did a great job with the remodel." I look at Grace, who's standing in front of the fireplace—and it brings me back to the first day we made love.

Months have passed since then, but God, it still feels like yesterday that I first laid eyes on her.

"You helped too," she teases before looking at Lily. "What do you think? Do you like it?"

Lily frowns. "It's okay, I guess."

"What's wrong?" Grace looks at me and hides a smile.

"Well, I was kind of hoping there'd be a special place for me when I visit."

"Oh. Well, hmm." Grace takes her hand. "Why don't you come with me?"

Lily looks my way, and I wink at her before following them up the stairs and down the hall.

"I think we might have missed a room when we showed you around." Grace places a hand on the knob, her eyes finding mine as she does.

When she opens the door and Lily's little hands dart to her mouth in shock, my heart swells.

"Is this really for me?" She rushes into the room, which has a Little Mermaid theme since Lily is currently obsessed with that movie.

I nod. "And it has an ocean view."

Lily runs to me and wraps her arms around my legs, squeezing tightly before she finds Grace and hugs her as well. "I love it!"

Lily takes in every toy, every inch of space. I walk up next to Grace and pull her tight against my side, breathing in her jasmine scent.

"Thank you," I whisper into her ear.

She reaches for my hand that's on her stomach and places hers over mine. "I love her too, Noah. You don't need to thank me."

Lily's studying the collection of princess dolls displayed by the bay window.

"Those were my grandmother's." She leaves my side and walks toward my daughter. "She was kind of like an evil queen in a Disney movie, but then her heart softened, and she became—"

"More like you?" Lily looks up, smiling. "A princess?"

"I'm no princess," Grace says while laughing a little.

"No, you're right." Lily's shoulders pop up. "You're definitely a queen."

Grace kneels next to her, smiling. "Mm. I'll be whatever you'd like me to be."

"Well, good. Because if you're a queen and you and Daddy get married, I get to be a princess!" She claps and leaves her hands clasped as she spins in a circle before purposefully falling onto the floor.

Grace tugs her lip between her teeth and looks up at me, her light blue eyes holding mine. "Come on, I'll race you downstairs."

Grace and Lily are on their feet, and Lily laughs as they breeze past me, their hair whipping up behind them.

"You coming?" Grace calls out to me, probably already nearing the staircase.

"In a moment."

I look around the room one last time, seeing the teddy bear with one eye that Cindy left behind at our house in Virginia when she left me.

So much has changed since she told me she was leaving.

So damn much.

And I have no regrets—absolutely none.

As I start down the stairs a few minutes later, I hear Miles Davis, and when I enter the living room, I still at the sight before me.

Lily and Grace are dancing together in front of the lit fireplace.

I look at the record player I gave Grace before I lean against the wall just inside the room, my hands in my pockets as I watch them, my heart so close to exploding. I never knew it could be like this—that it could feel like this.

Loving a woman like Grace has changed me. It's opened me up to a whole other world I didn't know existed. And now I want to give Lily sisters and brothers—hell, I want to fill this entire house with kids. I want to marry this woman. And I will. And this time, it's going to be forever.

Grace lifts Lily and spins her around before I join them.

"Took you long enough." She smiles at me as she puts Lily down.

And then Grace changes the record to a song with Spanish lyrics, and Lily starts to shake her hips and move around. I tip my head back and laugh as Grace imitates Lily's version of salsa dancing.

"I better see your hips moving too, mister!" Grace says.

I step in front of her, grab hold of her waist, and dance with her, showing her some of the moves I learned on an op in Colombia four years ago.

"Wow, Daddy, you should go on a talent show. You're good." Lily claps her hands to her cheeks and giggles. "Me next!"

I hold both of their hands as we dance to the music.

God, *we* dance.

All of us. As a family.

EPILOGUE

NOAH

"Did you approve the plans I sent you?" Bella's standing in front of my desk.

"I think we need to hire more people. I'm only one man." I cross my arms but smile.

"Oh, come on, you're like the equivalent of ten good men. Why spend more when I have you?" She laughs.

We've drastically expanded since we opened our own official business two streets down from where Grace's office used to be. Well, the office is still there, but Cade runs it. Grace hasn't worked there since that day we faced her father.

"Hire a few more architects, or maybe I will go work with Luke. Hell, it'd probably be easier than dealing with—"

Bella shows me her fist, squinting one eye. "Don't even think about saying me."

I glance at the clock on the wall, and my heart speeds up. "Shit. I gotta go."

"Oh, is it tonight? How could I forget?"

I nod. "See you there in an hour?" I power down my computer and grab my keys.

"You're going to change first before you pick up Lily, right?"

I'm in jeans and a T-shirt.

"And shave too."

"What?" I run a hand over my short beard. "Grace loves the beard."

Bella exhales. "This event calls for something a little formal." She chuckles. "Come on, don't waste time!" She shoos me away, flicking her wrists.

"Fine." I come around from behind my desk. "But no tie."

And then I stop walking, a smile sneaking up on me—an idea now trapped in my mind.

God, it's going to be a good night.

* * *

"SHE'S GOING TO GET AN A FOR SURE, DAD!" LILY CLAPS IN the seat next to me and attempts to whistle.

"I don't know if that's how they grade in music school, but you're right—she played beautifully."

I look back up at the orchestra on stage. Grace has the cello positioned between her legs, the bow in her hand—but her eyes are on me. It's as if I'm the only one in the crowd, and she's playing naked for me again—because I suddenly feel as though we're the only ones in the massive auditorium.

And after her next song, I stand and hoist Lily up onto my shoulders as she raises the bouquet of roses and waves them. Grace takes a bow, and Lily tosses the flowers as hard as she can onto the stage.

Once the crowd starts to disperse, Grace climbs down the side set of stairs and heads to our row where we're waiting.

"How'd I do?" she asks, and I lean forward and kiss her.

"Amazing," Bella says over my shoulder.

"You were the best!" Lily shouts.

Grace hugs her tightly. "Thank you." Her eyes are sparkling, and her long white gown reminds me a little of our wedding day last month. Grace smiles as she reaches for the navy-blue material at my neck and slides it through her hand. "You wore a tie?"

"Yeah, can you believe I convinced him?" Bella's lips split into a grin.

"Mm. Yeah, him and ties." A smile lights Grace's cheek, and that mischievous look in her eyes tells me she knows what I'm thinking.

God, I can't take my eyes off my stunning wife.

I still get breathless whenever I look at her. And I'm so damn proud that she's back in school, living her dreams—not just pursuing them, but actually living them.

And I am too, because I finally have…*everything*.

* * *

WANT MORE GRACE & NOAH? DOWNLOAD THE MINI **BONUS story** - available on my website: brittneysahin.com/bonus-content.

ALSO BY BRITTNEY SAHIN

A new action-packed **SEAL TEAM** series (Stealth Ops) is now live, starring Luke, Jessica, Owen, and other Navy SEALs. Plus, a surprise guest appearance from Noah & Grace!

Note: *Someone Like You* and *My Every Breath* take place in the time between the prologue and chapter one of the book, *Finding His Mark*.

*

Cade King's book, *My Every Breath*, is now live! This is a romantic suspense, which guest stars Noah, Grace, and Corbin - as well as Noah's buddy, the sexy SEAL, Owen.

*

Stealth Ops Series: Bravo Team

Finding His Mark - Book 1 - Luke & Eva

Finding Justice - Book 2 - Owen & Samantha

Finding the Fight - Book 3 - Asher & Jessica

Finding Her Chance - Book 4 - Liam & Emily

Finding the Way Back - Book 5 -Knox & Adriana

Stealth Ops Series: Echo Team

Chasing the Knight - Book 6 -Wyatt & Natasha

Chasing Daylight - Book 7 - A.J. & Ana (7/30/20)

Becoming Us: *connection to the Stealth Ops Series (books take place between the prologue and chapter 1 of Finding His Mark)*

Someone Like You - A former Navy SEAL. A father. And off-limits. (Noah Dalton)

My Every Breath - A sizzling and suspenseful romance. Businessman Cade King has fallen for the wrong woman. She's the daughter of a hitman - and he's the target.

Dublin Nights

On the Edge - Travel to Dublin and get swept up in this romantic suspense starring an Irish businessman by day…and fighter by night.

On the Line - novella

The Real Deal - This mysterious billionaire businessman has finally met his match.

The Inside Man - 4/30/20

Stand-alone (with a connection to *On the Edge*):

The Story of Us– Sports columnist Maggie Lane has 1 rule: never fall for a player. One mistaken kiss with Italian soccer star Marco Valenti changes everything…

Hidden Truths

The Safe Bet – Begin the series with the Man-of-Steel lookalike Michael Maddox.

Beyond the Chase - Fall for the sexy Irishman, Aiden O'Connor, in this romantic suspense.

The Hard Truth – Read Connor Matthews' story in this second-chance romantic suspense novel.

Surviving the Fall – Jake Summers loses the last 12 years of his life in this action-packed romantic thriller.

The Final Goodbye - Friends-to-lovers romantic mystery

* * *

A Stealth Ops World Guide is now available on my website, which features more information about the team, character muses, and SEAL lingo.

SOMEONE LIKE YOU PLAYLIST

Until You Were Gone, Chainsmokers
Castle on the Hill, Ed Sheeran
Stay with Alessia Cara, Zedd & Alessia Cara
Blue in Green, Miles Davis
Waves – Robin Schulz Edit, Mr. Probz/Robin Schulz
Everytime We Touch, David Guetta/Chris Willis
Someone Somewhere Tonight, Mark Blomsteel
Slow Hands, Niall Horan

CONNECT

Thank you for reading Noah and Grace's story. If you don't mind taking a minute to leave a short review, I would greatly appreciate it. Reviews are incredibly helpful to us authors! Thank you!

For more information:
www.brittneysahin.com
brittneysahin@emkomedia.net
FB Reader Group - Brittney's Book Babes
Stealth Ops Spoiler Room
Pinterest - Inspiration boards

Made in the USA
Las Vegas, NV
13 June 2021